I0659840

THE TRISKELION SERIES

TOMORROW'S NEVER PROMISED

LUNA EVERLY

Copyright © 1st Edition 2023 Luna Everly

All rights reserved.

No part of this book may be reproduced, distributed, or transmitted in any form
or by any means, including electronic or mechanical methods, without prior
written permission from the author, except as permitted by U.S. copyright law.

This is a work of fiction. Unless otherwise indicated, all the names, characters,
businesses, places, events, and incidents in this book are either the product of
the author's imagination or used in a fictitious manner. Any resemblance to
actual persons, living or dead, or actual events is purely coincidental.

Cover Design and Interior Design © Quirky Circe Book Design

Ebook 979-8-9881075-0-7
Paperback 979-8-9881075-1-4

To the one who told me to write the book:
I wrote the damn book.

TRIGGER WARNINGS

This book contains dark elements such as crime, violence, death, grief, drug use, underage drinking, cheating, and sexual content. Intended for those 18+

They say: 'lightning never strikes twice'...

Apparently—based on a quick web search–it can.

Multiple times. Usually, with things that are isolated and tall.

Like me.

This fact has me wondering if love can also strike you multiple times,

changing the beat of your heart each time.

So, what do you do when you feel an instant connection with Liam, the enigmatic bouncer with

his own secrets? What happens when he leaves you with no choice in the matter and not even a

second glance behind him?

You move on—only to discover that you are now dating his best friend. His partner in *crime*.

The same man who will soon be the leader of the Tri-State Syndicate.

I never knew passion this intense or temptation that delicious could stun me twice.

But it sure can.

Now, Liam is back, and he wants me back too.

It's too late for us. At least, that's what I tell myself.

He made *his* choice, but did I make *mine*?

PROLOGUE

MADISON

HAVE you ever questioned why the Universe puts certain people in your life only to remove them? Me too. I guess it's all about the lessons—but why do good people learn such hard lessons? *Maybe* it was the plan all along before we even incarnated. Some 'Divine plan'.

Then, there are what I like to think of as 'Divine detours'—rerouting our course without warning. Like a sailboat in a storm that gets lost at sea and ends up somewhere it never expected.

I constantly wonder, if the Universe didn't intervene, where would I be right now? It couldn't be healthy to live our lives thinking about the 'what ifs'—but what *if* we did? What if *one* thing, was done differently? Then what? Could it *change* our fate? *Could it have changed mine?*

He is gorgeous, he is mysterious and he is *mine*—well not technically—*but what if he still was?* That 'what if' was the only thing that kept me going in this crazy shit show of a relationship. *If you would even call it that.* The indescribable connection I shared with him was esoteric.

The kind of love that you see in movies.

The type you greedily soak up in romance novels.

The hot, *alpha male* type with the *big*...you know where I'm going with this.

Really, it was that knowing feeling—*even when it didn't make sense.* The deeply rooted knowledge that this man was meant to be in my life in one capacity or another.

There is one problem, however.

Okay, one *major* problem.

His best friend also makes me feel that way.

My roommate Leah and my bestie Alexis are the only ones who *knew* what this was and how complicated it became. I sit here and wonder if the grief messed with my head. Perhaps I lost touch of reality. It couldn't be possible to love two men at the same time? *Could it?*

I am about to fill you in on *all* the details: The good, the bad, and the *ugly.*

Let's call it our little secret.

You be the judge. Am I walking a dangerous line, or is this the most epic love story in the making?

Let's get back to where it all started...

NOVEMBER
2013

CHAPTER 1

MADISON

KE$HA is blasting throughout our off-campus house. Leah is preparing for another Friday night out after our shift at the hockey stadium. All our friends are about to meet at the local bar Schmitty's—which we like to call 'Schitty's'—due to how you felt the next day. *Cheap liquor and 2 dollar beers will do that to you.*

It is down the block from our house, making it a prime spot. Our broke asses can walk home without having to pay for an overpriced Uber. Schmitty's is the hot spot for post-game drinks and getting lost in the music or *someone* for that matter.

Leah pops her head in my room smelling like Victoria's Secret Love Spell perfume, hair spray, and *tequila*.

Oof, it's going to be *that* kind of night.

I'm sure I'll hear her stumble in later with one of the hockey players. Looks like she will be the next one to add her name to the 'getting pucked' list.

Yeah, I really just said that.

Since our school lacks a football team, the hockey players are the big eye candy around campus. And my roommate has made herself quite comfortable with the whole team.

I'm silently sending a prayer up to the sex gods to have the two of them end their night at the hockey house and not ours.

Leah is a loud lover—let's just say she can win an Oscar for her performances in the bedroom.

You go girl.

She is absolutely stunning. Leah has legs for days, curves in all the right places, wild short brown curls, and tattoos that scream '*come take a peak*'. She truly is my best friend; no matter how or *where* she chooses to enjoy her sex life. All I care about is that she stays safe and out of trouble.

I guess that's how my nickname "mama" came about. I am always cooking, helping with hangovers, and checking in on her and our friends. I used to be out on the town with them—except that all stopped a year ago when my life decided to crash down on me.

"You aren't going to get laid looking like that," Leah half laughs, eyeballing my messy bun and pajamas. She's been my rock this last year, and sarcasm is her way of getting some kind of reaction out of me.

I look up to see her charcoal-lined eyes, strappy heels, and tight black bodycon dress. She's holding two shot glasses filled to the rim with the bottle tucked under her arm. My eyebrow instantly raises at the sight and *smell* of it. *Yep—definitely tequila.*

She's up to no good tonight.

The *Mad Maddy* inside me misses the party animal while *Mama Maddy* clutches the bedspread tighter to her chest.

"I am *soo* not in the mood to go out tonight, Lee," I sigh. "I am freaking exhausted from work and I have a *huge* anatomy exam to study for." I pin her with a stern gaze, nodding my head to the open PowerPoint on my laptop. I'm praying she will just drop it. Although, knowing her, *she won't*. If there is one thing about my roomie—she is stubborn as hell.

She holds her hand out with the shot spilling over the rim as I laugh and shake my head. I place one of my headphones back in my ear, ignoring her. Lee sits on my bed and uses her elbow to shut the screen, completely shutting down my music, PowerPoint, and incognito tab. *The tab hiding my reactivated online dating account.*

I finished updating my new bio earlier this morning, trying to pack as much as I could into a small character limit.

Hey! My name is Madison. Some like to call me Maddy or Mama Maddy. I guess you can say I'm already wifey material lol. I love to cook, watch movies and snuggle up with some good books. Family is everything to me. I am currently studying to become a nurse. Traveling the world is at the top of my to-do list, especially if I end up on a beach. I would love to meet someone who shares similar values and interests as me. If you asked me where I see myself a few years from now, it would be getting married and starting to build my small army of kids... adding in a few fur babies as well. Oh, I may have a slight obsession with coffee...some would call it an addiction. I call it love.

Disclaimer: *Hearts break easily, so be gentle with mine...it already has a few cracks.

So far, there have only been some creepy men with no bio and Myspace-angled pictures. You *know* which ones—taken from below or above at that *certain* angle. The type of men living out their dreams in their parent's basement, still wearing Ed Hardy hats and ripped jeans.

One pleasant message did stick out, however—

Hello, sweetheart. My name is Killian. I immediately noticed your profile. It was something about your eyes...they hold the pain of loss. I also have experienced loss and heartbreak. Even the strongest of men have a couple of cracks in their armor, in the fortresses they've built around themselves. I think you could be the one to break down those walls. Perhaps we could get to know one another. Maybe two sad souls wandering this world and hardened by grief can feel a little less lonely. I look forward to speaking to you, and if not, I hope you find someone who can mend those cracks in your heart.

What the *actual fuck*. Is this for real?

I am intrigued now.

Not only are his profile pictures complete eye candy, but he is 28, owns his own business, and is *covered* in tattoos. Hello *Mr. Tall, Dark and Handsome.* Did I mention he lives in New York City? I grew up on Long Island.

I was about to respond before Leah closed down my laptop. *Guess it'll have to wait until later.*

"It's been over a year, Mad. You are too young to keep yourself cooped up here while we all go out. You are only young once, Maddy. You know Sean would want you to move on, to be happy, and not become *grandma* Maddy," Leah says, her voice cracking.

That sets me off, and now I start leaking the tears I've carefully kept at bay for the last few months. I told myself to be strong and focus on work and school. *And I did just that.*

"I promise you I will come out for a girls' night after these exams." I smile at her as I wipe a tear away.

Lee knows all the tricks in the book and decides to do a toast to Sean. How can I decline that?

"To Sean, we miss you, man." Leah's voice cracks as she

raises her glass to the sky. I grab the shot, clink my glass with hers and slam it back. *To Sean.*

"Ughh...*tequila*." I shiver as I close my eyes. Heat instantly spreads across my chest.

I lean over to place the empty shot glass on the end table. As I turn around, Leah is already filling her glass back up. Casually, she hops off the bed to refill my glass, placing the half-empty bottle where my glass once sat.

I *knew* she was up to no good tonight.

She hands me the refreshed glass and holds hers out for one more toast. "Tonight is the night your life is going to change. You are coming out with me no ifs, ands, or buts—" she starts but I interrupt her.

"I love you to death but I need to study," I mutter.

"And that exam is not until Monday!" she huffs. "You have been studying for the last week. Put it off for one night and come out with us! We are finally all twenty-one and it's Carly's birthday!" Carly is our coworker—she and Lee have been thick as thieves lately. I guess that comes with the territory of not going out anymore. The world keeps on moving even if I don't.

Part of me is screaming to just *do it.* It has been *so* long since I've let loose. I feel the tension starting to leave my body, thanks to *Mr. Jose Cuervo.* The other responsible side of me whispers, *I really do need to study.*

I sit in silence for a moment, calculating my next move. Grabbing my phone off the bed, I check the battery life—65% —*good enough.* What I do next, not only shocks me but shocks Leah as well.

I slam the second shot back and in my best *Grinch* voice, counter, "'But what will I wear?'"

Leah immediately jumps into action. She hastily takes her shot of tequila, shakes her head from the taste, and grabs my hand. Throwing the empty glasses on the table, she pulls me full force toward my closet. Within seconds, she is sifting through my clothes, mumbling yes and no to each dress.

It is the first week of November, and it's freezing already, especially in Connecticut. If I'm going out, I'm calling the shots on what I wear. And news flash—it *isn't* going to be a barely there, thigh-high dress.

"Lee, I am *not* wearing a fucking dress in this weather," I laugh. "Plus, you know there is no coat check. If we are walking to Schmitty's, I'll freeze my ass off before we even get there." I throw my hands up, contemplating staying home.

Leah bends down to the bottom of the closet, rummaging through its contents. I watch as she grabs a pair of my thigh-high, black suede boots with the studs on the side and tosses them onto the carpet. She strolls over to my dresser and pulls out my black leather leggings, a black lace long-sleeve shirt, black camisole, and a pink lace thong. *Can you tell that I basically only wear black?* The exception is always my panties. I love a good surprise.

The devilish grin Lee's fronting as she tosses them on top of my boots is further proof she's got plans for me tonight.

Fuck. Is *Mad Maddy* ready to make her debut again? My cheeks heat. I'd blame it all on the tequila, but I also *miss* feeling sexy and desired. This outfit will most definitely turn some heads.

"Put these on and your favorite hoop earrings, and meet me in my room when you're done," Leah says as she walks into the hallway.

I'm undressing when she pops her head back in with a big shit-eating grin on her face. "I'm proud of you, Mad. I know you're scared to get back out there, but I just have a *feeling* about tonight. Everything is going to change," she sings while sashaying away.

I laugh and smile back at her as I take Sean's oversized t-shirt off. For the first time in over a year, it feels like pieces of my armor are coming off.

His shirts were my safety net.

My way of living with his *ghost*.

It was time to *live*—and not just for me—but for him too. For a life lost too young. For a beautiful, kind soul that didn't get to experience all the amazing things this world has to offer. *Marriage. Children. A full night of sleep. Dreams. Stability.*

Instead, this beautiful human experienced the pain and trauma of war and the demons that followed him as a consequence. He was just a boy sent across the world, fighting to keep us safe.

I need to live *for* him.

Suddenly, it feels like a huge weight has been lifted off my shoulders. A chill runs over my arms and wraps around me as I take a deep breath. Goosebumps spring up over my skin, blanketing my entire body. *I miss you, Sean.*

I get ready with more enthusiasm, feeling so much lighter than before. I do a quick once-over in my full-length mirror on the back of the door, shake my hair out of its bun, and head to the bathroom Lee and I share.

Leah is sitting on the edge of her bed, her eyes laser-focused on her phone. That devilish grin is back as her fingers fly over the screen. She must be texting Chase—the Hockey God. I was never interested in any hockey players...but the bouncers at Schmitty's? Well, I should say *one* particular bouncer—always caught my eye. *I wonder if he'll be there tonight.*

I scramble through my makeup bag, deciding on a smokey eye and a nude lip. Makeup has always been my favorite part of getting ready to go out. I love being able to accentuate my features, especially my eyelashes. They are naturally thick and long, but add a little liner and mascara and watch the magic happen. Suddenly my eyes look huge and doelike.

I've nailed it down to a sultry look in less than ten minutes—

which is impressive for not doing a full glam look in a while. I dust some highlighter on my cheeks and nose and stare into the mirror for what feels like forever.

The girl staring back at me is one I didn't think I would ever see again, *but here she is.*

"You look hot, babe," Leah confirms as she leans against the bathroom door. She chuckles, and her eyes meet mine in the mirror.

"Jesus, Leah. You scared the shit out of me!" I shriek and throw my lipstick at her. "Put this in your purse tonight. I've got a small wristlet, and my phone takes up the whole damn thing."

"*Oooh,* the *sass* is coming out already!" She tucks the lipstick into the bag wrapped around her body and moves forward to hug me. "You got this, girl. Now let's go."

CHAPTER 2

MADISON

SCHITTY'S IS *PACKED*. Wall to wall is lined with college students grinding up against each other. Loud bass is pumping through the speakers, and the lights are going wild, painting the walls in a kaleidoscope of colors. The place reeks of stale beer, and the floor is sticky as fuck. Lee grabs my hand and drags us through the crowd to the bar. Her phone glows as she multitasks moving through the crowd while responding to a text.

Chase greets her when she reaches the bar. He gives Lee a once-over and licks his lips before shifting his focus to me—looking shocked. Leah pulls me closer, wrapping a protective arm around me. "Chase, you remember my roommate Maddy, right?"

Chase wraps a clammy hand around mine, giving it a hard squeeze. "Of course, so glad you came out tonight," he slurs with sympathy in his eyes. "Let's grab you ladies a drink. What's your poison?" He gestures to the female bartender.

"Cranberry, vodka, club, and lime," Leah chimes in. "Two, please." She winks at me, knowing it's my drink of choice as well. After living and working with this girl for three years, she knows almost everything about me.

I crane my neck and look around to see if my favorite

bouncer is here, but I come up empty. Disappointment floods me. *I could have used one of his big hugs right about now.*

Chase retrieves his beer and our drinks off the bar. He shoots a wink at the busty bartender. She smiles sheepishly and taps his hand. "I'll throw these on your tab," she purrs. I wonder how many women in this bar he's *fucked*? *He is the university superstar after all.*

He hands us our drinks and raises his own. "To the big win tonight!" He clinks his glass against ours while undressing my roomie with his eyes. The nearby crowd and his teammates go wild, whistling and hollering. All I can think is *this cocky motherfucker*. He isn't just talking about the win on the *ice*.

Leah's cheeks heat as she grabs my hand to tug me off to the dancefloor. *David Guetta ft. Nicki Minaj - Turn Me On* is playing. It's amazing how my body gets right back into the swing of letting the music guide my moves. It feels like a goddamn sauna in here, and the tequila from earlier is still running through my bloodstream. Beads of sweat form on the back of my neck, making my hair cling to it. Leah and I are reciting the words and falling back into our same ritual of singing into our invisible microphones.

It doesn't take long for Chase to find—or should I say *stalk* Lee down like a wolf on the prowl. Within seconds, their lips meet, and his hands are all over her ass. *Listen*, as long as she's having a good time—I don't care. He's a fuck boy, but she's just looking for a good time. It's not my place to intervene.

I dance by myself for a few more songs and start making my way to the bathroom. Do I really want to break the seal now? I will be peeing *all* night. I mentally curse myself for wearing leather. Such a stupid idea—already, the material is clinging to my legs. I finish my drink to cool myself off, but I'm still hot as hell.

As I approach the bathroom, I notice the line for the ladies' room is ridiculously long. *It's one thing I never understood.*

Women are organized and diligent for the most part. How hard is it to get in, pee, and get out? I guess the drinks make us chatty, and we end up socializing more than actually using the bathroom.

Forget it! I bypass the line and head straight for the back door. My eyes immediately land on the rugged man standing there. My heart skips a beat. *He's here.* His eyes meet mine, and a smile spreads across his handsome face. God, how long has it been since I experienced his warm welcome? *That smile can make any girl swoon.* Don't even get me started on his *eyes.*

"Hey there, *love.*" He picks me up in a big bear hug, lifting my feet off the ground. I genuinely smile for what feels like forever. I wrap my arms around his tatted neck as his beard tickles my face. *Ugh*, I missed his Irish accent, strong arms, and the way he calls me *love.* Never have I felt uncomfortable in his arms. If anything, they have always given me a sense of comfort and familiarity.

This man is *all* muscle, beard, and tattoos. He's gorgeous with his dark brown eyes and perfectly combed hair. He wears it slicked back with the sides buzzed short. His beard is trimmed neat but longer than most males in this bar, with exception of the other bouncers.

Let me tell you, the number of women in this bar trying to get this fine man home is off the charts. I don't think there is one woman here who doesn't know who *Liam Donelly* is. He's what the majority of the bathroom chatter is about.

Liam places me back down on my feet, steadying me with his arm on my lower back until I am stable. He has always been this way with me. Leah and I had many wild nights; some nights we even closed the bar down. I also had my fair share of nights where he had to toss my drunk ass over his shoulder and place me in an Uber home.

He may look super intimidating, but he's truly the *sweetest* man ever, always making sure I get home safe. And if I'm being honest, *he makes me feel safe* around him. His name is Liam, after all—which means protector.

We established this friendship my freshman year when Lee thought fake IDs could easily work to get us in if our charm—*or revealing dresses*—didn't. And it *did* work the first few times. Except one day, the new bouncer at the front door refused me entry. Lee got in with no problem, but of course, he stopped me. Then this *behemoth* of a man shows up to the commotion Lee was creating, grabs the ID from his peer, and asks me to state my name.

"Madelyn Marrone."

Then he asks my date of birth.

"3/11/1989."

He looks me up and down, asks me to smile, and then nods his head to the other bouncer.

"She's good." He winked at me as he handed me back my ID.

Since that day we both shared the unspoken knowledge that I wasn't of age until this year. Whenever I showed up, he would seek me out, whether it be by the bar or on my way to have a cigarette. Yeah I know, it's a *terrible* habit. I used to only smoke when I would drink. I'd usually bum one off Liam or buy my own pack for the night. After Sean died, I used it as a coping mechanism. Now, I'll have one or two when I'm super stressed.

Liam pulls a pack of menthols and a lighter out from his dark wash jean pocket. He grabs two, holding them up between his fingers, and raises an eyebrow at me. "Still smoking, lass?" he asks as he places his own between his lips and lights up.

I nod as I study him blowing the smoke toward the crisp night sky. *What is happening to me?* I've always appreciated this man for his looks and protective nature, but *never* have I felt *drawn* to him in this magnetic way. My eyes linger on his lips. It feels like I am seeing him through a new lens. He looks edgier —*dangerous* even. Enough to make tingles run up and down my spine.

It must be those damn tequila shots.

He places the cigarette in my mouth as our eyes make contact. I find myself searching those dark eyes. What I see there makes me shiver with a hunger I have not felt in over a year. My palms become slick, and desire begins to ignite in my core. *What the actual fuck?* Did Chase put something in my drink? I feel high off of Liam, lusting over him like I never have before.

The spark of the lighter breaks me out of my reverie. I inhale and take a step back, blowing smoke upwards. He gives me that lopsided smile I know all too well. I see it on many of my classmates' faces when they find out about Sean. *Sympathy.*

I make my way to the cushioned wicker couches by the gas fire pit, avoiding the familiar feeling of being felt sorry for. *I'm tired of people walking on eggshells around me.* I place my drink down, prop my legs on the edge of the fire pit and lean back to look at the stars.

The cushion beside me sinks in as Liam sits beside me, wrapping his burly arms around me. They are covered in Celtic tribal markings and intricate swirls. Heat radiates off him, putting the fire to shame. His delicious scent encompasses me— a mix of lavender soap and some sort of woodsy cologne. *Cedarwood, maybe?*

"I heard about yer man. I am so sorry, love," he says apologetically.

"Leah?" I question, knowing she was most likely the one who told him about my unexplained absence.

"Yeah," he sighs while tucking a stray hair behind my ear. "I thought you'd gotten sick of me and this bar full of idiots."

He releases me from our embrace and stares into my eyes. Once again, I shiver with these feelings awakening inside me and the loss of his warmth. *Get sick of Liam? How could I? He's always been more than kind to me.*

"When Leah told me about what happened to yer man, I asked her for your number. I wanted to extend my condolences, but she told me it wasn't a good idea." He takes a long drag of his cigarette. "She mentioned you were in a really bad place this last year," he eyes me cautiously.

I take my own deep inhale of smoke, watching the cherry glow at the end.

Exhale.

"We've got some catching up to do Liam…"

CHAPTER 3

LIAM

I AM BACK at my post at the back door after breaking up a fight by the outside bar. These kids are fucking out of control. Piss drunk and fighting over a fucking pint spilled on their pretty designer dress shirts. Give me a *fucking* break. Not one of them works. The majority have their parents' money to buy their drinks all night. And that is on top of the fancy dress shirts, the newest shoes, drugs, cars...you name it.

Don't get me wrong, I enjoy my luxury lifestyle—*not the drugs*—but I earned that with my *blood, sweat,* and *tears.*

As for the *real* rich kids—they found a business dealing the drugs we distribute out of the underground club of this bar. Their fathers provide them with the money and connections to do so.

The club offers high-stakes gambling—that many of the university elite attend—VIP rooms, and a few BDSM rooms. Lavish parties are held often, especially on the student's first day back on campus. That is when *all* the elite come out to play. A few *professors* too.

The other students are none the wiser of what goes on below. Part of my job is to keep it that way. It is soundproof—but even if it wasn't—with the noise of the music upstairs, *you would never know.*

I'm already in a shit mood. One of the little pricks—Chase, has got my blood boiling. I got word he's been placing ecstasy in the drinks of the women he's trying to take home. *And right now?* I don't give a flying fuck who his Da is or that he is actively doing business with us. We *do not* allow our drugs to be placed unknowingly in *anyone's* drink—*especially* in our fucking bar.

This gobshite is about to get a nice lesson on how this place works and just *who* he is dealing with.

I crack my knuckles and neck in an attempt to calm down. As I turn to make my way back inside to deal with Chase, I spot a stunningly beautiful brunette making her way to the door. The lights from the DJ booth catch her face just right, and I have to do a double take. My heart pounds in my chest like it would after a good sparring session.

It's *Madelyn Marrone.* I have not been graced with her beauty in over a year. But the memory of her sure as shit graced my fantasies in the shower. *Fuck me.* My cock pushes against my zipper as she gets closer. *I need to calm the fuck down.*

A bitter taste forms in my mouth as I mentally list all the reasons I can't make her *mine.*

She is seven years younger than me.

She still has university to finish up.

She just lost her fucking boyfriend.

My job is dangerous as fuck.

And most importantly, this woman deserves *so* much more than the life I could provide for her.

You see, I am a soldier like her man was too—but not the kind you may be thinking of. I work for the Kennedy family. The head of the Irish Mob here in the States'. Our territory consists of New York, New Jersey and Connecticut.

My job is to protect the brotherhood, those I took an oath for —*my family.*

How did I get involved in such a heinous lifestyle? My best friend's Da practically raised me after my Mum passed. She was a single mother, and I was an only child. My Da left us when I was born, which left me an orphan. I was only ten when she died. That was the age I learned that the man who took me in was in the Irish Mob. And not just in it, but *ruled* it. Although we lived in Ireland at the time, he was becoming needed more in the States'. We moved that same year, taking up residence in New York. From that point on, the criminal underworld became all I knew.

The Tri-State Irish Syndicate became the talk of the underworld, and Jack Kennedy was *ruthless*. His name and power quickly gained recognition and respect from the other syndicates and organizations across the globe.

At eighteen, I was already moving product and flying around the country on assignments. Jack taught his son and I all we needed to know to become the powerful men we are today. I would lay my life down for any of them. The Kennedy's are the only family I have left, and I'm beyond grateful for them. They gave me *everything* when I had *nothing*.

As of recently, Jack has been very ill. Three years ago, he was diagnosed with an aggressive form of pancreatic cancer. His son —the next heir, asked me to run the Connecticut business while he tackles Jersey and New York. The same day I started here three years ago is the day I met *Madelyn*.

I open the back door, and her familiar scent invades my space. As soon as she is outside, I waste no time greeting her.

"Hey there, love." I smile, picking her up and pulling her into one of our old hugs. *Damn this woman!* She smells just as good as I remembered. That perfume could drive a man fucking mad. I suppose that's where her nickname *Mad Maddy* came about. I heard her friends call her that a few times.

Her arms wrap around my neck, forcing her full lush breasts to press against my body. Silky tanned skin brushes against my face. I set her down, lingering my hands at her waist, afraid if I let go, she'll disappear again.

Am I going fucking bat shit? This woman leaves my life for a year, and the first day I see her, I start thinking like an eejit.

I've got it fucking bad for her. I told myself she had a man. I told myself not to use my resources to investigate her life—*and I didn't*—yet she's all I've thought about since the last time I saw her.

Seeing her today is like handing a man a glass of water after being parched for weeks. I didn't truly realize how much I was thirsting for her until now. All I can do is soak it all up, every succulent ounce of her.

Chase is *very lucky* that I've been distracted.

Her leather and lace look isn't helping my cock settle down. I reach into my jeans pocket and try to nonchalantly adjust it, while grabbing my pack of smokes and lighter.

I pull two from the pack and place one between my lips. "Still smoking, lass?" I ask, raising an eyebrow. I light mine, pulling the smoke deep into my lungs, hoping the nicotine will calm my nerves in her presence. You know, its funny, ask me to shoot someone in the foot, no problem. Ask me to converse with this goddess of a woman, and I'm the biggest *pussy* ever.

Exhaling, I see her nod out of the corner of my eye. I place a cigarette between her lips. A set of lustrous brown eyes with lashes for days study me. They are full of pain and sadness. A portal deep into her soul that shows just how much she's been suffering.

Maddy shivers and I instantly regret making her feel uncomfortable. I spark the lighter and cup my hand around the flame to light her cigarette. She deliberately takes a step back and retreats towards the couch by the fire.

I've always been her protector, yet, here I am, making her feel she needs protection from *me*.

She sits and places her head on the back of the couch to

22

observe the stars. It's pretty cloudy tonight. I'm not sure she'll see much. Smoke blows out of her mouth towards the sky as if releasing all the tension she's had built up. It probably wasn't easy for her to get back out here tonight. I suppose this is her first night out with the ladies—*and not one of them is to be found.*

I need to make this right. Maddy needs some form of comfort right now. I silently take my place on the couch beside her, and pull her into a tight hug. She instantly melts into me. This is what she needed. *Who am I to deny her comfort?*

"I heard about yer man. I am so sorry, love," I apologize, getting rid of the elephant in the room. A small sigh escapes her lips as she mentally confirms the source of the information she never disclosed.

"Leah?" she states more than asks.

"Yeah," I confirm as I place a strand of hair behind her ear. "I thought you'd gotten sick of me and this bar full of idiots," I blurt out, releasing her from my hold. Her body trembles. *Smooth, Liam. You are acting like the biggest pussy ever.* Now she's even more freaked out by my loose lips. Usually I'm very calculated, but with her, I feel unnerved.

I attempt to remedy the mess I've created thus far. The last thing I want to do is make her uncomfortable around me. "When Leah told me about what happened to yer man, I asked her for your number. I wanted to extend my condolences, but she told me it wasn't a good idea." I had wished Leah would have just given me her goddamn number. But knowing how she affects me, I wouldn't have been able to stop texting her.

"She mentioned you were in a really bad place this last year..." I trail off as I eye her, cautiously seeing if I officially overstepped our...*friendship.* I watch as she takes a drag of her cigarette and exhales what looks like smoke mixed with relief.

"We've got some catching up to do, Liam..." she looks at me as one corner of her mouth turns up in a half smile.

At least I didn't completely fuck up tonight. I just hope we can get back to the place we used to be. I want nothing more than to put a smile back on her face. Watch her eyes glow with the spark they once had. Hear her sweet laugh again and watch her dish out that *sarcasm* of hers...

I'll do whatever is necessary to protect her from anyone who could hurt her. *But does that include protecting her from me?*

CHAPTER 4

MADISON

I PUT out my cigarette while searching for my drink. It's empty of course. Getting up, I look back at Liam's large frame sitting on the couch behind me. He looks so out of place on such a delicate piece of wicker furniture. I'll need another drink for this if we are going to catch up. I reach for the glass and shake the remaining ice left. "I'll be right back, just need a refill," I smile at him.

He grabs the glass from my hand like the absolute gentleman he is. Our fingers lightly brush against each other, sending a wave of excitement coursing through me. *What would it feel like to have his fingers brush other parts of my body?*

"I've got it." He gets up and points to the couch. "Now, sit your pretty arse down."

While Liam is gone, my phone dings with a notification from the dating app. I scroll through and delete a bunch of messages that start off with **DTF?** *I mean, really?*

A notification chimes on my phone. I glance down to see who it's from. My face heats and my heart starts pounding wildly. The world even seems to be spinning. I open the message with shaky hands:

> I don't mean to come off so strongly, but I noticed you left my message on read, and you are online right now. I promise I'm not a stalker. I just know when a beautiful woman wants nothing to do with me. I want to wish you the best and hope you're having a lovely night. Cheers.

FUCK! I don't want to miss my chance. There is something about him that makes me want to know him. What kind of loss did he experience? He's absolutely gorgeous. Why is someone like him on a dating app? He must have women throwing themselves at him. With the liquid courage coursing through me, I throw caution to the wind and type my response:

> Hello, Killian. I was not ignoring you, more so giving myself time to craft a response. I found your messages to stick out amongst all the creepy ones! I don't think you're a stalker lol, just persistent. You don't seem the type to scare off too easily. I like that. I found your message to be equally charming and intriguing. I would like to get to know one another as well. Hope you're having a great night too.

I hit send, and pray I am making the right decision. I guess Leah's right—my life will change tonight...

And how right she was.

Almost immediately, my phone chimes with a response:

I'm flattered that I stand out to you amongst the 'creepy ones'. All sarcasm aside, I'm truly honored you chose me to get to know. A gorgeous woman like yourself shouldn't be broken-hearted so young. Life is crazy, unpredictable and intense, but that should never stop you from opening your heart again. Would you mind telling me about yourself? Or shall I go first?

Butterflies swirl in my stomach but the *warning* kind. I'm not sure why. Maybe it is the thrill of online dating or the fact that this man knows all the right words to say. Regardless, I start to type a response when Liam returns.

"Who's putting that smile on your face?" he jokes as he hands me my drink.

I glance down, noticing he got me my cran vodka. Trying to school my face—and failing miserably, I pat the seat next to me and place my phone back inside my wristlet. I take a quick sip and leave it on the table before folding my hands in my lap.

"So as I mentioned, we need to catch up," I pop the P at the end. He squints his brown eyes at me. Tonight they look darker than they usually do. *If that's even possible.*

"Woman, you'll be the death of me," he whispers as he walks around the couch. I would have missed it if the song didn't end at that *exact* moment.

Is it wrong I am turned on by him acting more protective—borderline possessive of me? I am starting to think tonight isn't one sided. *Great, Maddy. You get out for one night, and suddenly you've turned into the biggest hornball.* Flirting with a guy on the internet, and now the bouncer—who you've always had a great connection with, but haven't seen in over a year.

Liam takes a seat next to me, placing his arm around the back of my head. He keeps some distance between us as he rests his hand on the top of the cushion.

"I know how hard it was to get out here tonight, to try and be yourself again when it feels like nothing is the same...or ever will be. I lost my mum to breast cancer when I was ten. I know it's not the same as losing a boyfriend, but the grief is very much the same," he sighs, his gaze moving to the fire.

"My best mate, his da took me in when I had no one, and it was...it was an *adjustment*. I was angry, I was hurting, and I felt numb. I lashed out a lot as a result. His dad taught me how to channel my feelings. And how to turn pain into a tool to help power my success. I started to feel whole again. To feel like I belonged to a family again," he continues, turning back to face me.

He takes my hand in his and stares directly into my eyes. "You can allow the pain to destroy you or forge you, and Maddy —you are meant to be forged by the fire that is still burning inside you. You are *strong*, beautiful, and smart. One day when the time is right, a man will come along and set that fire ablaze —even if it means burning himself in the process."

A tear escapes my eye and slides down my cheek at his poetic words. Liam reaches up to rub it away with his thumb, twining his fingers in my hair. My mind is so confused right now—*fuzzy even*. I stare down at his lips while leaning my head into his hand. *It feels amazing.* Strong yet gentle at the same time. Everything about this man is a paradox. My tongue darts out to wet my dry lips.

As Liam leans in closer, my heart begins to palpate, forcing me to take a few breaths. He's going to *kiss me*. My vision blurs, and I realize I'm crying more than I was. Liam kisses my cheek, taking my tears with him as he approaches my lips. I place my hand on his scruffy cheek, preparing for his lips to claim mine. *He smells so fucking good.* I squeeze my thighs together to try and dull the ache between them, but that only makes it worse.

"Mad Maddy! Leah slurs, wrapping her arms around me. Oblivious to what was happening between Liam and I. Carly is right on her tail, stumbling in her heels as she makes her approach. *Impeccable timing. The Universe really has it out for me.*

I once again put distance between Liam and I before taking a huge swig of my drink. I need to cool this heat radiating within me.

"Come on. It's midnight—time to celebrate Carly's "official" twenty-first birthday with a round of shots!" Leah practically sings as she air quotes the "official" part.

Liam clears his throat and smiles up at her. "I'll pretend I didn't hear that, lass."

"Oh, Liam." Leah shifts towards him. He stands to help support her as she wobbles over to give him a loud kiss on the cheek. "You are the bessssttttt!"

Liam looks at me bashfully, red staining his cheeks. I send him a wink and pick up my glass. It's time to head inside with these crazy ladies.

Leah and Carly grab my hand, tugging me towards the inside bar as it starts to flurry. "See ya later, Liam." I wave awkwardly before the girls shuffle me away. *Smooth Maddy.*

CHAPTER 5

LIAM

I SPOT her at the bar, taking shots with her girls. They are already drunk off their arses. My eyes track her as they make their way to the dance floor. "Feel So Close" by Calvin Harris is playing and the dance floor is packed with sweaty kids rubbing up against one another. The girls form a circle, throwing their hands in the air and dancing like it's a private show.

Maddy has her eyes closed and head back, swaying her perfect hips to the rhythm. *Stop this, Liam. Stop it now.* Not only am I not allowed to fraternize with the students, but if I was to, Maddy should be the last woman I pursue. *She's too good. Too sweet. Too pure* to be corrupted by my criminal life.

I peel my eyes away from her in search of that bastard Chase. He's leaning against the bar with a circle of girls around him and his mates. I take one more glance back—*OH, FUCK NO.* Some arsehole has his hands wrapped around her from behind. He has his nose tucked into the crook of her neck and appears to be whispering sweet nothings to her.

She's grinding her sweet arse against him with her eyes still closed. Sloppy hands run down her lower back and over the swell of her arse. He grabs a handful first—followed by a slap. She slams her eyes open, looking disoriented. He turns her around to face him, his greedy fingers pulling her face towards him. *I'm ready to break his fucking hands off.* I don't think before my legs start moving towards them. *Abso-fucking-lutely-NOT* on my watch is this going to happen.

The rational part of me is saying I'm just protecting her from a drunk imbecile, the other part of me is *raging. Why does it feel like she's already mine?* It may not be right for me to interfere or cock block, but there is no denying we both felt something outside. *Hell, I felt something between us since the moment we met.*

Within seconds I get between them. The dickhead retreats immediately with his hands up in surrender. *Good. Get the fuck lost.*

I wrap both hands around Maddy's face forcing her to look up at me. The look she returns me is full of fire. That's when I notice her eyes—her pupils are dilated, and not just out of fear or excitement. She looks like a Powerpuff Girl. *Holy fuck.* How did I not realize this before? *Someone* must have slipped something in her drink.

"Sweetheart, did anyone get you a drink tonight besides me?" I press. I have a bad feeling that I know exactly who did. My hands begin to shake, and my molars are about to turn to dust. *I'm going to fucking kill him.*

Maddy runs her hands up my arms, lacing her soft fingers around mine. Fear has crept its way over her features. She knows there is something wrong. "Chase got me and Leah drinks when we first got here. Leah is probably going home with him tonight, so he put it on his tab," she says candidly. The wheels in her head start to turn. She looks over at Leah dancing with Carly.

"Love, I think you've been roofied by Chase. Do you feel okay?" I dig for more details. She releases her grip on my hands, wraps them around herself and takes a step back. *Once again, placing distance between us.*

"I felt off all night, but I chalked it up to not drinking in a while or getting laid," a small giggle escapes her lips at the last part. "I do feel dizzy, and my heart is racing, but my body feels *sooo* good, Liam—I've never felt like this before." Her eyes twinkle with lust.

I'm about ready to beat that little shit to the ground. Except that wouldn't be productive for anyone right now. I need to focus on Maddy first. "I'll drive you home, love. Gather your gals, and let's go."

Maddy turns to Leah and whispers in her ear. Her eyes go wide as her head whips around to Chase. *Damn.* I wouldn't want to be on the receiving end of the daggers she's throwing. Maddy grabs Leah's wrist, restraining her from going after him. *Don't worry, darling—I'll be taking care of him.*

I clasp Maddy's hand in mine and walk her and the girls to the entrance of the bar. I spot Conor at the front door. "I'm leaving for a bit. When I get back, we have some *things* to deal with." I nod my head in Chase's direction.

"You got it, boss. Should I tell Kieran as well?"

"No. And I would appreciate it if you didn't mention this to anyone else. I'll deal with the repercussions later," I sigh.

"Of course," he whispers while grabbing a patron's ID.

"Thanks, brother." I slap his back.

We step out into the cold November air. The snow has picked up a bit, already coating the street and cars. I autostart my blacked-out Audi S7, and it roars to life, the headlights illuminating the path in front of us.

The short walk is silent. I wrap my arm around Maddy in an attempt to keep her warm. These women are *nuts* walking around the way they do with barely a stitch of clothing on. She gratefully wraps her arms around me, letting me guide her to my car.

I unlock the doors and walk around to the passenger side to help Maddy in. The girls are already getting situated in the back, giggling and whispering about how sexy this car is. My chest vibrates with laughter as I help Maddy into the front seat. Being near her soothes me; she is the salve on my tough exterior. I still want to murder that son of a bitch, but I already feel better knowing she's safe.

I blast the heat when I get in. Maddy has closed her eyes and is resting her head against the window. I eye Leah in the rearview mirror, "Can you direct me to your house, please—and for the love of God, if you need to puke, let me know so I can pull over."

Leah laughs and directs me as I pull out of the parking lot. "Head towards campus. When you see the cemetery, we are the house across the street," she hiccups.

"You live across the street from a cemetery?" I ask incredulously, realizing they only live about a mile down the block.

"Yeah, it's kinda morbid. I like it," Leah hiccups again.

"That is...if you aren't afraid of a few ghosts," Carly chimes in theatrically.

You have no idea what morbid is, sweetheart.

IT TAKES me all of three minutes. I pull into their drive and park by the front door. Leah and Carly get out and walk up the porch towards the front door. I conceal a laugh as I watch Leah struggle to find her key in her purse.

I direct my attention to the gorgeous woman snoring softly in my passenger seat. Her features softened by sleep. The car's ambient lights highlight her stunningly beautiful face. I know I need to distance myself from her. *She can't be mine.* I just wish it could be different. I should be the one to set her fire ablaze. It should be me who helps her shine brighter than the Sun and Moon combined.

Guilt hits me hard, knowing that can never happen. She deserves a normal life. Getting involved with her will only bring more death and chaos into it. And dragging her beautiful soul into the darkness is not an option.

With a sigh, I get out and carefully open her door. I squat down to see if she's able to walk to the house on her own. She sits up, moving her hair out of her face. A delicate smile forms on her lips when she notices me. Her eyes close again as she lays her head on my shoulder.

"I've got you, darling," I whisper while leaning in to unbuckle her. I gather her in my arms and walk up the porch steps. Leah stands at the entryway waiting for us.

"Her room is the last door on the left," she points.

Brushing my wet boots off on the mat first, I advance down the hall. I nudge open the door with my foot, and use my elbow to hit the lights on. Briefly looking around, I take in her decor. It screams Maddy. *Classy yet cozy.* There is a small television, desk, and dresser.

The full-sized bed has a fluffy gray comforter and black sheets, along with twinkle lights that surround her bed frame. A white shag carpet with a gray bean bag covers the floor. Two plants sit on the windowsill above her desk that look well cared for. Her end table has two empty shot glasses and a half drank bottle of tequila on it. *I wonder if she needed some liquid courage to come out tonight.*

Shifting her into one arm, I remove her laptop from her bed and place it on the desk before pulling the comforter down. Leah and Carly are whispering something about 'letting me do this for her'. I've known Leah as long as I've known Maddy. She trusts me. The question is, *do I trust myself enough to do the right thing?*

As I lay her down, she sighs and cuddles up in the fetal position. *She's fucking precious.* I place her wristlet on her end table, before making quick work of removing her boots and earrings.

This will be the last time I get this close to her, feeling her soft skin touch mine. Next time I see her again at the bar, I'll make sure to keep myself busy. *She deserves better.*

I throw the bedspread back over her and place a gentle kiss on her forehead. *I might as well, if this is the last chance I get to touch her.* She turns over briefly, smiles up at me, and whispers, "Thank you, Liam."

I grab a pen and Post-it off her desk and leave my number and a note saying if she needs anything to call me. It doesn't matter if I can't have her. I will *always* protect her. I gather the empty shot glasses and tequila bottle and click the light off, quietly shutting the door behind me.

Leah is there leaning against her door frame across the hall. I'm not sure how long she was watching, but quite frankly—*I don't give a fuck* if she saw me kiss Madelyn's head. *Clearly, she was too drunk to notice we had almost kissed by the fire.*

I place the tequila bottle and glasses in her open hands. "Thank you, Liam. We appreciate your help tonight," she smiles drunkenly at me. "You know, you should ask her out. She's always had a great bond with you, and this proves that you are a good fit for her. Maddy needs a strong man like you. Someone who will take care of her when she falls apart." *Perhaps she is more observant than I give her credit for.*

I turn on my boot, making my way to the kitchen as she follows me. I try to leave before Leah convinces me of all the reasons I'm good for her best friend. Trying not to be a complete dick, I pop my head in the opening of the door before shutting it —"I'm not a good man, Leah. She deserves so much better," I say roughly. The words weigh heavy on my tongue. There's no doubt that I can be the type of man she needs. I could make her happy and feel loved in every way she deserves to be. But I refuse to allow my dark path to merge with her safe one. "Make sure you lock this door," I add more gently.

With those parting words, I get back in my car and prepare myself for what's about to go down back at the bar.

CHAPTER 6

LIAM

CONOR HAS him downstairs in my office, zip tied to a chair. I cross the door's threshold and take a seat at my desk, leaning back with my hands behind my head and feet up.

Chase's eyes grow wide as he realizes just how fucked he is. He begins to tremble, pulling at the zip ties on his wrists. "I'll take it from here Conor—thank you," I announce. Conor nods and shuts the door on his way out, taking post by the entrance.

My eyes never leave his as I contemplate how to go about this. He is the son of one of our most affluent business partners. His dad Alan is also friendly with the Kennedys directly—Mrs. Kennedy's childhood friend.

I'll probably get heat for this, but it has to be done. And It's not just about what he did to Maddy. It's entirely about the fact that this kid thinks he can walk on water. No matter how much power a man can have, no one is fully invincible. I stroke my beard for a few seconds, letting the bastard sweat it out a little longer.

Grabbing a pair of scissors off my desk, I stalk my way towards him.

"I demand to speak with my father. You do realize who the

fuck he is. I *know* you do. I've seen you at plenty of the Kennedys events," he says hysterically.

I am losing my patience with this little shit. I lean his chair back so that it's resting on the two back legs and get in his face. I press the scissor blades up to his freshly shaven skin, putting pressure under his right eye.

"I don't give a flying fuck who yer da is. You've been placing E in the drinks of the women you want to fuck for a few weeks now. I just caught wind of it today. And to say I wasn't happy about it is an understatement..." I trail off, running the scissors down his face, leaving a trail of blood. It's not significant enough to need stitches. Can't say for sure that it won't leave a scar.

I click my tongue and shake my head showing my disapproval. *This shit won't fly in my bar.* Sweat begins to bead on his forehead and his chest starts to heave harder.

"You do realize you roofied Maddy tonight instead of Leah," I continue, circling around him. "It seems you've set your eye on Leah for the night, thought you could continue your high after the game...make it easier to take her home..." I snarl.

"That whore wanted my cock without E! What the fuck are you talking about?" He growls, spittle flying from his mouth.

"I have the camera footage, Chase. At least be a man about it and admit you put ecstasy in Leah's drink, not realizing Maddy took it," I press on.

"Maddy could use it, don't you think? Her vibrator batteries probably died. That's why she came out tonight. If anything, I did her a favor," he smirks.

He turns his head from me like the little *bitch* that he is. That is when I lose it—I see *red*. Kicking my boot out, I let the chair crash to the ground. I lean over him and grab his face between my hands, forcing his head back to look at me. He *fucking laughs*.

I punch him once. "*That* is for all the women you and your mates take advantage of." Then a second time, hearing a crunch, and watching as blood splatters his shirt and the floor. "And *that* is for breaking the rules of your contract with the Kennedys— take this as your only *warning*." I cut his wrists free from their bindings and pull him up by the shirt.

"Get the fuck out of this bar. And if you even so much as look at Leah again, I'll find you," I snarl as I shove him against the wall. Blood is pouring from his nose and down his mouth.

"What about Maddy? She looks like she could use some comfort tonight..." he insinuates. *Does this kid have a death wish?* I guess he has bigger balls than I thought. My fingers lace around his throat, and I get in his face one last time before I cross a line I can't undo.

"Stay. The fuck. Away from her. She is *mine*," I spit. I knock twice on the door. Conor comes back in and grabs Chase by the arm, dragging him towards the elevator to the parking lot.

Sighing loudly, I sit down at my desk chair and run my hands through my hair. *What a fucking mess.* I stepped out of line over a woman I can't have. And honestly, I'd do it again.

My phone buzzes in my pocket.

K

Got an assignment for you. Call me when you can.

I throw my phone onto the desk, dragging my hands down my face. They are still covered in Chase's blood. I should take the assignment. It'll give me time to cool off and get my head on straight with Madelyn. I *want* her. There is no doubt about that. Tonight she seemed to have reciprocated my feelings. But I would be a selfish bastard to start anything with her.

I need some advice from my best friend. I send a quick reply back:

LIAM

Ok. Call you in a bit. I need advice.

I use my private bathroom to clean my face and hands with a damp towel. I drop it in the hamper before taking a piss. *The cleaning service is on our payroll, and all the employees are required to sign an NDA.*

My phone vibrates in my back pocket—it's *Killian*.

"Hey, brother," I answer.

"Hello, *sweetheart*," he jokes in a feminine tone. "I heard ya need advice, what's the *craic*?" he asks more seriously.

I sigh and run my hands through my hair while staring at the blood all over the floor. "I need to come clean about something... I met a woman. I'm crazy about her, man. Problem is, we met here at the bar. She's a student. I'm sorry Kil, I know we aren't supposed to fraternize with the students," I confess in a marathon of words. *I really could use my best friend right now, not my boss.*

His advice and history with women are better than my own. Killian was engaged once. His da set up an arranged marriage in an effort to strengthen our alliance with the Cubans. He and Selena had gone through a two-year courtship and they actually fell in love. At the last second, the deal was pulled due to rising tensions with her father. Kil was absolutely gutted after that, believing he'd stay a bachelor forever. He'd be content having one-night stands for the rest of his existence if he didn't need an heir to continue the family name and business.

There is a pregnant pause. "Damn Liam, *slow down*, you sound like a love sick puppy! Tell me about this goddess that's got you willing to break the rules," he laughs into the receiver.

I feel a moment of relief, but the anxiety is back again when I realize I should still do the right thing by her. Problem is, after tonight, I don't think I can stay away—*even if I tried*. She is like quicksand; the more I resist, the further she pulls me in.

"We met my first day here, three years ago. She is everything I want in a woman—a dark-haired, brown-eyed beauty. Not only that but she's got brains and knows how to use the perfect amount of sarcasm to keep me on my toes. Even her laugh is contagious. She's the full package. You'd love her, Kil. I'm just afraid to bring her into this life. It's too dangerous. Madelyn has been through so much already." I close my eyes and wrap up my thoughts.

"How's the sex?" he attempts to lighten the mood.

I clear my throat, embarrassment coursing through me. "We haven't yet".

"Liam, for fuck's sake. You're this crazy over the girl and you haven't even fucked her yet? I *need* to meet her," he implies. "Speaking of women, I actually met one as well. She's also a student—so don't feel too bad. Believe it or not, we met on a dating app," he cackles at the last part.

"No fucking way. The heir to the Tri-State Syndicate has an online dating profile? Did Hell freeze over?" I chuckle, thinking about the image of Killian sitting on his phone swiping left or right.

"Brother, don't knock it til ya try it. I'm finally getting back on the horse. Ya know my Da needs me to have an heir of my own."

My phone buzzes with a text. Pulling the phone from my ear, I see a number I don't know. I place Killian on speakerphone and open it:

> Hey, it's Maddy. Thank you for tonight. I know I may be a hot mess right now. I just wanted you to know that my feelings were there before alcohol or drugs were involved. If I'm being honest, the second I saw you tonight, I felt something shift between us. Something worth exploring. I wish you stayed. Maybe I'm being extremely bold here but come back after your shift. If you want ;)

Fuuuuuck. This woman isn't making it easy to stay away from her. I promptly add her name and number as a new contact.

"Liam, ya there?" Killian questions.

"Yeah, brother. Sorry, it's my girl," I sigh. "She wants me to go over there after my shift. I drove her home earlier because she was drugged. That's another thing I need to talk with you about." I come clean again. I respect Killian—not just as my boss—but as a brother too. He needs to know what went down tonight.

"I already heard about it. Conor told me when I checked in earlier. I'm fucking pissed you didn't ask me first. Now knowing it was yer woman, I understand. In saying that, why don't you go to her. Have the night of ya life, then clear your head a bit."

"I want to," I admit.

"Winter break is around the corner. The lass will be going home soon. Take the assignment I have for you in Miami and see how you feel when you come back. If you can't be without her after some time away, then you have my blessing. Don't let a connection that strong slip through your fingers. You know she'll be safe with us."

"Thanks Kil, I appreciate the advice. I'll take the assignment —send me the details. Oh, and good luck with yer woman, I hope it works out." I let out a sigh of relief. *That went better than expected.*

"You got it. I need you to be at the jet with Kieran by 10 a.m. tomorrow, so enjoy your night and stop gossiping with me on the phone. I've got my own woman to message. Have a good night, *sweetheart,*" he laughs before ending the call.

I'm still hesitant about subjecting her to the underworld. An angel like her doesn't belong there. I'd be tattooing her wings in black if I pulled her into my world—permanently sealing her fate. But Killian gave me the perspective I needed. *We* can keep her safe. Hell, there is an entire army to protect her.

Without getting back into it again, I pull my conversation back up with Maddy. I respond with the biggest shit-eating grin on my face. Perhaps, I can preserve her beautiful, flawless wings. I type quickly so I don't change my mind.

LIAM

Hello, beautiful. I was trying to be a gentleman and respect your boundaries. Especially since you were drugged, but the feeling is absolutely mutual. I wanted to ravish you all night. Hell, I've wanted to ravish you the moment I met you. Here's the deal. I am leaving tomorrow on a business trip and I may be gone for a few months. If I come over tonight, I won't have the restraint I had earlier. I want you. Badly. I'm leaving it up to you, princess. Are you sure this is what you want?

I watch with bated breath as the bubbles pop up on the screen.

MADDY

Please come. I need you. Even if it's just for tonight...I need to feel alive again. I feel safe with you and I trust you.

LIAM

I'll be right over, love.

CHAPTER 7

MADISON

HOLY SHIT. *He's actually coming over.* I throw the covers off my body and race down the hall like a bat out of hell. Leah's door is open. She stares at me like I awoke from the dead—which I guess I have. This whole night has awakened a part of me that was dead. As soon as I enter the bathroom, I throw the shower on hot, slightly lowering it so it's practically boiling but still bearable. I strip my clothes off in record time and situate myself under the hot stream, careful not to get my hair wet. *Ahh. It feels so good on my skin. That's not why I'm here.* Focus, Maddy. I quickly get to shaving all the essential parts, careful not to cut myself. Let's just say they had received less attention than they deserved. I hear the door creak open—

"I thought you were about to be sick," Leah calls out. I peek my head out of the shower curtain. She is sitting on top of the closed toilet seat. "I'm so sorry about Chase, Mad. I didn't know that *fucker* was like that," she admits.

"It's *fine*. I'm just glad Liam was there to help." I sheepishly look down. "I actually feel better tonight than I have in a long time." A smile creeps onto my face at the thought of what's about to happen.

"What's that look, Madison?" Leah stares me down. She

always knows when something is up. *I don't have a great poker face.*

"Did something *happen* between you and Liam?" she pushes for the dirty details. I close the curtain to shield my guilty face and begin pouring body wash onto my loofa.

"No, it didn't—thanks to your *perfect* timing, but even if it did, he's leaving for a few months," I sigh. *Timing is such a bitch.* "I asked him to come back tonight after his shift." I drop the bomb she's been waiting for. Bubbles gather on my body as I scrub quickly, knowing I am running out of time.

"You go babe. That man is going to *deliver.* I know it. Just look at him," she swoons, clapping her hands. "Are you feeling any better?"

"Yes, much better. I think the two giant bottles of water and some sleep helped immensely," I say over a mouthful of toothpaste.

I hear her walk out of the room. Knowing her, she's off to go get some freaky shit like handcuffs or bondage to lend me.

A few moments later, I hear footsteps again. Except this time, they are louder than before and *definitely* not Leah's.

Fuck me.

My heart starts beating out of my chest with anticipation, knowing exactly *who* they belong to.

"She's all yours," Leah announces, shutting the door behind her. He chuckles softly. *I am going to fucking kill her.*

"Hey there, love," Liam announces his presence, his alluring scent arousing my heightened senses.

I don't know what to do. Should I be bold and invite him in, or do I tell him I'll be right out? *Goddamn it, Leah. You could have had him wait for me in the living room.* I poke my head out, shielding my body with the curtain—a*s if we aren't about to do completely filthy things to one another.*

"Hey," I greet him seductively. It comes out shakier than sexy —*and he can tell.*

A tantalizing smile forms on his face as he makes the first move of removing his boots and socks. My eyes widen in surprise. Not because he's about to get in the shower but due to the large spots of blood splattered on his shirt.

"Oh my God! Liam, are you hurt?" I presume. He looks down at his bloodstained shirt and shrugs. *Yeah. Totally fine. No big deal.*

"I'm okay sweetheart, it's not *mine*. Chase won't be bothering you or any other woman—*ever again*," he declares, while lifting his shirt over his head and ceremoniously dropping it to the floor.

I scan his body to confirm he hasn't been injured and what I find are more tattoos covering his chest—two black, tribal ravens are perched on each of his pecs. Both his nipples are pierced, adding to his bad-boy look. Dark hair veils the center of his chest and dips low towards an impressive set of abs. My eyes dip lower, watching him reach for the buckle of his jeans. With steady hands, he swiftly unbuckles his belt, interrupting my exploration. Liam's fingers pause at the zipper. I look up at him and his eyes meet mine with resolve.

"You're sure this is what you want, love?" he quizzes me with an eyebrow raised.

I feel a wave of my own tenacity hit me. All my nerves go out the window and I loosen the death grip I have on the curtain. "You better get in before the water gets cold," I respond with finesse, letting the hot water cascade down my back. He chuckles again.

I grab the face wash, realizing the steam and water probably turned me into a racoon. *No wonder he was looking at me like that.* I close my eyes and scrub at my face, attempting to remove the dark circles of mascara and eyeliner. Turning back towards the shower head, I hear the *swoosh* of the shower curtain and start to shudder with anticipation. I run my face under the water as his two strong hands pull me flush against his body. They wrap around me like a harness and I am about to take the plunge. His erection presses hard against my ass.

Leah was right. This man will deliver–*I have no doubt.*

He twists me around to face him and runs his hands up my waist. I keep my head down, nervous to look him in the eyes, knowing damn well I'll see the same hunger that is coursing through me. *Holy...Jesus.* This man's cock is perfect. The girth is more shocking than the length of him; both equally formidable. A thick vein runs up his shaft to a swollen crown. I bite my lower lip with my teeth as I clamp my legs together. *By this time tomorrow, I am going to be deliciously sore.*

The knuckle of his index finger caresses my jaw, lifting my chin up. His hands wrap around both sides of my face as my eyes find his. "You look nervous," he points out.

I'm done talking about this. I yank his face to mine, locking my lips around his. He stills, unprepared for my ambush. It lasts only a few seconds before his tongue pushes past my lips. Liam presses my back against the tile and shoves my legs apart with his knee, putting pressure where I need it most. Boldness takes over me as I run my hands down his abs, placing one on his hip and grazing his length with the other. I open my mouth wider, granting him full access. Our tongues dance before I pull his lower lip in between my teeth and then retreat.

He lowers his head, leaning his forehead against mine. "Woman, you'll be the death of me," he groans. *He said the same thing earlier at the bar.* His lips find mine again, continuing his mission to devour me. Calloused hands slide down over my breasts. His thumbs roll my nipples to peaks, and my core starts to clench with the need to feel him inside me.

I grasp his cock in my fist as I moan into his mouth. He grabs my other hand, pinning it next to my head, and twines our fingers together. I tighten my grip on his growing length, pumping from base to tip. A growl escapes his lips as he mirrors me, matching my rhythm thrust for thrust. Liam grabs my face with his other hand, clenching my hair around his fingers and mercilessly reclaiming my lips.

I am heaving heavily when we break free. I've lost track of time. *How long have we been exploring each other?* He trails softer kisses down my neck and over my right nipple, circling his tongue around the tight bud. Then begins to lick and suck, forcing my body to squirm at the incredible sensation. I am already so sensitive, *it's all so much.*

The heat of the water rushing over us.

The pressure of his hips against mine.

His lips taking turns on my nipples and throwing my mind into a frenzy.

I have *never* felt this way before. *And it's not the drugs.* This chemistry between us has been building for years. It was always how he looked at me that drove me wild.

Liam licks his way back up my neck, peppering kisses along my jaw. I love how he goes back and forth between *savage* and forbearing. I remove my hand from his cock, sliding it up through the neatly trimmed hair. I walk my fingers over his abs and up to the center of his sternum, gently pushing him back—about to drop to my knees. He grabs my hand and throws it above my head while running his nose over my collarbone.

"Not so fast, beautiful," his whisper tickles my skin. Liam kisses me...

Once

Twice

A third time.

Each one with more intensity than the last.

He walks us backward toward the shower bench and sits down. I straddle him and wrap my arms around his neck, staring into the eyes of a man on a mission. The corner of his mouth lifts into a smile. One of his hands slides around my lower back while the other slips between us. His fingers run up and down my slit, building my need for more contact. I gasp and throw my head back—*God, this feels amazing.*

My hips buck at his touch and I squeeze my thighs tighter around him. He leans forward to latch his lips onto my throat, sucking at the delicate flesh. His fingers continue their pursuit deeper into my folds, circling his thumb around my clit and breaching a finger through my slick entrance. Working his finger deeper into my channel, my walls begin to clench around him. I close my eyes at the sensation and ride his hand, using his neck as leverage. His other hand drops lower to grab a handful of my ass, guiding my thrusts and encouraging my orgasm.

He adds a second digit, increasing the pressure building within me. Moving his thumb and palming my clit, he starts to crook his fingers at a relentless pace. My breath hitches in my throat and I see stars behind my eyelids.

"Open your eyes, sweetheart—I want your eyes on me when you come," he demands while he continues to bewitch me. I force my eyes open and ride his fingers harder until I fully detonate my orgasm. *And with it, the last piece of my armor falls off.*

"Liam!" I cry out before sagging against his body like Jell-O.

CHAPTER 8

LIAM

SHE'S FUCKING *gorgeous when she comes.* This woman is the definition of *perfection.* Her slick wet body against mine. Taking what she needs from me. Riding my hand to orgasm. I remove my fingers from her, placing them in my mouth and sucking them dry. Sweetness seizes my tastebuds. *She tastes better than I imagined.* I can't wait to feast on her...but that will have to wait 'til later.

I grab the condom packet I left next to us, rip the foil off with my teeth and spit it onto the shower floor. She lifts her head off my chest as I raise my hips up to sheathe myself.

I stand, hoisting her up and cupping her delectable arse. She wraps her legs around my hips and arms around my neck. My cock twitches against her stomach, more than ready to dive deep inside her. I want to fuck her hard and fast, but that's not what she needs. *It's not what I need.* This is all about savoring the time I have with her. That's the thing about time—*tomorrow's never promised.*

Maddy molds her lips around mine as I move us under the warm water. Long, dark brown hair pools down her back. I steal one more kiss, before pushing her up against the tile and placing my cock at her entrance. Her long lashes glisten with water droplets as she gazes into what feels like my soul. With just her eyes, this little enchantress has me feeling profusely vulnerable. I take a second to admire her beauty. She is naturally stunning without a stitch of makeup on. *Fuck me.* This woman makes me feel things *no* woman ever has.

I slam into her, slapping her arse against the wall. She cries out, muffling her scream by biting my shoulder. Shock, regret, and outrage hit me all at once as I am met with resistance. My mind is racing a million miles a second. *Is she a virgin? She had a boyfriend for almost three years. There is no way they weren't intimate.* My mind snaps me out of my tangent like a rubberband. *Fuck.* Did I hurt her?

"Maddy, are you okay?" I ask with a shaky breath. She looks up at me with a fiery expression on her face. Gone is my tremulous girl; a brazen goddess just replaced her.

"Don't you dare stop now," she demands, her eyebrows coming together. Her fingers grip my shoulders tightly. "I'm fine —*more than fine.*"

"We need to talk about this, *Madelyn.* I can't believe you let me take your virginity in a fucking shower," I raise my voice, realizing how much of a selfish prick I really am. I should have stayed away from her from the beginning. My intuition was spot on, and it usually is. She is *too good* and *pure* to subject herself to a man like me.

Gently, I pull out of her, and place her back down. I step out of the shower and toss the condom in the trash. The towels are on a rack by the sink. I grab one, drying off as quickly as possible. She's crying, but hasn't made any effort to follow me out. I dress promptly before I do something stupid again—like go back in there and fuck her 'til she can't remember her name.

I'm slipping into my boots when the water shuts off. The curtain flings open. Out steps Maddy, *a very flustered Maddy.* She grabs a towel and aggressively wraps it around herself. *She's pissed.*

"Liam, why are you so upset? I wanted this!" she shouts, barricading her body against the door. *It's cute as hell that she thinks her little frame will stop me from getting through.*

"You know damn well you deserve better than an arsehole bouncer like me taking your virginity. Especially after everything you've gone through and *especially* since you were on ecstasy," I hiss. I cross my arms over my chest to prevent them from reaching out for her. It's sick that my cock is still hard seeing her dripping wet and flustered. Her cheeks heat red with a mixture of lust and anger. *God, how I wish things could be different.*

"Liam, I haven't felt *this alive* ever. I mean it. Yes, Sean and I *never* had sex. He was deployed for almost our entire relationship. I was lucky if I got to Skype with him from time to time and even luckier if we found privacy to get each other off over the phone," she admits as tears slide over her red-rimmed eyes. I can't tell if they are angry tears with me or sad tears for Sean—maybe a combination of both.

Closing the distance between us, I walk over and wrap her in my arms. Wet arms wrap around me in return. She buries her head in my chest and starts sobbing. I run my hands in gentle circles around her back, trying to soothe her. "Shh...Madelyn..." I want to say it will all be alright. *But that would be a lie.*

"It's Madison, not Madelyn," she mumbles over my shirt.

"What's that?" I pull her back to look at her.

"My name is Madison. My fake ID says Madelyn." She holds her hands up in surrender and then places them on my biceps. "I promise no more *secrets*," she laughs. "Can we *please* start over, Liam?" The look she gives me is one of hope.

Fuck—this woman is so wholesome and innocent. I need to be strong for her sake. She can't be tarnished by my world. I pull her face to mine one last time and kiss her with every ounce of pain I feel.

"I'm no good for you, *Madison*," I say her name like a prayer. "There are secrets I hold that I can't tell you about—just know that I am a *dangerous* man, and you deserve better." I leave her standing in the middle of the bathroom. I force my feet to keep walking out of her home and out of her life.

ONCE INSIDE MY CAR, I lose it. I slam my fists against the steering wheel and shake it for good measure. A rush of profanities leaves my lips as I run my hands through my hair. And then, for the first time since my mom died, I cry.

Madison is *everything* I want in a woman. I want nothing more than to make her *mine*.

Memories flash across my mind's eye. *Her mouth open and her head thrown back in passion. The sight of her delicate hand wrapped around my cock. Her adorable smile—*

Then I remember the last memory I will have of her. *The look of betrayal on her face when I pushed passed her.*

I angrily swipe at the tears, start my car and peel out of her driveway. Not daring to look back in my rearview.

CHAPTER 9

MADISON

MY PHONE VIBRATES on my end table a few times throughout the night. I don't bother checking it. It doesn't matter if it's Liam. Whatever *that was*, whatever *we were,* or I thought we were heading toward—is done now.

Thank God for blackout curtains. My eyes are swollen and irritated from crying. Even the backlight from my phone is bothering me. It feels like I've been in my bed for days. *Who the hell even knows what time it is.*

I don't think I've cried this hard since Sean's funeral. It's strange. I didn't think it was possible to feel this way about another man, yet here I am, mourning another loss. It was over before it even started. Liam meant so much more to me than I ever realized. Last night, I opened up entirely to the possibility of what we could be; of what was right in front of me for so long— only to be sorely mistaken.

Fuck him for making that choice for me. 'Dangerous man'... because you smack people around at a bar when you need to? I think I can handle that. *Who is he to decide what I want?*

A knock on the door interrupts my reflections. "It's Leah. Can I come in?" she asks softly behind the door.

"Yeah." I pull the blankets tighter to my body. *I'm still naked.*

After he walked out, I went straight to my bed and have been here ever since. The hallway light illuminates part of my room, revealing Leah with a styrofoam takeout container and a large iced coffee. She sits on my bed and pats my legs under the covers.

"Did Liam put you into a sex coma? It's almost dinner time," she giggles and then stops short, taking notice of my swollen eyes. "Jesus, Maddy. I haven't seen you like this since Sean's funeral," she gasps. "What the fuck happened? Is it because he is leaving today? Are you going to miss him? Is it the drugs wearing off?" Lee rambles on, ultimately getting the wrong idea of why I'm crying.

I sit up and take a sip of the coffee Leah hands me, letting its magic wake my taste buds and energy. "I had the most incredible time with him in the shower before it all went to *shit*. He freaked out when he found out I was a virgin. We didn't even technically have sex before he stopped and left. He said that I deserved better, and he has secrets that he can't tell me..." I rehash the memories in my mind as I tell Leah. "Also, something else about being a 'dangerous man'..." I trail off, looking to her for possible answers.

She shrugs her shoulders. "Maybe, he's in the *mob*," she jokes.

"Oh yes, I'm sure he lives a double life. Mobster by day, college bar bouncer by night," I find myself laughing with my best friend at the ridiculous notion.

"You'd make a *hot* mob wife," she continues our outrageous conversation.

My stomach growls, prompting me to take a peek at what Leah brought me. Opening the lid, I am delighted to find our favorite Chinese takeout. She hands me a plastic fork and I dive in, stuffing my face with fried rice.

"Has he texted or called you?" she inquires, nodding a head

to my phone on the end table. I pop an entire fried dumpling in my mouth before grabbing my phone to check.

Scrolling through my notifications, I see drunk texts from my best friend Alexis. She is currently studying at Arizona State but will be home for winter break as well. I need to fill her in on everything that's transpired soon. She already knows about my crush on Liam. Scrolling some more I come across a new message alert for my online dating account.

Killian.

Nothing from Liam.

I shake my head at Leah because my mouth is too full to talk. She gives me a sympathetic look. "Maybe it's for the best Mad, let him be a big bad gangster. He'll come running back when he realizes what he lost—guaranteed. Why don't you reactivate your online dating app in the meantime and find someone who is DTF? You know the best way to get over someone is to get under them," she wiggles her eyebrows at me. "Plus, I am sure you have the biggest case of lady blue balls. What an asshole to leave you high and dry—or wet in your case."

I take another big sip of my coffee. I feel more human and level-headed, now that I've had some food and caffeine. Leah's presence always helps too.

She's right. *It's Liam's loss.*

"About that. I actually reactivated my dating app. Before we left for the bar yesterday, I was talking to a man named Killian. Ironically, he sounds Irish as well—just my luck," I laugh at the pun. "Anyway, he's TDH, 28, owns his own business, and lives in New York City. Here look—" I show her his profile and watch her facial features as she scans through his pictures.

She whistles and licks her lips, "He is wicked *hot.*"

I notice that there is a message from him and it hits me. I was busy with Liam last night and didn't get the chance to respond to Killian. Would it be wrong to continue talking to him? If I am being a hundred percent honest, I am *livid* with Liam but I am nowhere near *over him*.

"He is looking for a commitment, Leah. And he seems like a really nice guy. I don't want to hurt him by getting involved with him. Especially considering how strongly I feel about how things left off with Liam." I push my rice around with my fork. "I mean it *was* nice talking to him. He did experience his own heartbreak, so maybe he'll be more understanding and actually respect me and my own choices. Hopefully, his job isn't 'dangerous' like *Liam's*." I scowl at the thought. *Clearly, I'm still bitter about last night.*

"Honey, you are *single*. That means it's perfectly okay to casually date. Hell, date someone else too! Liam didn't claim you. Going on dates doesn't mean you're marrying the guy or that it will even work out in the end. Just see how it goes. Killian may even make you realize you are better off without Liam," she declares while stealing a piece of General Tso's chicken.

"I'll message him back in a little while. I just need to get some fresh air first." I'm becoming more and more confident with the plan we've made.

Liam, who?

I place my food and coffee on the end table and secure the lid. Sliding my towel around my body, I make my way over to the dresser and grab whatever is on top. I'm pulling on my neon pink hoodie when Leah gasps.

"Oh my God, Maddy. This will be the last I bring up Liam— for now—but you have to *see* Chase's face!" She presses her hands in prayer over her lips and starts laughing—*snorting*, actually.

I raise my eyebrows at her and toss my towel in the hamper. "Okay..." I wait for her to continue.

"Liam must have fucked him up good. Both his eyes are black and blue, and his nose is broken. He's got a cut under his eye and his wrists are all scratched up. His Facebook post says he got jumped last night coming home from the bar. The University's Facebook page is advising students to be extra vigilant when walking home at night." She snorts again. I stare at her for a few seconds, processing it all.

The blood on Liam's shirt.

'I'm a dangerous man.'

The mysterious business trip.

'Chase won't be bothering you or any other woman ever again.'

'There are secrets I hold that I can't tell you about...'

What if he *actually is* in the mob and Chase fucked with the wrong man?

"Earth to Maddy. Are you okay?" she asks nervously, waving a hand in front of my face. I snap out of it and walk her through my unsettled thoughts.

"I mean...it's not a completely ridiculous theory..." Leah trails off. "Would that change your perspective of why he left you?" *Would it? Would I still have chosen to be with him if I knew the truth?*

"He makes me feel *safe*, Leah. He's always protected me. I don't think he'd ever intentionally hurt me. I...I don't think it would bother me. Is that bad?" I confess.

She gets up and walks to the door. "I think you should message Killian back," she says firmly, leaving me to my thoughts.

CHAPTER 10

MADISON

I WALK OUT of my last class of the day. I'm excited and *more than ready* to be getting a week off for Thanksgiving break. I was supposed to be heading home to New York, but my mom got stuck in Florida on her vacation. A Nor'easter is the cause of her canceled flight. Connecticut is projected to accumulate the highest snow totals. I highly doubt she is disappointed to be spending another few days with her girlfriends in Miami. I don't mind though, I get the house my roommates and I share to myself. Oh, and I am meeting Killian for the first time in person.

Yeah, you read that right.

Since the day after Liam left, Killian and I have been talking nonstop. It's insane how much we have in common. In such a short time, we've discussed everything under the sun, from our favorite foods to our biggest fears in life. His biggest fear is losing his dad, which means he'll take over the family business.

My phone has been glued to my hand. Even in class or at work, I find myself sneaking my phone out for a fix. The damn thing is constantly needing a charge.

I just about fell off my bed when he called me for the first time. *What is it about men with accents—especially Irish ones—*

that turn me on? I think it's a husky voice and terms of endearment that do me in.

My phone rings in the back pocket of my skinny jeans. A smile forms on my lips as I take in the caller ID. I wrap my knitted scarf more securely around my neck. The flurries are starting to come down more heavily now.

"Hello?" I answer, pretending I have no clue who is calling.

"You haven't put my name in your contacts yet? Do I mean that *little* to you, love?" he plays as his gravelly laugh fills the line.

"Oh Killian, I didn't realize it was you..." I continue our little game. "All jokes aside, I have you saved in my phone as *Darth Vader* and your ringtone is already "The Imperial March.""

"I'm cool with that, as long as you are willing to come to the *'Dark Side'* my Queen," he banters.

I wholeheartedly laugh, which he makes me do—often. We are in the habit of fueling each other with sarcasm. He has been nothing short of kind, funny, and an absolute gentleman since we began talking. We even Facetimed a few times. Mostly before bed. Let me tell you, he is just as handsome as his pictures painted him to be.

His life is definitely mysterious. That's for sure. Killian has hinted many times that he owns many different kinds of real estate—including the bar we frequent. Schmitty's. *Small world.* I have been wondering if he knows Liam. I just haven't found the courage yet to ask him.

"What time will you be here?" I ask on a more serious note. Butterflies swarm my stomach—again—the *warning* kind.

"I just got in the car as we speak. Should take me about an hour and a half. An hour if I drive the way I like."

I approach my car in the parking lot and get in, cranking the heat and throwing my backpack on the passenger seat. "You better make it to me in one piece, or there will be hell to pay," I threaten.

His laugh comes through my car's audio. "Sweetheart, there is nothing to worry about. I am a fantastic driver. I'm just eager to see you, that's all," he discloses.

"I am too. I'm *especially* interested in seeing this 'special entrance' you speak of at Schmitty's." He told me that we would be going to my favorite bar for a few drinks. He also informed me I would see a side to it I'd never seen before. "Will my normal 'night out' attire work? Or is there some special handshake and dress code I need to know about?" I half-joke, curious as ever.

"As for the handshake, none needed—I own the place. Everyone knows who I am," he says sardonically. "As for the attire...a little black dress always works just fine."

I suddenly feel very anxious. *Am I making a huge mistake here?* I don't even know this man, *really*. We've talked every single day for the last few weeks. We learned a lot about our families, our careers, dreams, goals...but *I don't know him*. I *know* he was engaged before and that it fell through due to family drama. I *know* his dad is dying from pancreatic cancer, and he's taken over more responsibilities of the family business...

"Madison, are ya there?" his voice breaks through my mini panic attack.

"Yeah. Sorry, I was focusing on the road," I white lie.

"No worries. I'll let you go so you can *focus,*" he clearly knows something is up with me. "I've got another call coming in. Madison...*relax*. I promise you are safe with me. There is no pressure tonight...I'm not trying to sleep with you on the first date—if that's what you're worried about," he speaks more softly.

His words were exactly what I needed to calm down. *I may have been freaking out a tad.* "Thank you, Killian. I'll see you in a little while. Please drive safe."

SIPPING MY RED WINE, I give myself a once-over in the full-length mirror. *I may or may not have had half the bottle.* I settled on a simple knee-length, long sleeve black dress. The front dips into a nice V, revealing just the right amount of cleavage. Black stiletto heels with small rhinestone bows on the back wrap around my feet. *I look hot but still classy.* My phone buzzes on the dresser with a text from Killian:

KILLIAN

15 minutes until your chariot awaits my Queen...

I am so fucking nervous. Not only am I meeting Killian in person, but this is my first time back at Schmitty's since I was roofied. That knowledge alone brings about a whole collage of memories. Good ones and bad. *What if Liam is there?* Fuck. I didn't even think about that possibility—considering he's been completely MIA.

No calls.

No texts.

Leah said he hasn't been at the bar either. I take the remaining swig of my wine and leave the glass on top of the dresser. *I am a terrible person.* The thought of possibly seeing Liam again is now driving me mad with anticipation. More so than meeting Killian for the first time.

I skim through my jewelry rack and find a nice pair of diamond earrings to pair with a tennis bracelet. Tonight is going to be a simple look. I have a feeling this isn't going to be the typical *Schitty's* night. It's Thanksgiving Eve. The night everyone floods the bar for a drink with their old friends. I'm sure it will be packed with locals and those who stayed on campus instead of heading home for break.

I apply my nude lipstick and liner and toss them in my black clutch. My eyes linger on the pack of cigarettes on the desk, but I think better of it. I haven't smoked since my last night at the bar. *It's probably best I avoid the smoking section out back anyway.*

I grab my phone off the dresser and shoot a quick text to Alexis. She's all caught up on my dating life and the events that occurred earlier this month:

MADISON

Killian should be here any minute! Wish me luck. Also, I am sending you my location in case I go missing lol.

LEXI

You got this girl. Send me a picture of your outfit!

I snap a picture of myself in the mirror and send it.

LEXI

You look fucking hot. He won't be able to keep his hands off you. Enjoy yourself. Don't overthink everything like you always do, just enjoy the night and see where it leads...

There is a knock on the door. He's here. *Deep breaths, Maddy.*

I send one last text and share my location with Alexis before tossing my phone in my bag.

MADISON

Thanks, Lexi 🩶

WITH ONE LAST glance in the mirror, I hit the lights and grab my jacket and scarf.

I see him through the glass-paneled door. He has one hand in the pocket of his gray overcoat. The other is wrapped around his phone. His head is down, and he's laughing to himself. *I wonder what is so funny?* I take a minute to study him before opening the door.

CHAPTER 11

KILLIAN

I PULL INTO HER DRIVE, already knowing which house it is. I've passed it many times on the way to Schmitty's (which is only known as *Schmitty's* upstairs). Those who know my family and the elite members who frequent the exclusive underground club know it as *The Triskelion*.

I wasn't sure how bad the roads would be, so I drove the Cadillac Escalade. The snow has been coming down pretty heavily. Most of the highways are pretty slick. I park by her front door and leave the engine running, making sure to keep the inside toasty warm for her.

My black dress shoes crunch along the snow blanketing the ground as I approach her door. That's when I remember my plan to lighten the mood of our first introduction. I knock twice on the door and quickly scroll Youtube to find the "Imperial March (Darth Vader's Theme Song)" by John Williams. I laugh, feeling lighter than I have in a long time.

The door swings open, and *my god*, she is a sight for sore eyes. Lately, the only people I've been around are corrupt men and cranky middle-aged nurses. I have barely left my father's side in our New York City home.

I take a moment to really take in her beauty. My eyes roam

over her from head to toe. A tight, low-cut dress clings to her curves. The kind that dips into cleavage I've been dying to explore. I like how she listened to my suggestion of a little black dress. The hem of it lands just above her tan, muscular legs. Shiny black toenails peep through a pair of black suede 'fuck me' heels. *Most men are turned on by red or even white nail polish but black is hot as sin.*

Her silky brown hair is curled and pulled to one side. And her makeup is minimal with just a winged liner and dusting of sparkled shadow. She looks like a goddamn Queen. *The nickname suits her.*

Madison's eyes meet mine with a devious smile, knowing this game we are playing has only just begun—*and I fucking love it.* I stand at the threshold of her door and take notice of the bottle of red wine on the kitchen counter. *Ahh, she needed a little liquid courage to take the edge off.* Her cheeks heat a beautiful pink when she realizes where my gaze has gone.

"I was nervous...and wine always...calms me..." she trails off as I pull her into a hug, unable to keep my hands off her.

"I already told you, there is no reason to be nervous around me. You are safe with me, love. I promise you," I try to reassure her. She relaxes her shoulders, releasing all that tension she was holding. Leaving her hands linked around my back, she pulls away slightly. Gorgeous brown eyes look up at me with more confidence than she was sporting prior.

"It is nice to '*officially*' meet you, Killian," she giggles. "Even though it feels like I have known you for years."

"It's a pleasure to '*officially*' meet you as well, Ms. Marrone," I agree while running my hands down her arms. *I already know so much more about her than she knows of me.* I take her hands in mine and give them a gentle squeeze. "Ready to go?" I nod towards the car in the driveway.

"Yes. I can't wait to see what Schmitty's looks like with the owner on my arm," she winks. *Oh sweetheart, you are in for a surprise*. She grabs her leather jacket off of the chair, slips it on, and wraps a Burberry scarf around her neck. I step outside, giving her space to lock up the house.

She pulls the handle closed after locking the door from the inside. I wrap my arm around her waist and help her down the few steps off her porch. I guide her to my murdered out Cadillac, open the door for her and help her in. I'm about to close it when a ridiculously adorable laugh escapes her plump lips. Pausing, I hold the door open just enough to lean my head in.

"Is something funny, *my Queen*? Is this chariot not up to your standards?" I inquire in the most proper voice.

"Oh no, *sir*. It is *very* accommodating. It suits *you* perfectly. You know...with the whole...'Darth Vader' thing you got going on—that's all," she snickers again. *Damn this woman and her sarcasm. Don't even get me started on what it did to my cock, when she called me sir.*

WE ARE PARKED by the back entrance. Madison's eyes go wide as she notices two of my men walk toward us. I get out to greet them.

"Sir."

"Killian," they say in unison, nodding and shaking my hand. I am about to open Madison's door when she opens it and gets out herself. *One thing she will need to learn while she is with me is that she'll never open another door again.* I take her hand in mine and walk us to the door. This time placing my hand on her lower back and opening it for her.

"Maybe it would be fun to make up our own secret handshake—just for shits and giggles," she smirks at me while entering the building. *Jesus, this woman is so sassy. I fucking love it.*

I wrap her hand in mine, curling my fingers around hers. I

caress my thumb over her soft skin, bring her knuckles up to my lips and place a gentle kiss. "How's that for a handshake?" I beam.

Madison looks at me, raising an eyebrow when I press the button for the elevator. She has been curious as ever since I alluded to there being another side to this bar. When it arrives, we step in, and I punch in a code to access the lower level.

"Can you keep a secret, lass?" I turn to her as the elevator makes its descent. Her eyes light up with eagerness. She nods her head once while gnawing on her lower lip.

The elevator doors open to a large corridor. Two more of my men stand at each set of doors at the end. I place her hand back in mine and walk us to the entrance of the underground club. The doors on the left go off to mine and Liam's private offices; the doors on the right open to the club. I push open the door on the right and usher her in—

"Welcome to *The Triskelion*, beautiful."

CHAPTER 12

MADISON

"IF I LOSE MYSELF" *by OneRepublic and Alesso* is playing through the speakers as we walk in. I lean over the glass balcony to look around, amazed at the sight in front of me. *There is no way Schmitty's is upstairs.*

Don't get me wrong, Schmitty's isn't a hole in the wall, *but it's not this.*

There are two levels with staircases on both sides that lead down to the dance floor and a wall-to-wall bar. The DJ is performing from a large, central stage, slightly raised above the dance floor. Half-naked dancers are in clear birdcages on either side of the stage. A huge chandelier hangs from the industrial ceiling with exposed beams and more laser lights.

The upstairs is a U shape. There are sections of dark couches and tables spread throughout. They appear to be VIP areas. A few closed doors line the walls of each side—frosted glass obscuring what hides behind them. Lights and smoke scatter the room as I scan the faces of a few of those dancing. Quite a crowd has gathered here. All of them seem to be thoroughly enjoying themselves. Wait. *Is that my anatomy professor?*

The bar is directly across from the stage. A giant waterfall wall with neon underlighting cascades from behind it. The top of the bar is sparkly white quartz, and the base is some more frosted glass. *This place is fucking awesome.* I wish Leah and Lexi were here to see this right now.

I feel his *eyes* on me as I process this all. "What do you think?" He asks, casually leaning against the balcony railing—like the *God* that he is.

Dark dress pants cling tight to muscular legs, leaving little to the imagination. *Holy crap.* His white dress shirt is tucked into his pants, with the top two buttons open, exposing his chest. And a simple black leather belt with a silver buckle wraps around his hips. His dark hair is neatly brushed back and buzzed on the sides, with a few grays scattered throughout. Five o'clock shadow peppers his strong jawline. Damn, *he is the definition of Tall, Dark and Handsome—that's for sure.*

I walk over and wrap my hand around his upper arm. "Killian, this place is incredible," I shout over the music. The smile I get in return is one full of pride.

A scantily dressed waitress comes up next to us. "Would you like a drink, Mr. Kennedy?"

He turns to me, paying no mind to the waitress at all. "Would you like something to drink, love?" he whispers in my ear, wrapping a hand around my waist and pulling me flush against his hard body. His clean, refreshing scent floats in the space around us.

"Sure. I'll take a glass of Prosecco, please." I look up at him, curious what he'll be drinking. My heart begins to beat wildly. I am finding it hard to be near him without being extremely turned on. It doesn't help that I'm pressed up against him.

He gently tugs the scarf around my neck, slowly pulling it loose. My pulse picks up even more. He shrugs out of his jacket and then helps me take off mine, handing them to the waitress. "I will have an Old Fashioned, and Ms. Marrone will have a glass of our finest champagne. Please have a couple of bottles delivered to VIP suite two. Thank you, Olivia."

"Would you like me to bring an NDA as well?" she asks, directing her attention to me.

"That won't be necessary," he says firmly. With a nod, Olivia walks away, but not before giving me a nasty look. She is not pleased that I am here with Killian. I hold back the desire to be a two-year-old and stick my tongue out at her. *Bitch.*

KILLIAN TAKES me to a secluded room behind one of the frosted doors on the left. We are sitting on an elegant suede couch. A glass table holds our drinks and two more bottles of champagne in an ice bucket. A vacant stripper pole is in the center of the room. White tufted walls with blue ambient lighting line the ceiling, making it feel more relaxed and private than the main room—which is the complete opposite of how I feel at the moment. *NDA? And why are we in a room with a stripper pole? He said he wasn't trying to sleep with me on the first date.*

"I can see your mind running a million miles an hour," he rubs my knee. "I didn't have you sign an NDA because even though we just met, I *trust* you." He tucks my hair behind my ear and lifts my chin until we make eye contact. I've been avoiding looking at him since we came in here.

"Why would I need to sign an NDA?" I ask harsher than I intended to.

He sighs, removes his hand, and takes a sip of his drink. "There are many high-profile people who come here, including celebrities. We have all our guests sign them."

The butterflies are back, assaulting my stomach. Warning me something is not right here. I take a few sips of my champagne with the hopes it will help.

"Madison, look at me."

I do and what I see there are a set of kind, warm eyes. "Ask me anything at all, I promise to tell you the truth. If you feel uncomfortable or don't think this will work, I will take you home and you won't ever have to see me again," he declares.

"You aren't just an exclusive underground club owner, are you?"

He finishes off his drink and returns his full attention to me. "No. I'm not. My Da is the head of the Tri-State Syndicate and I am next in line to run the organization."

"Meaning..." I trail off, already knowing what he is going to say.

"Meaning, I am about to become the head of the Irish Mob in the Tri-State area," he confirms.

My mouth goes dry. *Fuck. Fuck. Fuck. Here I was worried about Liam being in the mob when I am literally dating the fucking head of it!* I grab my glass and drain the rest of its contents. I know I said I wouldn't care, but that was when I was seriously lusting over Liam. Rose-colored glasses had tinted my vision. *I am so naive. So stupid.* The signs were there. I just ignored them and my intuition. *What have you gotten yourself into Maddy?*

CHAPTER 13

KILLIAN

SHE'S SCARED. I don't *blame* her—*she should be*. I just dropped a huge bomb on her. If I am being honest, I am already falling for her. Her looks are a *bonus*. It's her mind, her drive, and her passion for the people and things she loves, that make me want her.

To prevent both of us from future heartache and complications, I needed to be completely candid with her. *Madison needs to know what she is getting herself involved in.* I don't want to hide my life from her. Certain things she may need to stay privy to, while others may be better left unsaid. But not the fact that I am a very dangerous and powerful man. If we continue this, she'll have my security following her whenever I'm not around.

I pop open another bottle of champagne and grab myself an empty glass. I pour myself some before pulling her shaking hand closer to mine to refill hers.

"Why would a *mobster* like you want anything to do with a girl like me? Look at this place," she says, fanning her arm out. "You have gorgeous women all around you." She takes another large sip of her drink, her eyes shooting daggers in my direction.

A deep, boisterous laugh escapes me. I haven't been called a 'mobster' *ever* in my life. "Sweetheart, do you realize how much this lifestyle bothers me? The majority of the women here are fake as fuck and don't hold a goddamn candle to you." Clearly, this woman doesn't see how amazing she is. She is the full package. *How can she not see that?* Men would kill to be in my position right now—women too.

When she doesn't say anything, I try to explain myself better. "I never wanted to take over my Da's position. I *envied* those working a 9-5 or those with a 'normal' career. As a lad, I wanted to become an engineer. Find a wife one day, get married and build a family. A simple life. But I wasn't born into a *simple life*, love."

Her eyes reach mine again. *There she is.* "Will you kill me if I walk away?" she whispers.

Another laugh slips out, and she stares at me like I've grown two heads. "No, Madison. I won't *kill* you. I told you, you're safe with me. And I meant that. I care about you a lot."

The tension dissolves from her face before she speaks. "*If* —she holds up a pointer finger—"and this is a *big if*. If I decide to continue dating you, will I be able to finish my nursing degree and get a job in a hospital?"

She is too fucking cute, worrying about a nursing degree after what I just told her.

"You can have whatever you want, sweetheart. Whatever makes you happy. But you don't need to work if you don't want to. You'll be taken care of."

"I want to help people, Killian." She contemplates, biting on her black polished thumbnail.

"Then you will," I promise. My thumb slides over her flushed cheek. "Please give me a chance, Madison," I beg, feeling more vulnerable than I ever have. *I don't beg anyone. Ever.*

"Alright."

"Alright," I repeat with a huge smile forming on my lips. I

pull her closer to me, moving in for a kiss when she places a gentle hand on my chest—

"But I need more time." My smile falters from the blow. I tilt my head and kiss her on the cheek instead.

"Time is all we have." I pull her into a hug, and she willingly wraps her arms around me. Madison lays her head on my shoulder and lets out a huge sigh. I hold her there, stroking her hair for a few minutes, enjoying the stillness I rarely get.

"Killian?" She pulls back to look at me with eyes that burn with a fire I haven't seen yet.

"You can kiss me now," she smiles coyly.

And I do just that.

I've wanted to do this since I first laid eyes on her. So I kiss her with every built-up emotion I've held onto over the years. *A failed engagement. Rivals. My Da on his deathbed.* Her kiss reassures me that, together, we can make it through the darkness.

I pull her on top of my lap, letting her straddle me. She kisses me again, dipping her tongue in my mouth, and rubbing against my erection. *The little vixen was worried I was going to move too fast.* I grow harder beneath her and there is no chance she isn't feeling it. My hands roam the exposed skin on her thighs then over the swell of her perfect arse. I lick my way up from the dip in her breasts to her neck. Her dress bunches at her thighs, giving me a great view of her black lace panties. She tilts her head back, granting me better access to latch on to her throat. My hands move to her waist and over her tits, giving them a gentle squeeze.

She lets out a throaty moan, and it's my undoing. The animal inside me is clawing its way out. I lower the neckline of her dress to expose her black lace bra. Her pink nipples tease me through the delicate material. I pull one nipple taut through the lace, procuring another moan from her gorgeous lips. She is watching me now as I give her other nipple attention.

Madison is lucky I don't rip this dress in half and take her on this couch like I'd like to. I am *trying* to restrain myself. She was worried about having sex on the first date prior to the alcohol. I am trying my best to honor that and she isn't making it easy. *No woman has ever had this instant effect on me—including Selena.*

I am about to feast some more on those gorgeous breasts when my phone rings in my pocket. I have to answer it too. "Saved by the bell, sweetheart," I tell her as I pull her dress back up and retrieve my phone. She goes to get off my lap, but I grip her arse, firmly holding her in place.

The caller ID is private. Most likely one of my men on a burner phone.

"Hello?" I answer as I rub my thumb against her plump lips.

"It's done, Kil." Liam's voice comes through the line.

Madison takes my thumb between her lips and sucks. *Fuuuck.* She is not making this easy at all.

I clear my throat. "That's grand. You just made me a *very* happy man," I say into the phone as I look into the eyes of the beautiful queen in front of me. That elicits a smile from her.

"Plan on staying for another month to make sure that there is no immediate threat of retaliation. We'll be in touch soon, *sweetheart,*" I laugh while hanging up. Madison raises her eyebrows in what seems to be confusion mixed with...*is that jealousy?*

"Sorry about that. Business as always," I say, ready to pick up where we left off. She tries to get up again, but I pull her back down. "What just happened, Madison?" I ask, worried about her change in demeanor.

"'*Sweetheart*'?" She repeats my conversation with Liam.

I throw my head back and laugh. "That was one of the brothers, love. He and I joke with each other like that. I'm sorry, you must have thought I was on the phone with another woman." I pull her face to mine and give her a chaste kiss.

"*Know this.* There are *no* other women in my life–besides you, Madison Marrone."

My phone buzzes with a weather alert. I tap open the notification and see that there is about to be a heavy band of snow moving into our area. The blizzard warning is in effect until tomorrow evening. "I hate to cut this short, but we need to get you home. The storm is about to get pretty bad.

CHAPTER 14

MADISON

WE ARRIVE BACK at my house after a treacherous drive home. The roads are a disaster. Snow is coming down heavily, and the visibility is horrendous. A good amount has already accumulated since our time at The Triskelion. Killian took extra caution, driving extremely slow. I'm sure he would not have been as careful if I wasn't there. He parks by the front door and leaves the car running. Before I even have a chance to get out, he's there opening my door for me. He scoops me up the way he did in the parking lot earlier and places me on the porch. *True gentleman.*

"Thank you for a lovely time. Tonight went so much better than I had hoped for." Snowflakes start to dust his hair. "I'll make sure you get inside safely, but then I need to head to my hotel. The roads are going to continue to get worse."

"Killian, that is ridiculous. You're not driving in this weather! The roads are already bad. Plus, I have all this food for Thanksgiving tomorrow and no one to share it with." I look up at his gorgeous face, his nose is already red from the wind.

He looks back at the Cadillac idling and then back at me. Indecision marring his perfect features.

"You're sure?" His features morph into that of hope.

"Positive. Who am I to deny you a warm place to stay and *ride* out the storm?" *Ride.* Thoughts of us back at the club resurface in my mind. *Him licking up my neck. His thumb in my mouth, his strong hands gripping my ass.* My lace thong is already soaking wet.

He raises a brow, clearly picking up on my double entendre. My cheeks flush at the realization that I will wake up next to this man tomorrow. *Yes, I know that I was hesitant to sleep with him earlier.* It's as if the danger of the situation I find myself in is fueling my desire for him. I don't want to be Mama Maddy tonight. I've been taking the safe route my whole life. I want to be Mad Maddy tonight and take this giant leap of faith. I don't let him respond. I unlock the door with my school ID and leave it open for him.

Killian closes the door behind him and locks it, wiping his feet off on the mat. He places an overnight duffle bag next to the door and removes his jacket. I reach for it, draping it over my own on the kitchen chair. He bends down and gently removes each of my heels, leaving them by the door.

"Here's the deal, love," he starts, pulling me flush against his warm body. "I will stay tonight, *but* I'll take the couch." Disappointment floods my face. I step out of his hold, putting some space between us.

"I know I made it seem earlier that I wasn't interested in sleeping with you—" he holds his hand up to stop me.

"You said you needed time, and I respect that. I am *trying* to do the right thing by you, Madison," he sighs.

"The couch is a piece of shit. You aren't sleeping there." I point towards my bedroom down the hall. "You can sleep in my bed. It's only a full, but I'm sure you won't mind," I try my best to persuade him.

A beautiful smile graces his lips as he pulls me back against him. "Fine, but we are going to *sleep* in that bed. Tomorrow we can have ourselves a day cooking and getting to know each other more."

I look up at him, "I was wrong about you."

He looks down, staring into my eyes with a curious expression. "How do you mean?"

"I said you were *Darth Vader*, but I was wrong. Killian, you are *Anakin Skywalker*." I rub my thumb over his lips. His eyes become glassy and fill with unshed tears. He swiftly wipes the moisture away, kisses my forehead, and walks down the hall toward my bedroom. *Men. Always afraid to be vulnerable.*

"You coming, sweetheart?" He turns around to wink at me.

I open the door to my room and make space for him to enter. He looks around, takes in my bed, and touches the twinkle lights wrapped around my bed frame.

"Nice touch," his lips curl into a smile. He stalks towards me and pulls me into a passionate kiss. Leaning his forehead against mine, he lets out a sigh. "Thank you for saying that, Madison. You don't realize how much it meant to me," he whispers.

I brush a strand of untamed hair off his eyebrow. "You don't have to wear a mask around me, Killian. I see the real you. It's okay to be vulnerable around me."

He kisses me again, and we go at it, not coming up for air. Our hands roam all over each other. Our teeth nip and clash. We are entangled and clumsy, which results in us bumping into my dresser. Of course, my empty wine glass comes crashing to the floor, interrupting our fun.

"Don't fucking move an inch!" he commands. He picks me up and throws me over his shoulder, swatting my ass in the process and laughing. Where is your vacuum?" he asks while depositing me on my bed.

"I can clean it, Killian. Just grab me my slippers," I point to the bottom of my closet.

"Absolutely not. Stay in that bed, beautiful." He schools me with a *not to be fucked with* look. "Now, where is the vacuum?"

"In the hallway closet, the second door on the right." I shake my head and smile at his need to be the perfect fucking gentleman.

"ALRIGHT," he says on his return from putting the vacuum away, "where were we?" He gives me a mischievous look.

"You were just about to unzip my dress," I get off the bed and turn around, placing my hair over my shoulder.

He whistles while approaching me. "Is that so?" Warm hands brush over my shoulders and down my bare back. He reaches for my zipper and drags it down inch by inch, brushing sweet kisses over my neck and shoulder. "Madison..." he says my name in warning.

I let my dress fall to my feet and spin around to face him. I unbutton his shirt, trying to be hasty before he changes his mind. He helps me by holding up each arm so I can unbutton the cuffs. I step back and watch with eagerness as he continues undressing. *He unbuckles his belt and pops the button before lowering his zipper with excruciating slowness.*

Killian toes off his shoes and leans down to discard his socks. On his return, I push the dress shirt off his shoulders, letting it fall to the floor. He lowers his dress pants and steps out of them. A snug pair of gray boxer briefs cling to his hips. My attention directs to the outline of his erection pressing against his thigh. *Woah.*

I boldly lead him to my bed and drag the comforter down. Laying down on my back, I spread my legs, inviting him to join.

"What am I going to do with you, Madison?" He stares at me in awe before claiming my lips again.

Killian kisses my neck as I rake my nails down his back.

Tattooed arms surround me in a warm cocoon. His hand reaches between us, rubbing circles around my clit through the fabric. I lift my hips, adding more pressure to where I need it most. He continues lazily stroking me as goosebumps erupt over my skin. Lifting his head, he looks at me, his brows coming together again. He wants this just as much as I do. Removing his hand, he hooks his thumb into the side of my thong.

"If we do this, I won't be able to stop myself. I'm using all the restraint I have left to do right by you. Tell me to stop, and we'll go straight to bed."

"Don't stop," I lean forward, whispering against his lips. That's all it took for him to rip my thong on both sides. He runs his two fingers down my wetness, exploring deeper. Breaching my entrance and capturing my lips in his, he pushes them in all the way. I sigh into his mouth and buck my hips forward, hitting his palm.

"You're so wet for me," he whispers while thrusting his fingers inside me at a deliciously torturous pace.

"And so fucking tight."

He continues his expedition until I am clinging to his biceps and riding out an incredible orgasm. I sprinkle kisses all over his collarbone and neck while removing his boxer briefs. I add them to our growing pile of clothes on the floor.

"I didn't bring a condom, love," he groans, pausing his mission of unclasping my bra. He lowers his head onto my breasts. The feel of him sans boxers, teasing my already sensitive skin, is driving me mad with need.

"I'm on the pill." I lift my hips and guide him to where I need him. I don't want to stop now. We *can't* stop now. *Been there, done that. Can't a girl just get laid?*

After a moment of contemplation, he unstraps my bra, tossing it behind us victoriously. "I am clean. I get checked regularly, and it's been a while, honestly," he confesses, running himself up and down my slickness.

He leans one arm on the pillow above me, the other wrapped around my hip. In one motion, he thrust all the way in. A moan escapes my lips as he becomes fully seated. The feel of him bare inside me is such a different sensation. This time it doesn't sting. Not the way it did last time. He begins to rock into me. Tenderly. Slowly.

Savoring my body.

Worshiping it.

Kissing him, I meet him thrust for thrust as his pace begins to quicken.

"Fuck, you're perfect. Come for me, beautiful." I cling to him as I feel another orgasm building deep inside me. This one is different than I've felt before. It's a slow burn, building, and building. It's like being on a rollercoaster—

The butterflies you feel the last few clicks before you creep over the edge.

The giant breath you inhale right before the big drop.

Feeling weightless on the descent.

In that moment, I realize the butterflies are a warning of the risk I am taking and the danger right in front of me. I know he will keep me safe, and that's all I need to enjoy the ride.

Stars invade my vision as a full-body orgasm takes me over. "Killian!" I scream out, *not giving a fuck*. No one is home but us. He follows right behind me, pulling out abruptly. I watch him grind down on his molars above me. He strokes himself once from base to tip before his abs flex. He leans over me, depositing his warm release on my stomach.

"Goddamn, Madison. I am a lucky man," he breathes out, crashing on the bed next to me. He snuggles me in closer and kisses me. "You. Are. Amazing."

"That was...*wow*." I let out a deep breath, my heartbeat whooshing in my ears. We take a few minutes to catch our breath, not saying anything. It's just the soothing sound of the wind, our heartbeats, and his hands rubbing up and down my arms. He eventually gets up and finds his way to the bathroom, returning with a warm washcloth.

Killian cleans my stomach off and throws the towel in the hamper. Getting back in bed, he pulls my back to his front and wraps his arms around me. "Sleep now, sweetheart. You're safe in my arms," he says, kissing the back of my head.

CHAPTER 15

KILLIAN

I WAKE up to the wind whipping noisily outside. The blizzard has been at it all night—like Madison and I. It's not expected to stop until later this evening. I glance down at the sated, sleeping beauty in my arms. My face beams with memories of last night. I can't even recall the last time I had a good night's sleep.

Removing my arms from our embrace, I lean over the bed and grab my pants. I fish through my pocket to retrieve my phone. A few text notifications are there as well as multiple weather alerts. I check the time—7:30 a.m. *You'd never know with these blackout curtains.* Madison stirs next to me but doesn't wake. A soft light is casted on her face from the string lights above. She is the most gorgeous woman I have ever met. *Inside and out.* Her heart is *pure gold.*

You can hear it in her words.

See it in her actions.

Feel it in her touch.

This woman could ask for the whole world on a silver platter, and I would provide it for her.

I place a gentle kiss on her forehead and slip out of bed. I collect our clothes on the floor, quietly sorting hers from mine.

Draping her dress and bra over her desk chair, I slip out of her room, leaving the door open a crack.

BACON IS FRYING on the stovetop griddle. Coffee is brewing in the Keurig (my second cup). I glance at my phone behind me on the kitchen island—8:30 a.m. Princess Maddy is still sleeping soundly down the hall. There hasn't been so much as a peep in that direction. I've already responded to quite a few calls, texts, and emails; went over a few contracts. It was a treat to sleep in today.

I am finishing up with the western omelets I made us when she pads down the hall, yawning. She has on a pair of black and white plaid pajama bottoms and an oversized gray sweatshirt.

"Good Morning, sweetheart," I say while plating the omelets. Her cheeks blush, and she smiles, taking in the breakfast plates on the counter.

"He cooks too! *Am I still dreaming?*" she laughs while pinching herself.

"Not dreaming," I pull her to me, about to place a kiss on her lips. She throws her finger up, pressing it against my lips.

Alarmed eyes meet mine."—I need to brush my teeth." She darts away to the bathroom.

Women and their worries over minuscule things. It's ridiculous. Newsflash: we don't give a fuck about your morning breath.

While she is brushing her teeth, I set the table. I'm not used to being domestic like this. Everything has been handed to me my whole life. There were always maids, housekeepers, chefs, and drivers.

My mum would cook when I was younger. Those are the only good memories I have of her. She left us around the time Liam came to live with us. My Da was having an affair. Mom wanted out of their loveless, tainted marriage. Her final straw was taking on another child—it was too much for her. She still lives in Ireland with her new husband. I haven't met him nor do I want to. I've maybe spoken to her a handful of times since she left. Birthdays have always been consistent. A card will get sent to the house—which now goes unopened.

"Want some coffee, love?" I shout over the water running in the bathroom.

She opens the door and pops her head out over the door frame, vigorously brushing her teeth. Her mouth is full of toothpaste foam, "Is that even a question, Kil?" she mumbles over the toothbrush. That eyebrow of hers is raised again. *The sass.* If she keeps it up, the toothbrush won't be the only thing in her mouth. My cock twitches at the thought of it.

Her on her knees.

Her soft lips wrapped around my shaft.

I head over to the Keurig, pull out the drawer of K-Cups and pick which one I think has Madison written all over it. *Pumpkin spice.* I load it in, place a mug below and hit start. The bathroom tap shuts off, filling the room with the irritating noise of the machine brewing.

Two warm arms wrap around my torso as she lays her head on my back. "How'd you know I like pumpkin spice?" she asks innocently.

I turn around and shrug. "Wild guess." I place a chaste kiss on her lips. "You and every girl in America have this strange obsession with pumpkin spice." I gather her in my arms and pull her into me. "I mean fuck, is it true they have pumpkin spice scented Ugg boots?"

She actually looks perplexed, wondering if a pair out there exists. Normally, I have a great poker face but with her, it seems to falter. It doesn't take long before my laughter comes pouring out.

"Are you calling me a *basic bitch*, Killian?" she giggles against me.

I plant a kiss on the top of her head. "You, my dear, are anything *but* basic."

MADISON PLACES our empty dishes in the sink and leans back against the island. In an exaggerated display, she rubs her stomach and stretches her arms over her head. Her sweatshirt lifts, revealing her tanned skin.

"Damn, that was delicious. I'm stuffed. Thank you for making breakfast."

My eyes don't stray from her exposed skin. Her own travel to where mine are glued.

"Funny, because I'm still hungry..." I slide my chair back noisily. I stride her way and grind my erection into her sweet spot.

She moans and pulls my lips into a kiss as I hoist her onto the counter. I push her back gently so she leans on her hands. Slowly, I untie her pajama bottoms and pull them over her arse and down her legs. They fall to the floor, leaving her bare to me. *Fuck. This woman went commando.* Her pussy is trimmed neatly above her slit.

I slide onto the bar stool and pull her to me, wrapping her legs around my shoulders. I run my nose up and down her folds, making her wiggle away.

"Killian!" she reprimands, attempting to scoot away from me. *But that won't do.* My fingers grip her arse and I pull her back towards me. "I haven't showered yet!" Red stains her cheeks with embarrassment.

"You have no reason to be self-conscious, sweetheart. Not around me." I take a deep inhale. She must have cleaned up earlier. Her pussy smells like a flowery feminine wash.

To prove my point, I flatten my tongue against her opening and slide it up. My tongue circles around her clit a few times as the sexiest sound spills from her mouth. I continue my pursuit by dipping two fingers inside of her, lazily going in and out. Her walls clench around the invasion. I suck her clit into my mouth, and she begins to writhe against my face.

I start to fuck her with my fingers.

She pulls my head closer to her core and rolls her hips against my face. I take turns, alternating my tongue and fingers, before stroking her precious bead and sucking it into my mouth.

"Damn, that feels so good..." she trails off, moaning and thrashing on my face. Her head is thrown back and her eyes are squeezed shut. Her legs start to quiver around my head. *She's close.*

Like a vice, she tightens around my fingers. Removing them, I dip my tongue into her channel and pinch her clit. Liquid sweetness explodes all over my tongue as she screams her climax to the ceiling. I lap at her, licking her clean as she shakes with aftershocks. Her fingers rub circles on my scalp while she comes back down to Earth.

I stand up, shove the stool back, and throw my black sweatpants down. She opens her eyes and stares at my cock greedily. I lift her arse up and slide into her. Her body is still trembling, post-climax. This isn't going to be like last night.

It's going to be hard.

And fast.

I pound into her, my knuckles turning white as I grip the edge of the granite. Madison clings to my biceps as I rock into her. The sounds of our passion and our bodies slapping against each other fills the air. Our breaths are uneven and frantic. I kiss the hell out of her.

"Touch yourself," I demand. She scrunches her eyebrows together but obeys. Shaky fingers circle her already sensitive clit. Within minutes she is clenching around me. I roar out my own climax, emptying my load inside her.

Pulling her face back to mine, I kiss her over and over again.

"Mine. Mine. Mine..." I whisper over her cheeks, her eyes, her chin, her jaw, and back to her lips.

Without a doubt, this woman has become my everything. She's all that matters. Every other worry or fear I had went out the window. She is *mine*.

CHAPTER 16

MADISON

TODAY IS the last day of the fall semester. *Hello,* winter break! I still need to complete a J-term, but then I can officially graduate with my BSN. I have enough credits to graduate a semester early—which is fantastic. This May, I will be walking for graduation alongside my peers.

Things with Killian have been amazing. We still talk non-stop since he was here for Thanksgiving. He stayed the entire weekend and even helped me cook a wonderful Thanksgiving dinner. If we weren't cooking, talking, or drinking—he was *feasting* on me. We had a ton of sex. When he left, I was extremely sore, but in the most satisfying way.

Since then, we have been apart, making it work over Facetime and texts. Some nights are sexier than others. And by that, I mean this phone sex isn't cutting it. It's driving me insane. I'm craving his touch in the worst ways.

I've felt a void since he's been back in New York. He's been extremely busy at home dealing with his dad in hospice. Mr. Kennedy's health has declined steadily over the last few weeks. I feel terrible that I can't be there for Killian, but I think he wants privacy as well. I can tell it is stressing him out. His eyes have dark rings underneath them on most days. He's been working late nights to make sure all is in order for when his dad passes.

Work and studying have been my life lately. Thank god for winter break. I need a breather. Leah and I are meeting for lunch at the cafeteria on campus before we head home for the holidays. I am leaving straight from campus. My car is already packed with items I will need over the break.

I MAKE a salad at the salad bar and grab a french onion soup. Leah is already diving into her panini at our favorite table by the television. *Jerry Springer* is on. It's been one of our favorite past times together since we met. We'd grab lunch between classes and watch the drama unfold.

"Hey, girl!" She gets up and pulls me into a hug. We've been so busy with finals that we barely had a chance to catch up.

"Hey, pretty lady." I give her a squeeze and rock us back and forth.

We sit, and Leah continues eating. She'll be heading home to Massachusetts for the break, and I'll be catching a ferry from Connecticut to Long Island in a few hours.

"How have things been with Killian?" she asks over a mouthful of panini.

"His dad is not doing great. It's getting close now," I scrunch my face up in sympathy.

"That sucks. Are you nervous that you are dating..." she looks around before throwing a hand up to shade her mouth, whispering, "... the head of the Mob?"

A nervous laugh escapes my lips. "A bit, but he makes me feel cherished and protected. I know that he would never let anything happen to me. It's crazy how I feel about him already. Sean was my first love, and Liam, well, that didn't even get a chance to take off the ground..." I trail off, taking a sip of my soup. Its contents taste bitter on my tongue.

She takes another bite of her panini and raises her eyebrows at the mention of Liam.

"Did you see him at the bar this weekend?" I ask her over a bite of Green Goddess salad, curiosity getting the best of me.

"No," she says, wiping her lips with a napkin. Shame stirs inside me. *In a way, I was hoping she would have said yes.* "You still haven't heard anything from him?"

"No. I would have told you," I say a little more harshly than I intended.

She stares at the TV, watching two women fight over a guy. Her thumb jabs towards the screen. "This shit is unreal, two women fighting over one man."

Her attention comes back to me. "Remember when we were worried that Liam was in the mob? And here you are dating the heir to the Tri-State Syndicate," Lee whispers again. "What a crazy world we live in." She shakes her head.

"Yup." I move my salad around my plate, no longer interested in eating. Memories of Liam have made their way to the surface. I carefully held them at bay for the last couple of months. Don't get me wrong. Killian is incredible. To be honest, I think I am falling in love with him. But there are still moments when Liam comes to mind. *I'm only human.* I can't help but think what could have been if he didn't leave.

What would he think of me now if he knew I was dating Killian?

If he knew just how dangerous Killian is.

"Babe, I can see you thinking way too much over there." Leah breaks me out of my pointless thoughts. It doesn't matter now.

I'm happy with Killian.

"You were thinking about Liam, weren't you?" she pushes for my dirty little secret.

My cheeks heat, feeling guilty for thinking about Liam when Killian has been an absolute gentleman. "I was, but it doesn't matter. He's gone, Lee. He chose his path."

She slides her hand across the table and places it on mine. "You are happy, right?"

"Yes. I am." And I mean those words. I haven't felt this alive —probably *ever*. Okay...that's a lie. *Once*. If I am being one hundred percent honest. *Ugh, Liam. Get out of my head!*

I AM BLASTING music and dancing on my drive down I95 toward the Bridgeport Ferry. The EDM music makes me reminisce.

Killian and I dancing in my kitchen while cooking for Thanksgiving. Me straddling him in the VIP room at The Triskelion. Liam about to claim my lips outside by the fire.

Fuck. I really need to stop this. He's only coming up in my mind because Leah brought him up, I try reasoning with myself. *Another lie.* He crosses my mind at least once daily. I'm always wondering if he'll ever message or call me.

I check my rearview mirror and get off the exit for the ferry. The same damn car has been following me since I left school. It's probably just another student taking the ferry home. *Wait. Liam has a black Audi. This one is almost the exact same. With dark-tinted windows and rims. It couldn't possibly be him. My mind is just fucking with me.*

I pull up to the dock and hand them my ticket before following the instructions to board. The car behind me must have gone up the opposite ramp of the ferry. I shrug it off. *Guess it was another student.*

As soon as I reach the upper deck, I get in line for a coffee. You'll be here forever if you don't get in line fast enough.

I sit in one of the booths, pop my headphones in, and hit

shuffle on my music. Scrolling through my phone, I open the Kindle App and start to read a book. Nothing like diving into a romance novel for the next hour and twenty. My eyes scan the crowd, wondering if there is a chance Liam could be onboard, but feeling ridiculous. *What are the chances of that being his Audi?*

A young bearded man wearing a leather jacket and beanie is about two booths in front of me. He is facing me, scrolling through his phone. He looks familiar, yet I can't place him. We exchange glances every few minutes. Warning signs fire away at me. He is watching me. *My intuition is telling me something isn't right.*

I try to stay calm and continue reading my book, looking up every few chapters. I don't want to bother Killian. There are plenty of people onboard as witnesses.

WE ARE PULLING into port when the speaker announces it is time to get back in our cars. I follow the crowd down the stairs, checking behind me to make sure *beanie dude* is not following me. *He's gone.* Maybe I have become paranoid because of who I'm dating.

I get into my car and hit the locks. *You can never be too careful these days.* Scanning the crowd—as the people watcher I am—I spot beanie dude getting into the black Audi across from me. *The same car that was behind me since I left school. Guess that solves that mystery. It's not Liam—but it's still strange.*

The ferry docks and begins unloading cars. My lane goes first. I pull onto the main road and head towards my home, anxious to see my family and tell them about Killian. Well, maybe not *everything.*

My rear view is clear. No Audi in sight. *It was probably all in my head.* I only get a few miles down the road before the black

Audi shows back up behind me. My heart beats widely in my chest, warning me of real danger. My fingers fly over the screen of my phone, calling Killian. It rings once before he picks up.

"Hello there, my *Queen*. Are you almost home? How was the ferry ride?"

"Killian," my voice is quavering and filled with anxiety. "I think someone is following me. They have been behind me since campus and got on the same ferry. Some guy sat across from me on the ship and kept looking at me, and now—"

His soothing yet commanding voice interrupts me. "Sweetheart, take a breath. He's one of my men. His name is Conor—big guy with a bushy beard? Drives a black Audi?" his gentle voice comes through the speakers of my car.

"Yes!" I let out a sigh of relief, sagging into my seat cushion a little more. Anger replaces my fear. "Why the hell do you have someone following me, Killian? Why didn't you tell me?" I raise my voice at him.

He laughs. *Fucking laughs.* "Killian, this isn't funny!" I shout again. He attempts to contain his laughter. "You are a spitfire, sweetheart. *I absolutely love it.*"

Silence fills the car when I don't laugh or say anything. "It's to keep you safe when I can't be with you, Madison. I want to be. Trust me, I do. You don't even know how fucking bad it's killing me that I can't be with you right now. Things are just difficult around here lately. Conor isn't going to interfere unless he needs to."

I can't tell if I feel comforted by that fact or mortified. "So he's going to be spying on me," I groan, like a petulant child.

"No. He isn't going to *spy* on you. Conor will not be reporting back to me on your every move," he laughs. "I don't need my men ogling over you."

"What are my parents going to think, with his car parked outside my house?" I say, tapping my fingers on the steering wheel apprehensively.

"He will not be seen, but *know this*—you *are* protected. The only time you will see him will be if you are driving somewhere...he may tail you."

I let out a sigh. "Fine, but you could have told me."

"I could have, but I don't want you to feel like you are being babysat—because you aren't. I would never forgive myself if anything happened to you. If I didn't have someone there to protect you."

"Kil, I miss you so much." I sound so needy.

"I miss you too, baby. *So much.* I'm *trying* to get some shit in order, so I can try and spend Christmas with you. Don't forget—New Year's Eve, you are *mine*. There will be a masquerade gala held at my home."

"That sounds amazing. I have never been to a *gala*—let alone a masquerade before. I'm looking forward to it."

"I'm looking forward to tearing that dress off you at the end of the night and fucking you in my bed." I squeeze my legs together, feeling the desire for him pulse through me at his vulgar words.

"I've got to go, sweetheart. I need to take this call. Facetime me when you're all settled in at home.

"I will... *I L*... I'll let you go." I hang up quickly. *I can't believe I almost told him I loved him.* I mean, I *think* I do. This is what love feels like, right? *Safe, secure, happy, adored.*

I dial Lexi's number next. We are meeting up later for a few drinks, and I'm more than excited to see my bestie. She and I are both home for the next few weeks. It sucks that with school, we rarely see each other anymore. The rest of the ride home, I bring her up to speed.

CHAPTER 17

MADISON

MY MOM WAS THRILLED to see me when I pulled into the driveway. It's been a few months since I've seen her. Our communication has been limited as well. Both of us have been busy with work and school respectively. It will be nice to finally catch up with her—I haven't told her about Killian yet. I don't think I will explain it all to her...just the 'need to know'. My mom is very conservative. I'm sure it wouldn't go over well if I told her Killian's profession.

"Have you called your dad to tell him you're home?" Mom asks while helping me take my bags from the trunk of my Jeep.

My mom and dad have been divorced since my senior year of High School. Truthfully, I think they still love each other. They just got married too young. My parents are better off living separate lives. If anything, they are much happier now than when they were together. Dad has his own apartment on the other side of town, and Mom got the house.

I will need to check in with him while I am home. If Mom doesn't hound him on his health, my sisters and I do. We usually spend Christmas Day with him and Christmas Eve with my mom. New Year's Eve has always been with friends, but this year will be an extra *special* one.

"Not yet, Mom. I just got home!" I laugh as I drag my heavy ass suitcase up the steps and through the front door. Damn me for packing so much shit. *A girl can never be too prepared.* We always need options.

My ten-year-old chihuahua wobbles her way over to greet me. For a teacup, she looks like a mini meatloaf. I drop my bags at the front door and toe off my shoes. Mom's always been one of *those*–the type who is anal about shoes in a basket by the door. I toss my sneakers in the wicker basket then pick up my sweet girl.

"Hey, Roxy! How's my little chunk?" I baby-talk her, letting her lick my nose.

Mom pulls the dog and I into a warm embrace. "I know you'll probably meet up with Lexi tonight. How about you come and have a drink with me first? I've restocked up on wine now that you and your sister are home," she rolls her eyes at me.

Roxy squirms out of my arms, scurrying off to the living room. Most likely she'll find her favorite spot on the couch to sleep.

I take a seat at the kitchen island while Mom pours me a glass of cabernet sauvignon. "Hope you're hungry. I ordered pizza," she smiles gently. There's one thing you need to know about my mom—she always makes sure we are fed. Knowing her, it won't just be pizza—rather, a whole spread of Italian food.

"Thank God. I'm literally starving!" My fifteen-year-old sister makes her appearance. She comes over and gives me a huge hug. "I missed you, Maddy."

"I missed you more, Mel." I rock her in my arms. She's looking more and more mature every time I see her. I have always been *overly* protective of my little sister. Like a second mom—*but way cooler*. At such a young age, she took the brunt of my parent's divorce. That's why I made it my duty to always include her on my shopping trips and coffee runs. When I'm away at school, I text her as often as possible.

The front door creaks open, interrupting our reunion. The dog starts yapping and running towards the door. *Chihuahuas.*

"Mikayla!" My mom runs to the door. *Can you guess who her favorite is?* I am the oldest, but not by much. My sister Mikayla was born eleven months later—Mom didn't exactly listen to the six-week abstinence rule. My sister and I, visually, are polar opposites. Mik is a blue-eyed, blonde-haired stunner. A beauty mark the same as Marilyn Monroe adds that extra allure to her beautiful face.

Men have always been interested in my sister. For good reason too. My *Irish twin* is gorgeous. *The irony is not lost on me.* I call her my Sun; she calls me her Moon. Mik is all light and sunshine, and I am all dark and... *moody?* We used to be completely different as teenagers. She was into sports. I was into science and music. As we got older, we became much closer.

Frequenting our town bar.

Hanging out with the same crowd.

House parties.

*Half-priced apps at Applebee*s.

She even went to college a few towns over from me so we could stay close.

Mom is in her glory right now. You can see it in the way she smiles. "I just love having all my girls home!"

Mikey sits beside me, casually ruffling my hair as she walks by. We get to see each other frequently while we are away at school. She was always checking up on me when Sean died. "What's up sis?" she grins as Mom pours her a glass of wine.

Mom fills herself a glass and raises it to the ceiling in a toast: "to all my girls being under one roof." Moisture begins to pool in her eyes. *Ahh, Mom.* She's always been so emotional.

We clink our glasses together. *"Salute,"* we say in unison. Melanie cups her hand and air clinks with us. There is no doubt she is drinking by now. Just not around Mom.

MIKEY DECIDES to come out with me for drinks. It's a hole-in-the-wall bar in our town that offers darts, beer pong, and the most *delicious* buffalo wings you've ever tasted. I bet Killian would love them. *He loves anything spicy.*

Lexi is meeting us here in a few minutes. Mik and I decide to order a celebratory shot now that finals are over. Our favorite bartender is working tonight, so we know the drinks will be cheap. His adorable chocolate lab sits behind the bar, making all the female patrons swoon over him. *The dog, I mean.*

Jake places two coasters in front of us. "What'll it be, ladies?"

I am about to say Jameson when Mik responds with, "two shots of *tequila,* please."

"I'd rather have Jameson," I tell her firmly. She looks at me and then back at the bartender with a shrug. I send out a silent prayer that Mikey will drop the fact that I declined tequila. The bell on the door rings, and in walks Lexi.

I jump out of my stool, almost knocking it to the ground. We practically tackle each other. Lexi and I hop up and down while squealing like a bunch of psychopaths. The entire bar is watching our ordeal. *My best friend just got home from Arizona. Sue me for showing emotion.* She shimmies out of her leather jacket, placing it over the back of her stool.

I get Jake's attention. "One more Jameson shot, please." I hold my index finger up. Jake pours another, and we clink our shots together and toss them back. Warmness spreads down my throat and across my chest. I've already got a slight buzz from the wine.

"Did you not get tequila because of *Liam*?" Lexi blurts out. *If I could facepalm myself right now, I would.* I shoot Lexi a quick look to zip it. Mikey raises an eyebrow before looking at me. She knows about the infamous bouncer Liam. I told her about *that* night when we got lunch in early November.

"Don't even tell me you are still stuck on that *dickhead*, Madison!" She grabs my arm. "He fucking left you when you finally opened your heart again."

I feel the need to defend him. "He didn't really have a choice in leaving."

"*Bullshit*. The way I see it is he fucked you and then left you. He made you feel like *you* did something wrong. Not only that, but he didn't even give you a chance to choose," she huffs out, signaling the bartender for another round of shots.

My heart hurts right now. *Her accusations aren't wrong.* And she is just being a protective sister. What she doesn't understand is that it was more than just *fucking*. There was something there, *something real*. Something deeper than some superficial love. It was on a soul level. No, he didn't give me a chance to choose. But the anguish on his face when he left me makes me think he hurt himself just as much as he hurt me. There was hesitation there. I could see it in his eyes that he was battling his own demons.

"I'm over him. I *swear*." I hold my fingers up in Scout's honor to get them off my fucking case. I want to stop talking about Liam. It's making my heart race and my head spin. *Or maybe, it's the alcohol.* "In fact, things took off with Killian. The guy I met online. We are dating now," I smile, despite being bombarded by my sister's opinion of Liam.

The bartender walks over with bottles of tequila and Jameson. "We will *all* have tequila," Mik says, sending me a look of 'prove it.'

Fuck it. *It's just tequila, Maddy. You'll be drunk texting your boyfriend a half hour from now.* I try to imagine Liam with a busty blonde wrapped around him. Hoping it would make me frustrated and want to forget him all over again. If anything—it makes me *jealous. Hypothetically jealous and angry.*

I slam the glass to theirs, sloshing tequila over the rims, and bang the shot back. I am seething over the 'what ifs' again, and it's pissing me off.

"I need a cigarette," I announce, darting straight outside. My body is buzzing, and my mind is reeling over my feelings for Liam. *Why can't I just let him go? Killian makes me so happy. He is who I see myself marrying one day and raising a family with. So what is the problem?*

Lexi comes outside and grabs her pack from her purse, offering me one. "You need, or you have?"

"I need one." I grab one and hand the pack back to her. "I quit after Liam left. I couldn't bring myself to smoke without memories of him and I. *It was our thing.* Fuck, Lex. My head is all over the place right now," I confess.

She lights hers and mine. I take a long drag, letting it sit in my lungs. I exhale over my shoulder, spotting my sister inside. Mik got roped into a beer pong game with a guy she graduated with.

"I'm sorry I brought up Liam. I know it still stings, Mad." Lexi pulls me into a hug.

"The tequila is just a reminder of our time together. That's what got me out of the house that night in the first place. Without the liquid courage from the tequila, I probably would not have gone out. I wouldn't have recognized my feelings for Liam, and we wouldn't have had sex—well...kinda. Sorta. For two seconds. Which technically means I wouldn't have lost my virginity to him," I groan.

"Many women regret their first sexual partner," Lexi shrugs.

"That's the thing, Lexi. I don't regret him at all. If we never had sex that night, I would have continued talking to Killian, and I wouldn't be thinking of Liam right now," I sigh into her shoulder.

She releases me and takes a drag of her cigarette. "I'm not sure that's true. You've always been drawn to Liam." Smoke cascades over her lips as she speaks. "Have you tried reaching out to him?"

I shake my head and take another drag. "No. It's not right to do that to Killian," I exhale. "Even if I did, I'm sure he wouldn't answer."

"I think you need closure, Mad." Lexi flicks her cigarette into the parking lot. "I really have to pee," she says, heading back inside. "You should text him. Tell him how you feel. Tell him he missed out and you have a new boyfriend. Maybe, you both moved on."

I don't plan on texting him any of those things.

Lexi leaves me to my thoughts. Liquid courage courses through me, making me feel bold. I retrieve my phone from my crossbody purse. Keeping my cigarette tucked in the corner of my mouth, I type out a text to Liam:

MADISON

Hi.

Before I can chicken out, I hit send. My heart palpitates in my chest with anxiety.

Bubbles pop up, showing he is typing.

Then they disappear.

I pull another drag of my cigarette in. Then blow it toward the clear night sky.

I wait.

And then wait a few more minutes.

But nothing comes back.

I feel stupid now. I should have left well enough alone. Dropping my cigarette in the sand bucket, I walk back inside. Liam wants nothing to do with me. I just need to accept the loss.

"Let's go, Maddy! We are up next," Lexi screams over the jukebox playing. *At least I won't lose in beer pong.* We are always the champs. I smile and try to forget about Liam once again.

CHAPTER 18

LIAM

I'M on the private jet home to New York when *her* text comes in. An electric current runs through my body as I see her name light up my screen.

Madison.

There has not been a day since I left that this woman hasn't crossed my mind. There have been numerous times I typed an entire paragraph out—just to erase it. Fuck, I miss her.

Her laugh.

Her smile.

Her smart mouth.

But that's just the physical. I miss all of her. I miss her mind, her heart, the way she cares for everyone in her presence.

> **MADISON**
> Hi.

I go to respond without thinking. My heart overriding my mind.

> **LIAM**
> Hi there, love. Are you okay?

THEN I REMEMBER what I had just done a few weeks ago. Killed a man who we have been rivaling with. *Selena's father.* Head of the Cuban Syndicate in Miami.

That right there is the reason we can't be together. Why we *shouldn't* be together. She deserves better than this. Better than me.

Regretfully I erase the message and slide my phone back into my jeans pocket. *Out of sight, out of mind. Right?* I take a sip of whiskey, lean my head back on the leather seat, and close my eyes. My mind wanders with ideas of what she could be doing right now. *Where is she? Who is she with? What did she want to say to me?*

THE HOUSE LOOKS FANTASTIC, *as usual.* Christmas decorations are distributed throughout the space. It smells of sugar cookies, pine—and the familiar scent of *home.* Jack has an exceptionally talented designer who decorates every year for the holidays. Just wait until you see how they decorate for the gala.

Our butler Andrew takes my bags from me when I walk through the door. "I'll bring these to your room Mr. Donnelly."

"Thank you, Andrew." I look around for Killian. "Any idea where Killian is at?"

"He is with his father. Killian requested the staff set up Christmas dinner there due to Mr. Kennedy's condition. I nod—knowing we are on *borrowed time.*

I enter the large room on the upper floor of the triplex penthouse. Jack is all set up on the chaise. A light blanket covers his frail body. He looks pale and much weaker than when I had last seen him. But leave it to Jack Kennedy to wear a full suit for Christmas Dinner in his condition. That man has so much pride. I have always been in awe of him. Of his strength. His dedication.

"Liam, my boy," he says weakly. "Come take a seat. I was just telling Killian there are some important matters we need to discuss."

Killian stands to hug me, slapping me on the back. "Welcome home, *sweetheart*," he jokes.

I laugh and pretend to punch his face. "Merry Christmas, ya gobshite."

He pours us some whiskey, and we take a seat by Jack.

"I know this will be my last Christmas with you both. I hear the whispers. I've got a few weeks left in me if I'm lucky. I've already gone through how the transition of power works with Killian. There are still a few other things you two need to know."

Killian and I exchange curious glances.

"There is no easy way to say this," he coughs. "I had an affair with your mother, Liam. She was the love of my life."

He turns to Killian, "I met her many years before I met your mother, Killian."

Another round of coughs leaves him trying to catch his breath. "Aoife and I had an arranged marriage. To build a stronger alliance between our families. *She knew about your mother, Liam.*" He turns back to me. "We showed face to everyone that we were happily married. But there wasn't a night I wouldn't go to your mum's house before I went home."

Killian and I look at each other dumbfounded.

"Aoife gave birth to Killian two months before Liam's mother, Aisling, did." *What the fuck.* My mind races with putting the pieces together. So that makes Killian and I...

"*Brothers.* You two are brothers. Not just by the oath we take but by the blood that runs through each of your veins. You both are *Kennedy's*," Jack finishes.

We are all quiet for a while, processing this huge, life-changing moment. *I'm a Kennedy.* I swirl my whiskey around my glass. Killian thrumbs his fingers on his legs. My eyes find Jack's. A look of peace is on his face from his admission.

Killian is the first to break the silence. "Thank you for telling us Da. I'm sure it's been weighing heavily on your heart."

"It has. I would have told you sooner, son," Jack says to me, "but I promised your mum I wouldn't tell you about this life. It was hard to do that when she passed. I knew I needed to take you in. I brought you into this life but as a foot soldier. Everyone always respected your authority because you've always been a son to me, Liam. No one else knows other than Aiofe and my lawyers. Both you and Killian will hold great responsibilities when I pass. *I need you to take care of each other.* Let our legacy carry on for years to come."

I get up and shake my Da's hand. Tears spring from his eyes. This is the first time I've ever seen this man cry. "Thank you for telling me this, Jack. I appreciate the life you've given me," I say, getting choked up myself.

Killian approaches me and clasps the back of my head, pulling me into a hug. He slaps my back. "You were always a brother to me, but now it's official."

AFTER DINNER, we let Jack get some rest. He barely made it through dinner without needing to be placed back in his bed and on oxygen. Hospice is already fully set up here. Nurses have been in and out checking on him regularly.

Kil and I head outside for some fresh air on the patio. There is a heated inground pool and hot tub. The views of Madison Square Park, The Empire State Building, and the Hudson are incredible. I lean over the railing, inhaling a deep breath of the frosty December air.

Killian hands me two fingers of whiskey in a crystal tumbler. He leans a hip against the railing, and we both take a sip of our drinks. "Well tonight was..." he blows out a breath.

"Yeah," I agree, finishing the rest of my drink. I place the empty tumbler on the cocktail table next to me and feel around my pockets for my smokes. Placing one between my lips, I hold the pack out to offer Kil one. He shakes his head—he's not big on smoking cigarettes. He will however, indulge in a good cigar here or there.

The smoke penetrates my lungs, delivering nicotine to my racing mind. "How are things going with your woman?" I attempt to break through some of the awkwardness. I exhale, letting the smoke take away some of my stress.

Killian's smile grows wider than I have ever seen it. He is genuinely happy, and that makes me so fucking happy for him. If anyone deserves it, it's him. My mood lightens significantly.

"My God, Liam. She is amazing. Absolutely the most caring, loving, sarcastic woman I have ever met. I am falling in love with her."

"That's so great to hear, man." I take another drag of my cigarette, hating how *lonely* my love life is in comparison. I wish more than anything I could have that with Madison right now. The holidays should be a magical time, and it feels anything but. "When do I get to meet her?" Smoke swirls around us, dissipating into the night sky.

"She'll be at the Masquerade Gala on New Year's Eve. How are things with your lady? Did you get with her before you left on assignment?" He waggles his eyebrows seductively.

"Yeah, we went at it like two horny teens—until I found out she was a virgin."

"And ... that is a problem...because?" he pushes.

"Because it's another reason I shouldn't have been there in the first place. She is too good and pure to be corrupted by all this, Kil."

"Women are able to handle a lot more than you think, Liam. My woman is like that too, but she's a fighter. She's strong. She can handle this life. She chose to be a part of this. I gave her a choice, and she took it—knowing the risks."

"Maybe you're right," I contemplate. I didn't even give Maddy a chance to choose. I just made the *choice* for her. Perhaps I'll text her back tonight, see how she's been. That's if she even gives a fuck about me after the way I left her.

"Look at our Da. He chose true love and was one of the best leaders. Why can't we do the same?" Killian slides the final puzzle piece of my scrambled mind into place. I finally see the bigger picture here.

Now that I've had her in my arms, I can't live without her. I don't want to. And the only thing that's been stopping me —is *me*.

I need to tell her.

CHAPTER 19

KILLIAN

THERE ARE ONLY a few minutes left of Christmas as I pull up to her family home. The lights are off inside. I get out into the frigid December night, and make my way down the driveway towards her bedroom window. There are a few acorns on the ground left over from fall. I grab a handful and start tapping her window with them. A light turns on, but no sign of movement just yet. *She wasn't expecting me.* I told her I had to stay with my family for the night.

My phone vibrates in my hand.

MADISON

I wish you were here with me tonight. I keep hearing weird noises outside. It's freaking me out! 😣

I wait a few seconds longer before responding.

KILLIAN

What kind of sounds? Do you want me to send Conor to check it out?

My chest vibrates with a cough in a poor attempt to stifle a laugh. The bubbles jump across the screen as she immediately writes a response.

MADISON

> No! My whole family is asleep! They don't need to know I have a bodyguard…or a super hot mob boss boyfriend.

I toss another acorn at her window with a little more force. I watch a shadow cross the room. Her perfect features silhouette the curtains before her head peeks out behind them. Frightened eyes scan the driveway then land on mine. She slides the window open and sticks her head out. "Killian! she whisper-shouts. "You scared the shit out of me!"

"I told you that you are protected, love." A smile builds on my face just seeing her in person again. My life has been so busy and hectic lately. We've only been able to Facetime and text, and that's not nearly enough for me.

"Merry Christmas, Killian. Looks like I got my gift afterall." She glances down at her phone, holding it up. "And with one minute left of Christmas."

"Merry Christmas to you, my beautiful, amazing, *sexy* woman." It's incredible that I get to call this woman mine. She knows the life I live, yet she looks past my rough exterior, seeing the sides of me no one else does. The parts of me I can't show anyone…especially if I am to be respected as the next leader of the Tri-State Syndicate. *Softness is a weakness*. Madison allows me to be vulnerable. And it feels *so fucking good* to take off the mask for a while. To remove all the heavy armor. "Get your arse down here. I need to kiss my woman—and wear something warm!"

I lean against the hood of my car and wait for my gorgeous girl. Within minutes the front door opens, and a small dog starts barking in the background. *Damn it*. So much for trying to be quiet.

She closes the door behind her and runs towards me like a teenager sneaking out. Her hair is still perfectly curled, and light makeup dusts her face. A black winter jacket with a fur lined hood wraps around her. She is wearing Christmas themed pajamas and slippers. *It's fucking adorable.*

I meet her halfway and pull her into me, claiming her lips. Her body against mine makes me think of all the filthy ways I can take her over the hood of my car. Unfortunately, it's winter, and we probably have an audience. I continue ravishing her lips by drinking her in and not coming up for air. Cold hands run up my body. She pulls my face closer to hers, moaning in my mouth.

We break apart breathless and heaving clouds of condensation into the air.

"I missed you, Kil," she says as she rubs a thumb over my tingling lips. Her own are swollen and red from my kisses, and her eyes...those eyes hold enough heat to keep us both warm in this weather.

"I missed you too, sweetheart. Now, get in the car. We are going on an adventure," I gesture towards my Bugatti Veyron. Her eyes widen with delight and a bit of mischief.

WE ARE PARKED at the top of the bluff. It overlooks the Long Island Sound and has views of the Connecticut skyline all lit up. A few fireworks are going off, and she intakes a breath in awe.

"You remembered this was my favorite place," she says, tucking a piece of hair behind her ear. "But how was it not locked? After dusk it is *always* locked up."

I raise an eyebrow and cock my head to the side. "You do remember who your *man* is, right?"

She giggles and cups my chin between her hand, leaving a swift kiss on my lips. "Right. How could I forget, Mr. Kennedy?"

Madison is distracted, taking in the views. I reach behind her seat to retrieve her gifts, then place the neatly wrapped boxes on her lap. A black lace mask with gold Swarovski crystals sits on top. She slowly unties it and holds the masquerade mask in her hand, turning it to let the light catch the crystals.

"It's seductive and classy all at the same time," she winks at me. "I have the perfect dress for this."

I smile and let that part slide. The day of the Gala, I have plans for her. But that's another surprise for another day.

She places the mask on the dashboard and continues to open the smaller box on top. Her fingers delicately slide through the paper, revealing a small velvet box. Madison shoots me a look of *this better not be what I think it is*... which has me thinking about how close we've gotten in only a few weeks. With trembling hands she opens the lid and gasps. Emerald diamonds form the shape of a triskelion and hang from a gold chain.

"This is... Killian..." Her voice is thick with emotion.

Madison gathers her long hair and pulls it to one side. I remove the necklace from the box and secure it around her neck. My fingers linger there before slowly dipping down to her breast bone. I grip the pendant between my thumb and index finger..

"Emeralds mean many things. They represent royalty, unconditional love, balance and patience. You have given me all of those things. These last few weeks have been everything. I want you to know that you are my *Queen*. I will love you—*I do love you*—unconditionally. You have been more than patient with me as I navigate my ever unfolding life. Thank you so much for that," I say, cupping my palm to her face.

I rub my thumb over her cheek as tears slip out. "Thank you for trusting me, for giving me a chance that I'm sure I don't deserve. I promise that I will always try my best to give you the life you asked for. A balance between your life and mine. We cannot change our past, but we can make a better future. You are my future, Madison."

I realize I'm getting teary eyed myself. Her soft hands caress my face, and her lips lock around mine. Our kiss starts off salty from our tears, but she sweetens it. "I love you, Killian Kennedy," she declares against my lips.

A permanent smile has etched it's way across my face. I release Madison from my grasp, and my fingers strum over her final present. She slips a finger through the wrapping paper, and raises a delicate eyebrow at the logo. Removing the lid, she breaks out into a laughing fit.

A pair of brown *Ugg* boots sit in the box. She takes a sniff of them and shakes her head in wonder. "No fucking way, Killian! How did you manage to pull this off? I actually looked online for them after Thanksgiving."

I clear my throat and chuckle at how cute she is. "Your man has a lot of connections. I told you, you can have anything you want."

She reaches into her jacket pocket and retrieves a small wrapped box. Handing it to me she lets out a sigh. "It's kinda hard to buy a gift for someone who can have anything they want." My Queen is shy now, looking embarrassed. I give her hand a reassuring squeeze.

"You are all that I want." I remove the wrapping paper and open the small box. There is what appears to be a coupon book. I flip through it, and my eyebrows raise in appreciation. They are coupons of *pleasure.* My cock jumps to life at the different positions and acts described.

The corner of her mouth goes up in a clever smile. "These can be redeemed whenever...or *wherever* you like," she adds, her voice just a whisper.

I browse through the book, finding the perfect one—*blow job in the car.*

I rip the coupon out with my teeth and slide my seat all the way back—more than eager to redeem.

CHAPTER 20

LIAM

I RETREATED to my room after Killian left to see his woman. I stroll into my walk-in closet and start unpacking my suitcase. My tuxedo for the gala is hanging on a clothing rack. A simple black mask sits on top of the dresser next to it. *Would Madison come if I invited her?* She should be on winter break by now, likely home on Long Island with her family.

I *need* to tell her how I feel, but this isn't something I can text or discuss over the phone. The thought of reaching out to my IT guy crosses my mind. It would only take him a few seconds to look up her location. That wouldn't be fair, though. Invading her privacy like that. With a sigh, I strip my clothes off. It's been a long day, and I need to get cleaned up.

The hot water pours over my aching muscles as I step into the shower in my en suite. Steam fogs up the glass and swirls around me. I stand under the spray for longer than needed, letting all my anxiety drip off me and flow down the drain. Closing my eyes, I see Madison's beautiful face.

I fantasize about her in an elegant ball gown. A seductive mask caresses her face. Long black eyelashes flutter from beneath it. Plump pink lips wrap around a glass of champagne, just begging to be tasted. My hand pushes her petite frame against my body as we get lost in the music. Her height difference gives me the most unbelievable views of her cleavage. I run my lips down her neck and drag her into the bathroom, slamming her up against the door. Reclaiming what is mine.

I wrap a hand around my cock, stroking it harder with every passing thought. I can still hear her moan my name. Feel her delicate hand, like satin, clutched around my shaft. Leaning an arm over the tiles, I pump myself harder, building my arousal. A frustrated growl escapes my lips. *Her tongue dancing with mine, her arse smacking the door with each punishing thrust. I close my hand over her jaw, and close my lips over hers, stifling her cries of pleasure.*

My body trembles with an impending climax. I beat the fuck out of my cock.

Our moans echo off the walls. Maddy throws her head back, and her chest heaves with her own euphoria. That gorgeous pussy clamps down on my cock. I explode my release onto the shower floor, banging my fist against the wall.

Fuck.

I need to make this right.

Steam permeates the bedroom when I open the bathroom door. I grab my phone off the end table and lean against the headboard, scrolling back to the message between Madison and me:

MADISON

Hi.

That one little word has been burning a hole into my retinas *all damn day.* I want to call her right now, but it's already a quarter to twelve on Christmas night. It wouldn't be right to disturb her and her family.

Maybe I won't need my IT guy to look up her address...I guess it would be harmless to stalk social media like the rest of this generation does. I follow Leah on Instagram—mostly to keep an eye on Maddy when she took a year hiatus from the bar scene. It turns out, Leah rarely uses Instagram. Only a few pictures are posted on her page.

Against my better judgement, I cave and browse Leah's page. I must be one lucky bastard. Leah just tagged Madison in a post, wishing her roommate 'a very Merry Christmas'. *Bingo.* I click on her handle and her profile fills my screen. I tap her latest picture (which was posted 4 hours ago) at an Italian restaurant. Pulling up my browser, I do a quick Google search. *Found ya, princess.*

I decided to ask her to the Gala. The only way I can possibly get her to say yes is if I give her a few hours' notice. Everyone sees the side of Maddy that is controlled and calculated, the one that doesn't take risks. But I get the pleasure of seeing the side of her that is spontaneous, that is dying for adventure. The part of her that wants someone else to take control, so she can let go for once.

It's worth a shot showing up unannounced. I'm not below groveling at her feet and am prepared to do just that on New Year's Eve. I'll show up at her front door and pray to God that she won't slam it in my face.

IT IS New Year's Eve. I have been on edge *all day*. It could be the three cups of coffee I already had. Most likely, it's about me confessing my truth to Madison. *God, I hope she says yes.*

The event organizers and staff are scattered around the penthouse, transforming it into a goddamn winter wonderland.

At two p.m., I grab my keys off the dresser and sprint down the stairs. I pass Killian, heading in the opposite direction with a questioning look on his face.

"Where are you off to in such a hurry, brother?" His hand lands on my shoulder.

"I'm going to get my woman back." I swirl the keyfob on my index finger, feeling uncertain but excited.

"Good for you, Liam. I'm assuming you're asking her to the gala tonight?" He pats my shoulder twice.

"That's the plan...unless she slams the door in my face. Which I *deserve*." A tremulous breath escapes me. I haven't given much thought to what my night will look like if she wants nothing to do with me.

"I hope it all works out." He holds out his hand.

"Thanks," I shake it and pull him into a hug, slapping his back. "I'll see you later, Kil."

I PULL up her driveway and take notice of the few cars parked there. I spot her Jeep, feeling confident that this is her house. I remember seeing her car in the driveway of her Connecticut house the night I came over. The black rhinestone license plate and crescent moon decal confirm it's hers.

Wiping the moisture from my hands, I walk up the steps to her front door and ring the bell. *Deep breaths, Liam.* Doubt creeps into my mind as I think of what I am going to say to her. *'Hey, Maddy... I just wanted to say I was a real dick. I should have given you a choice. Please come with me to a gala tonight...I can't live without you.'* I'm certain she'll slam the door in my face. *Fuck.* I run my hands through my hair as the front door opens.

A blonde middle-aged woman greets me, holding open the storm door. "Hello," she says warily, taking in my leather jacket, black aviators, and motorcycle boots. "Can I help you?"

"Are you Mrs. Marrone?" I take my glasses off and tuck them into my jacket pocket. She looks even more concerned than she did before.

"Yes...what can I help you with?" she asks a little more rigidly.

Realizing I am already making a terrible impression on her mother, I reach my hand out, smiling. "I'm a good friend of Madison's from Connecticut. I was in your neighborhood and wanted to stop by. Is she around?" My pulse accelerates with the thought of seeing her again.

Mrs. Marrone's body visibly relaxes. Her eyes soften, "Oh, you just missed her! Maddy went out with her girlfriend to the salon. She is getting all dolled up for an event she is attending tonight with her boyfriend."

My smile falters. And my heart sinks in my chest. She has a *boyfriend...fuck. I'm too late.* She should be kissing *me* at midnight—not some drunk college kid. My mind begins making up scenarios in my head. Some eejit with his hands all over her, giving her sloppy kisses as the clock strikes twelve. *Great job, arsehole. You let the best thing to walk into your life slip through your fingers. Only you are to blame for this.*

"Will you also be attending the party tonight?" Her mother inquires, breaking me out of my downward spiral.

"I don't believe we are." My voice cracks at the end, with raw, ugly emotions threatening to surface. "Thank you, Mrs. Marrone. I'll catch up with Madison another time." I turn and trudge back to my car, feeling totally defeated.

CHAPTER 21

MADISON

I WOKE up on New Year's Eve the way a kid would on Christmas morning. Full of excitement and impatience. *Tonight is the gala.* It is thrilling that I'll be going to Killian's home in New York City and meeting his family and friends. Knowing what I do now about him, there are some nerves rattling my bones as well. More suspense than anything. *I can already feel his lust-filled eyes on me when I walk through the door.*

Gowns are scattered across my bed along with different shoe and jewelry options. The gorgeous mask Killian gave me on Christmas is sitting on my bookshelf. I tap my index finger on my upper lip indecisively. There will be many people in attendance which means I need to look and feel my best.

My phone rings on the bed underneath the chaos of sparkles and satin. I dig around, attempting to hone in on the location of the ringtone. I finally find it after tossing half my dresses on the floor. Killian's handsome face lights up my phone's lock screen.

"Hey, sexy," I answer, lowering my voice in a seductive tone.

"Hello, my beautiful Madison," Killian practically purrs my name.

"What do I owe the pleasure of this call?"

"Mmm...after Christmas night in my car...I *owe you* some pleasure tonight."

A small moan falls from my lips. *I can't wait.* I'm hooked on him. It just gets hotter and hotter each time our bodies intertwine. I'm tempted to touch myself to relieve the yearning.

"I'm so hard for you right now. I can't wait to fuck you all night long in my bed—I hope you slept last night," he says with conviction.

"Looks like you'll be waiting until next year then," I tease in a pathetic attempt at a joke.

He howls out a laugh and then becomes extremely serious. *I can feel him through the phone, backing me into a corner to take what he needs from me.*

"Oh sweetheart, I plan on stealing you away before midnight. Know, when you leave my place, you'll feel me on every inch of your body for the rest of the week." His promise makes me desperate for his touch. I blow out a breath and fan my heated cheeks.

"I have a surprise for you," he whispers.

"What is it?" I whisper back, still thinking we are on the topic of sex.

"Make sure you have your overnight bag and belongings— don't forget your mask. My driver is waiting outside for you. He already picked up Lexi. You two are going to the spa. My designers will be there to get you both set up with gowns and accessories for tonight."

My mouth drops open with a gasp. "Killian..." I am at a loss for words at his kindness. "You are...*amazing*." *How did he get Lexi's number? Oh yeah. Look who I am dating.* "Thank you, Kil."

"I love you. I can't wait to see you later. My driver will take you girls to the spa in Manhattan and then to my place. Now get your arse to the car and have fun," he chuckles before hanging up.

I grab my already-packed overnight bag and tuck my phone

charger into the side pouch. Not forgetting my mask off the bookshelf, I close my bedroom door and book it down the stairs. *I wonder how Lexi feels about all of this?*

The driver gets out and opens the back door of the black Cadillac. Immediately I'm met with Lexi's shrieks of excitement. As the driver shuts my door, I turn to her and pull her in for a hug. "I can't believe he planned this all, *and* my best friend gets to come with me to a gala!" I clap my hands together.

She hands me a glass of champagne and lifts her flute to mine. "Cheers to ringing in another New Year with my bestie." We clink our glasses together and take a sip.

Lexi hooks up to the Bluetooth and starts playing *"Girls Just Want to Have Fun" by Cindy Lauper* as we cruise out of town.

THE SPA IS SERENELY STUNNING. No one is here but the staff and designers. There are racks upon racks of designer gowns. Shoes and purses line one end of the salon to the other. A buffet is prepared with salads, bagels, snacks, and refreshments. A table is lined with a black velvet tablecloth and diamonds galore. Lexi nods her head towards the table and mouths 'wow' at me. I couldn't have said it better. I feel like a Kardashian.

A blonde woman with long legs, a black leather pencil skirt, and a white satin blouse approaches us. She reaches her hand out to shake mine. "Ms. Marrone, my name is Rebbeca. I will be assisting you in your preparations for the gala tonight. My assistant Ellie will be helping you, Lexi." She turns abruptly, so we follow her.

She opens a large red door to a room with a private bathroom and wooden lockers. A black terry cloth robe and a pair of matching slippers are handed to us. "Change into these and head down that hall there." She points past the bathroom. "You will each be getting a body wrap and facial. After that, my assistant and I will help you select your outfits for this evening. Your hair, makeup, and nails will be done before we get you dressed and on your way." She pivots on her stiletto, leaving Lexi and me in awe.

"Holy fuckballs," Lexi says, grabbing my shoulders. "Girl, you need to introduce me to Killian's friends tonight."

I giggle and grab her shoulders in return. "When I meet his friends, I'll be sure to do that."

THE SPA TREATMENTS WERE *INCREDIBLE*. My skin feels like a newborn, soft and moisturized. Lucky for us, we get a goody bag to take home with new creams and serums. *They say money can't buy happiness, but it can buy good skincare.*

Rebbeca and Ellie meet us in the main space of the salon. They split in different directions, and we follow suit. I turn around and blow a kiss to Lexi before giving her a thumbs up.

We start at one section of the racks, except these aren't gowns. They are all *lingerie*. Rebbeca's impassive face breaks into a grin. "Mr. Kennedy requested you wear these under your gown."

I skim my hands over the delicate materials, looking at the tags. *La Perla*. Jesus Christ. *And here I was, thinking my bras were expensive.* I pause over a set that catches my eye. It's a black, scalloped lace bustier with a stockingless garter belt and a strappy mesh thong to go with it. "We also have that in emerald green," she says, holding it by the hanger for me to see. *Emerald green*. Like the necklace Killian gave me.

I nod as my eyes glow with an idea. She places it on the empty table behind her. "Rebbeca, I would like to wear an emerald green dress tonight. I also have a necklace I would like to pair with it, if possible." Her smile widens into a full-blown grin. *Ahh, this woman actually smiles.* "You will look stunning in a satin emerald gown. We absolutely can work with that."

I stare into the three mirrors in front of me, in awe of my reflection. A seamstress is finishing up my hem as I stand on the round pedestal. She needed to take a bit off on the length and take it in at the waist.

The A-Line, emerald green, satin ball gown dips low into my generous cleavage—thanks to the bustier. Regal sleeves petal from my breasts and fall off my shoulders. They wrap delicately around my biceps. A high slit runs up to my thigh, just kissing the straps of my garter. The gown is absolutely stunning.

A strappy black stiletto Louboutin is placed on my freshly pedicured foot. I went with OPI *Lincoln Park After Dark* for my nails and toes. *My favorite.* Killian's necklace sits proudly between my collarbones. I selected a pair of tear-drop emerald earrings to complete the look.

My makeup is flawless, with inspiration from Old Hollywood. Thick, winged liner and long black lashes outline my eyes. A slight smokey shadow adds to the seduction of this whole look. Candy apple red lipstick coats my lips like velvet. And my foundation is painted on like a second skin, which is smooth and lustrous from the facial.

Oh, and the best part? My hair took a dramatic turn. The stylist recommended doing something different and fresh for the New Year. I told her to have at it—she is the professional, after all. Dark auburn hair curls in big waves around my face. I've never had any other hair color besides my natural dark brown. I welcomed this new color—the whole look, really.

I am taking on a whole new persona tonight. Something wild and adventurous vibrates through me. *Wait until Killian sees.*

LEXI IS TWIRLING around in her dress—a navy blue, strapless, sequined ball gown. Her breasts are on full display as the back is a corset. Freshly highlighted blonde hair is done up in a low bun to one side with a braid weaved through it. Diamond safety pin earrings dangle from her ears. *My bestie looks hot!* She may just meet one of Killian's friends on her own tonight.

"Well, ladies, it has been a pleasure." Rebbeca shakes our hands. "Have a *safe* and healthy New Year," she says, holding the door open to the street. We step out into the chill of the December night, exchanging pleasantries. I inhale deeply, feeling the rush of cold air fill my lungs. *It smells like snow.*

Our driver assists us into the car, and we immediately pour ourselves another glass of champagne for the short ride to Killian's. I take a decent sip of my bubbly. My anxiety is at an all-time high now that we are getting closer.

"Your man is going to eat you alive tonight," Lexi says, grabbing one of my curls. "This color is badass." I shoot her a wink and take another sip of my champagne. Lust coils in my womb, thinking of Killian's reaction to my new hair.

We pull up to the curb of a luxurious building on Fifth Avenue. A red carpet lines the sidewalk from the curb of where we parked to the doors. At least ten men in suits and simple black masks surround the door. I crane my neck up to get a better view of the skyskraper. *So this is Killian's fortress.*

Lexi's hand squeezes mine, and I down the rest of my champagne. We help each other tie our masks in place. I slide my phone into my pocket (*yeah, my dress has pockets—how fucking cool*) as the driver opens my door. I spot Conor—aka *beanie dude.* His familiar stature and beard stand out to me almost immediately.

Conor helps Lexi and me out of the Cadillac and guides us to an elevator. We take it up to the top floor in silence. The doors open to a small corridor leading to tinted glass doors. There are men stationed at these doors as well. What hides behind them is an insanely luxurious, triplex penthouse. *This place is magnificent.*

It's like a winter wonderland in here. Crystals and clouds hang from the ceiling. Smoke blows out from hidden machines in the clouds. The blue and white lighting creates the feeling of an ice castle in the sky. Speaking of ice—there's a few ice sculptures arranged around the room. Let's not forget to mention the raw bar, sushi bar, and charcuterie station.

Just like his club, everything I've seen so far is clean edges and glass.

Modern cream furniture is styled throughout the first floor. Artwork hangs on some of the walls; also very minimalistic. Wait staff walk around with silver platters of passed hors d'oeuvres and fancy drinks.

"Mr. Kennedy is on the back patio with a few clients. He asks that you meet him outside," Conor says, pointing to the glass sliding doors off the kitchen. They lead to a white tent covering the outdoor space.

"Thank you...what is your name?" Lexi asks, already spotting a potential prospect.

Conor gives her a small smile, extending his hand. "Conor. And what about yours, angel?"

She places her hand in his. "Alexis, but you can call me Lexi."

He brings her hand up to place a kiss on the top of it. "That's a beautiful name for a beautiful woman. Save me a dance tonight, Lexi." He winks at her before leaving us.

Lexi grins from ear to ear as we approach the patio.

I hear his laugh, and my eyes find him by the bar. His eyes meet mine within seconds. Both of us are completely in sync with the other. Like a moth to a flame, I start gravitating toward him. His eyes never leave mine as I approach.

Killian's clients are still talking to him, but his body has shifted to face me. He casually leans an arm on the bar, a dark drink clutched tightly in his hand. His tongue darts out to wet his lips, and he crosses his large hands over the erection he's now sporting.

A black Armani tuxedo clings to his toned body. His muscles look extra firm and delicious in that fit. *I want to peel the damn thing off him right now.* A simple white mask curves around his eyes and over the sturdy bridge of his nose. His dark hair is slicked back, not a piece out of place.

As I get closer to him, he abruptly finishes his conversation. Like a wolf, he stalks toward me with precision. My pulse quickens, and my breath hitches at each step he takes my way. A few more strides of his long legs and he is pulling me into a kiss. One hand lingering on the small of my back, the other wrapped around my face.

"What did you do to your hair? He looks pleasantly surprised. "Are you *trying* to miss the whole gala?" He runs a thumb over my red lips. The need in his eyes matches my own. He leans down to whisper in my ear. "You know how badly I want to take you up to my room right now and never let you leave?" His teeth rake over my earlobe in his retreat. "You are such a gorgeous woman." He moves lower, kissing my neck, and runs a finger down to my necklace, placing it between his fingers. The back of his hand grazes the top of my breasts, leaving a fire in its wake. Goosebumps prickle my skin, and my breathing becomes labored, itching for him to touch more of me.

"You wore it," he peers directly into my eyes. His gaze has shifted from lust to adoration...or is that *love*?

"It was the inspiration for my entire outfit." I grip his bow tie, pulling him in for another chaste kiss.

He stands back and does another once-over, stopping at the deep slit in my dress. A wicked smile forms on his face. Killian runs his index finger slowly up my bare thigh stopping just shy of my garter. He slides his hand further up to cup my hip, his long fingers splaying across my ass. "Goddamn, Madison. I am one lucky man," he whistles out.

CHAPTER 22

KILLIAN

I AM deep in conversation with a few of our suppliers when one of my men taps me on the shoulder. "Excuse me, sir. *Padmé* just arrived." I smirk at the code name I gave my men for her.

"Thank you. Have Conor direct the girls outside to the tent while I finish up here."

A few moments later, a green goddess enters my peripheral. The chatter becomes distant as I turn my head towards my queen. Her hair is trimmed and dyed auburn. *The things I want to do to her right now...*

Her girlfriend takes notice of the intimate moment and makes herself scarce by the bar.

Madison struts her long, sexy legs my way with a newfound look twinkling in her eyes. That slit in her dress goes deep into territory that belongs to me. I lean against the bar, gaining a better view of her, and clutch my whiskey—about to crack this glass.

My lips twitch with the need to taste her sweetness. *Right. The fuck. Now.* I run my tongue over them preparing to claim hers in about two seconds. My cock is straining hard against the zipper of my tuxedo pants. I clasp my hands together over my crotch to shield the rest of the world outside of our little bubble.

It feels like we are the only two in the tent right now. I have maybe said two words to the suppliers this whole time.

I can't wait a second longer to touch her. "Excuse me, gentlemen. My woman has just arrived." My feet move, and I stalk toward her, meeting her halfway.

IT IS NINE O'CLOCK, and the gala is in full swing. Family, friends, and clients are drinking and socializing around the penthouse. A live band plays in the heated tent outside. Some guests have already gathered around the stage to dance.

Lexi and Madison are already tipsy, and by the looks of it, are thoroughly enjoying themselves. They are absolutely stunning. The both of them are laughing and smiling over their inside jokes. *Reminds me of Liam and I.* Practically my entire syndicate has their eyes on these two. Except for one. *Where the hell is Liam?* I need him to meet Madison. We haven't spoken since he went to win his girl back this morning. Either they are off somewhere fucking right now or he's nursing a stiff drink at the bar. And I don't see him at the main bar downstairs.

I guess now would be a good time to give Madison a *tour.* Perhaps we'll find Liam along the way. Lexi hangs back with Conor—he seems infatuated with her. *The kid could use a sweet and spunky lass like her.*

Hand in hand, Madison and I ascend the staircase to the second floor, where the bedrooms reside. I take her down the right side of the hall and open the door to the guest room Lexi will be staying in. "This will be Lexi's room this evening." She scans the room and then follows me to the door at the end of the hall.

"*This is my room,*" I rasp, innuendo laced heavily on my tongue. She smiles coyly as I swat her arse and nudge her in, closing the door behind us. I cup her face between both hands and kiss her with fervor, sliding my tongue into her mouth. She clings her fingers around my forearms, kissing me back with the same heat. Our tongues dance while I back her up until her arse hits my king-sized four-post bed.

Gently, I push her back until she rests on her elbows against the mattress. My wanton goddess bunches her dress above her thighs and opens her legs wide. Green straps cup her thighs and run up to a lace garter belt. A flimsy, mesh g-string acts as a barrier between what I crave and my face.

Leaning one knee on the mattress between her thighs, I bend over her and plant kisses along her neck. I run my fingers down over her freshly waxed pussy and cup her heat. I work them lower and down through her folds. "You are so wet for me, Madison." I swirl my middle finger in circles over her clit. Her back arches off the bed, allowing me to bite and suck the curves of her breasts.

"Killian, I can't take it anymore. I need you *now*."

"I told you, you can have anything you want..." I trail off as my face snakes down her body. I kiss and nibble on the inside of her thigh, licking the crease there, between her pussy.

Dropping to my knees, I lift her legs over my shoulders. My hands grip her thighs, dragging her arse off the bed. I slide my index finger down her slit and roam down over the rim of her tight hole. It puckers at my touch, and she tries to squirm up the bed. My grip on her thigh tightens, keeping her in place. "I *will* claim this one day," I state, looking up at her, making sure she is still with me. Her eyes blaze with an inferno I've yet to see. *She is turned on by the idea of it.* I smile innocently at her before moving my finger back up.

Hooking my finger over the g-string, I pull it aside and replace my tongue where it once sat. Madison gasps on contact. A tremble vibrates her body as I continue to lick and suck her. She is mewling and moaning as my tongue plunges in and out of her dripping entrance. My hands find her thighs again, and I tighten my hold around them, securing her closer to my face and spreading her wider.

"Ahh, that feels so fucking good," she breathes out as I slip two fingers inside her and suck her clit.

"Killian...I am so close...so...ahhh." Designer heels dig into my shoulder blades, and her walls clench around my finges. Her knuckles begin to turn white as she grips the comforter and arches her back.

She is gorgeous when she comes.

I lap up her juices and slide her thong back in place. Madison relaxes against the comforter and closes her eyes. Her hand rests over her heart as she breathes in and out.

I adjust my bulging erection and reach a hand out to help her up. *It's going to have to wait 'til later. We've got all night.*

WE REJOIN Lexi downstairs at the patio bar. She and Madison are whispering and giggling—most likely discussing the events of our absence. *I swear women talk more about their sex lives than men do.* Conor is still lingering next to them, drinking a pint and enjoying some oysters.

The band is playing more lively music as the New Year approaches. Madison runs her hand down my shoulder and squeezes my hand. "Lexi and I are going to dance. Would you like to come?"

Conor gets up and takes Lexi's hand, twirling her onto the dance floor. *Good for him.* The lad is super romantic. He could use a good woman by his side. I'm sure Madison won't mind.

I take my own lady's hand and spin her towards the stage. The lights are reflecting off the crystals on her mask. She looks like royalty tonight. An outfit designed for a queen. *My Queen.* I pull her back towards me, her body landing flush with mine. She steadies herself by gripping my biceps. Those gorgeous chocolate eyes find mine as I loop her arms around my neck.

We once again fall into our little bubble. The noise becomes dull and distant. It is just our breathing, the touch of her warm hand around mine, and the music. I grab the nape of her neck, latching my lips to hers. My hand slides slowly down her back and over the swell of her arse as we dance. I hold her body tightly against mine, devouring her lips. My cock strains against her thigh, letting her know *just* how ready I am for tonight.

Someone clearing their throat breaks me out of the trance I'm in. I place one last kiss on the tip of Madison's nose before we break apart. Madison turns towards Lexi, talking nonsense, embarrassed of being caught in an intimate moment. The waitress hands her a glass of champagne, and she takes a long sip, fanning her face and laughing.

Liam stands in front of me, looking like a goddamn trainwreck. His tuxedo is wrinkled and unbuttoned at the top. His hair is dishevelled. My guess is he didn't get his lady back. He finishes his double shot of whiskey in one swig and slams the tumbler onto the waitress' tray as she passes. *Fuck. He's tanked.* He only drinks like this when shit gets heavy.

He grips my shoulder with force. "Kil, ya gonna introduce me to yer woman?"

Madison whips her head around mid-laugh. Her eyes go wide like she's seen a ghost, which I guess she has—*he looks like the undead tonight.*

Liam stumbles back. "Damn, Liam. You're a fucking mess!" I grip his shoulder to steady him. "I take it you couldn't get her back?" I soften my voice.

"No." He runs a shaky hand through his hair. "When I stopped by her house this morning, her mum told me she had a *boyfriend*," he explains, his voice laced with disdain.

"Soo...are you going to introduce us?" He gestures his pointer finger between himself and Madison.

"Madison, I'd like you to meet my best frien–my *brother*–Liam," I say while pulling him to me and slapping his back.

She turns to me with a curious look on her face. "Brother? I thought you were an only child." Her hands reach up to play with her necklace. I wrap my hand around her waist and pull her to my other side.

"I thought so too," I laugh, giving Liam a squeeze. "We just found out on Christmas that we share the same Da." I kiss her on the top of her head. "I'm sorry I didn't tell you, sweetheart. It was a lot to take in."

Liam sticks his hand out a short distance, considering we are all huddled together—"Lovely to meet you…"

"Madison…Madison Marrone." She grips his hand and shakes it, pulling back immediately. My poor girl is probably terrified of him and his erratic behavior. He's not acting like himself.

He must have really loved her.

"It's a pleasure to meet you, Madison. Killian is a lucky guy to have a beautiful woman like you on his arm." He pulls away from me. "Excuse me, the bar is calling my name," he gruffs before sulking towards the bar.

Madison plays with her necklace some more. This is the first time I've seen her this uncomfortable.

"I'm sorry, love." I lean down and whisper in her ear. "From the looks of it…he's been drinking all night. He's not always so rude." I rub my hands over her arms to relax her. "This morning, he went to try and win back the girl he fell in love with. Poor lad looks destroyed." She nods and looks over to where Liam is leaning against the bar.

"Liam is in charge of our Connecticut business. He takes care of the Triskelion and Schmitty's. I'm surprised you've never seen him before. That's where they met. Madelyn attends your school as well—perhaps you know of her."

She finishes her champagne, and I take the empty glass from

her. "I'll drop this off at the bar and check on Liam. I lace my fingers through hers and we make our way through the crowd to the bar.

"Would you like another drink?" I ask as we settle in next to Liam. His head lifts to look at us.

"Actually, I need to use the restroom first before my bladder explodes," she laughs apprehensively.

I am about to show her the way when Liam offers first. He must have come to his senses and remembered his goddamn manners.

"I'll show you where it is. I have to take a piss anyway." He holds his arm out like a gentleman instead of the caveman he's been already.

"Shall we, Ms. Marrone? Or perhaps you prefer Madison or maybe, *Maddy*?" he laughs, as they start walking towards the doors.

"Madison or Maddy is *fine*." I hear her say in a clipped tone.

She turns back to me. "If Lexi is looking for me, just let her know I went to use the bathroom. I hope she is okay. I don't know where she went."

I look around for Conor and Lexi, but they are nowhere to be found. I hold back a smirk and level my voice to not give it away. "I'm certain she is *just fine*."

CHAPTER 23

LIAM

I'VE BEEN HOLED up in my room, nursing whiskey after whiskey. The noise of the gala downstairs has grown significantly louder. I guess the party is poppin'.

Killian's voice echoes through the hallway. Our rooms are adjacent to each other. Sounds like he is showing someone his room. *Lucky bastard.* That could have been me tonight, but I fucked it up.

The door slams shut, followed by a bang and heavy sighs. I scrub my hands over my face and take a deep breath. Some food will help absorb some of this alcohol, and get me the fuck away from the panting and moaning that's growing louder.

I run a hand through my hair and swing my legs off my bed. It's time to face the music that I am a lonely—*single man.*

Glancing at my reflection in the mirror, I realize what a mess I am. I attempt to smooth out the wrinkles in my tux before donning my black mask and adjusting my bow tie. "Fuck this." I rip the damn thing off and fling it to the floor. I pop the top three buttons of my shirt to reveal my raven tattoo, remembering its significance. The dark black ink is my reminder of strength after loss, and to always let the truth set you free. And the truth is— Madison has moved on. I need to accept that.

"I am so close...so...ahh." The feminine voice seeps through my walls. His woman is about to climax. Her high-pitched desperate voice is eerily similar to Madison's. Flashbacks of our time in her shower blind my vision. *This is sick. I feel like a fucking creep.* I need to get out of here. *Now.*

DOWNSTAIRS LOOKS INCREDIBLE. Everything is done just the way it always is, to a perfect T. I spot my favorite chef in the kitchen and make my way over to her. Her mum was the head chef for quite a while until she took over the reins.

"Hey there, Lainey." She's plating and running back and forth from the stove to the large island. Her eyes light up when they see me. I think she's always had a thing for me, but I never felt that way about her. We grew up together. Don't get me wrong, she is gorgeous, and a fantastic cook, but there's no spark. Not like the dynamite explosion I felt when I was around Madison.

"Liam, what can I do for you?" She smiles at me while her eyes laser-focus on my chest and then my lips.

"What do ya have to absorb all this alcohol in me?" I drop my eyes from hers and steal a piece of bread from the baskets in front of me. I devour it quickly, reaching for another.

She slaps my hand away. "Don't just eat *bread.*" Turning around, she grabs a plate of steak, asparagus, and mashed potatoes from the warmer. *Mmm, it smells delicious.*

"I prepared this for Mr. Kennedy, but he isn't feeling well enough to eat tonight." Her smile falters.

She points to the breakfast stool. "Sit and eat." I chuckle at her demands and do as she asks. Silverware wrapped in a cloth napkin slides across the granite towards me.

"Need anything else?" Lainey starts plating again.

"Yeah. A time machine," I mumble over the mouthful of food I just dug into.

THE DANCE FLOOR is packed with happy couples drinking and dancing. The complete opposite of what I want to be doing right now—*other than the drinking part.*

I make a beeline through the crowd to the bar. It's acceptable to drown my sorrows in more whiskey now that I've eaten. I'll give myself tonight to throw myself a pity party. Tomorrow is a new day, a new year and I will have to move on from her. I wanted her to have a safe life and find a good man. Now I need to honor that.

I sip my drink and lean against the bar to people watch. Conor has his arms around a beautiful blonde in a blue sequined dress. *Go Conor.*

Killian is out there too. He's dancing with a woman in an emerald green gown. Her back is to me but I can make out her tan toned leg that is exposed through the large slit of her dress. I strain my neck over the crowd to try and see the rest of her, but I can't get a full glimpse. Killian has his hands all over her arse, and they are packing on the PDA, lost in each other. Her dark red curled hair sways along with their movements.

I sip my drink once more and start to move through the crowd. I haven't seen Killian all night. It would only be right to check in on him and introduce myself to his woman. Slipping back into the crowd, I navigate towards them and clear my throat when I reach the happy couple. His girl turns away, clearly embarrassed. She starts chatting and giggling with Conor's girl.

A bolt of electricity shoots straight through my heart, nearly stopping it. The palpitations continue as panic starts to creep its way into my soul. *I know that laugh.* I can pick it out of a crowd anywhere—except this woman is a redhead. There is no way in hell Madison is *Killian's woman.*

I study her as a glass of champagne is handed to her. She tilts the glass and takes a sip, fanning her face with the other hand. The waitress is heading my way. I bang back the rest of my drink and slam the tumbler harder than I had wanted onto the tray. She looks startled, and I feel like a dick now.

I place my hand on Killian's shoulder. He is looking at me like I am a wild animal. *I need to see for myself that this isn't Madison.* Maybe my mind is so fucked today that I've started to make up scenarios that don't exist.

"Kil, ya gonna introduce me to yer woman?" I slur, realizing how much alcohol I've consumed today.

That's when *she* stops laughing with her friend to turn around. Her chocolate-brown eyes meet mine. To say her expression said it all is an understatement. *It is Madison.* A mask can't hide her gorgeous face from me. I stumble back in denial. *Did I blackout? Is this just a drunk dream?*

Killian lands a hand on my shoulder to steady me, thinking I'm drunk—*which I am*—but this moment just sobered me up real fucking quick. "Damn, Liam. You're a fucking mess!" Concern and irritation roll off him.

"I take it you couldn't get her back?" He softens his tone.

Madison is staring at me with her big doe eyes. Is she afraid I am going to say something? *Am I going to say something? Fuck, this is so fucked.*

"No." I run a hand through my hair, keeping it from doing something dangerous, like reaching out to touch her lips. "When I stopped by her house this morning, her mum told me she had a *boyfriend*," I say, eyeing Killian. I can't even believe that out of all the people in this world, *he* found *her* on a dating app.

Her posture shifts as she takes in this information. I can't tell if she wants to strangle me, slap me, or kiss me right now.

"Soo... are you going to introduce us?" I wave a finger between her and I. "Madison, I'd like you to meet my best frien —*brother*—Liam," Killian says proudly, pulling me to him and slapping my back.

She turns to him, looking confused as ever. "Brother? I thought you were an only child." Her hand reaches up to her necklace—*a triskelion.* She is fidgeting with it, like she needs something to do with her hands. Killian must have gifted her that.

He pulls her to his side so that we are now huddled together like a football team. Madison's breath hitches at my nearness.

"I thought so too," he laughs, giving me a firm tug closer. "We just found out on Christmas that we share the same Da." Kil leans down and kisses the top of her head. "I'm sorry I didn't tell you, sweetheart. It was a lot to take in."

This is all too much. Seeing his hands on her is driving me nuts.

That should be me.

I inhale her scent, and her eyes flash with a second of lust before they harden again. *She smells so fucking good.* Her enticing perfume involuntarily draws me closer to her. The need to touch her is becoming a problem.

I stick my hand out to 'introduce ourselves properly'...*well, I guess just to touch her...* since I have already been properly introduced to every inch of her body.

"Lovely to meet you..." I trail off knowing that I am unfairly making her squirm.

"Madison...Madison Marrone," her grip is tight around my hand, basically telling me to stop fucking around. She shakes it and pulls her hand back like she's been burned—but we both know that's *not* what we just felt.

"It's a *pleasure* to meet you, Madison. Killian is a lucky guy to have a beautiful woman like you on his arm." I suddenly feel overwhelmed. This whole situation is *so* beyond coincidental and crazy. I can't be around her right now, or Killian will discover she is my '*a rún mo chroí*'—secret of my heart.

I move out of Killian's embrace. "Excuse me. The bar is calling my name." I trudge back to the bar and don't look back.

A few moments later, Kil and Maddy appear in my peripheral. I let out a silent sigh. So much for trying to avoid them. Killian places her empty champagne glass on the bar. *Looks like we are both parched, darling.* I stare at them. She is playing the nervous game, the one she's good at. I can *guarantee* you she's itching for a cigarette right now. *I know I am.*

"Would you like another drink?" Killian rubs her hand with gentle strokes.

"Actually, I need to use the restroom first before my bladder explodes," she laughs, shakily attempting to mask her nerves.

I know now is my time to get her alone. I straighten my back, towering over her. "I'll show you where it is. I have to take a piss anyway." *I bet her eyebrow is raised under that mask at my suggestion.*

I hold my arm out to her—like the gentleman I am—*or am supposed to be.* She reluctantly wraps her arm around mine and my body buzzes with satisfaction.

Satisfaction I don't deserve.

"Shall we, Ms. Marrone? Or perhaps you prefer Madison or maybe, *Maddy*?" I tease her some more. It feels good to get under her skin again.

"Madison or Maddy is *fine*." Irritation radiates off her. *She is pissed.* Her black nails dig into my tux sleeves.

Oh my sweet spitfire, *I've missed you.* I can't hold back a chuckle at the insanity of how the hell we got here. We make a few strides towards the house when she swivels her head back to Killian.

"If Lexi is looking for me, just let her know I went to use the bathroom. I hope she is okay. I don't know where she went." *Oh Maddy. Always worrying about others.*

He scans the crowd. Looks like Conor and his lady in blue are missing. A hint of a smile tugs on Kil's lips. "I'm certain she is *just fine*."

She nods and I lead her to the doors leading to the house with more force.

CHAPTER 24

MADISON

I ABRUPTLY RIP my arm away from him nearly a second after we walk through the sliding doors. I wrap it around my center to control my shuddering and calm the butterflies swarming there. The worst part of it all is *I can't figure out why. Is it anger or desire?*

I am so fucking angry with Liam for leaving me. And I'm furious with myself for not trusting my intuition—the one telling me there was a connection between Killian and him. Of course, I didn't bother to ask about it.

I also feel like an addict right now.

My body is betraying me by responding to him—so easily turned on by a look, a simple touch, *his smell.*

He places a hand on the small of my back, guiding me through the kitchen and toward the staircase. *I stop in my tracks.* There is definitely a bathroom on this floor. I turn around and stare him down, my anger now escalating. *What is his game?*

"Why are we going upstairs? I'm sure there are half a dozen bathrooms down here." I stomp my heel for good measure.

"Lower your voice," he commands, looking around. "Stop making a scene, and I'll tell you."

We climb the stairs with his hand still lingering on my back.

He pulls me down the same hallway Killian took me earlier. With hesitant steps, I keep walking in the direction of Killian's bedroom until Liam throws open the door adjacent to it.

He ushers me in and slams the door shut. Caging me in with his muscular arms stretched over my head. My breathing becomes shallow and intensified. Heat radiates off him; his breathing is labored by my neck.

"What the *fuck* are you thinking, Madison?" His face is only inches from mine.

I slam my fists into his chest, trying to move him. But he's a bolder, and I'm an ant in comparison.

A smile crosses his face before his gaze becomes lethal. "You do realize who Killian is, correct? *Who I am*. He moves his hand down to wrap a strand of my hair around his finger. "Nice hair color, by the way—but I prefer you as a brunette," he winks.

I want to smack that smug look off his face. Instead, I slam my fist at his chest again. "Get *off* me, Liam," I laugh. Hysteria starts to build inside me. "I wanted you!" I shout as I keep hitting his chest. "You had your chance, and you *left me*. Just left me without a fucking trace." Hot tears build behind my eyes, blurring my vision.

Liam eases back and drops his hand from my hair. I duck under him and walk toward the open door. Hoping it is his en suite. *I assume this is his bedroom—it smells just like him— lavender and cedarwood.* Relief floods me when I confirm it's a bathroom. Slamming the door behind me, I slide my body down it. I claw at the mask and toss it onto the tiled floor. Tears fall as I press my fists to my eyes. Violent sobs begin to rock my body.

I hear a thump on the other side of the door and recognize he is sitting on the opposite side. His head thuds against the wood, and he releases a sigh.

"Maddy...you have to understand...it was never about not wanting you. I would have done *anything* for you. I just couldn't be selfish with you. You are smart, beautiful, and pure. The life

—*this* life isn't cut out for you. No matter how much we can protect you, things can go wrong. It's too dangerous."

"I don't care, Liam," I say between sobs. "You made me feel more alive than I have ever felt in my entire life. I was willing to face anything—as long as you were by my side. You didn't even give me a chance or the choice. *Killian did.* And that's why I am here."

"I realize that now. When I went to Miami on assignment, I was miserable. I typed out text messages to you every night just to delete them. I couldn't subject you to this life. It wasn't fair," he says more calmly.

I need to see him. I have spent countless days wondering when or if I would ever see him again. And now he is here, telling me he does want me.

What shitty timing, Universe.

Getting up, I open the door and look down at him sitting on the floor. He looks up at me, and my anger melts away. The black mask he was wearing rests on his forehead. He spins around to face me, reaches a hand out, and starts caressing his knuckles along my exposed calf. "You hold this power over me, Madison. It is *so wrong* to want this still. Killian is my blood. I *can't*—I shouldn't still want you, but I do."

His confession makes my heart soar, but then I think of Killian and how amazing he is. Liam is right. We *can't* do this. We shouldn't even be around each other.

"Did you know?" I sniffle.

Liam gets up off the floor and reaches around me to grab a tissue. He hands it to me, and I hold it up to my nose.

"Know what?" He wipes my tears away with both of his thumbs. Gently, he twines his fingers into my hair and cradles my face.

"That Killian started dating me."

He directs my head up from staring at his chest, making eye contact. "No, sweetheart. I didn't. It was just as much of a shock to me tonight as it was to you. For the first time in my life, I thought I was having a heart attack," he chuckles.

God, he's still just as handsome. His hair is even sexier, all dishevelled. The open buttons of his shirt expose his ravens' tattoo and the hair that sits there.

He grabs my hand and places it over his chest as if reading my mind. Strong fingers wrap around mine, keeping it in place. A rapid heart beats beneath my palm, scarily in sync with my own.

"I'm not telling you we need to cheat—because that would be awful for everyone involved—but I'm not giving up on us, Madison. A connection like this...*and I know you still feel it too*... doesn't just burn out or go away. No matter who you move on with. Even if that person is my brother."

I shake my head. *This is so fucked up.* I love Killian—but I also have this undeniable feeling I can't shake about Liam. It's magnetic. He is the gasoline to the fire inside me. *If we let these feelings spill over, we will all go up in flames.*

"You went to my house this morning?" I take my hand off his chest and back away from him and his intensity. That only makes him inch closer, so he's standing at the threshold of the door.

He points to the toilet. "You pee, I'll talk," he smirks.

"Are you *insane*? You're going to get us both killed!" I hiss.

"Fine, then *I'll* piss *and* talk." He breezes past me to the toilet, tugs his zipper down, and sets himself free.

I spin around, shielding my eyes, but it's too late. *Thoughts of Liam thrusting into me in my shower come to the surface.* I dig my nails into my palms to stop these thoughts from roaming down a dangerous path.

"I did go to your house this morning. I planned on begging you to take me back— and I mean beg. I was willing to wrap my arms around your legs and ask you to go with me to the gala. I wanted to tell you how sorry I was for how I left you. The memory of your face when I left still burns in my mind."

He clears his throat, which is thick with raw emotion. "My idea was to shield you from this life, but I realized quickly that a connection like ours has no boundaries. Nothing could keep me from you, even if I tried. I couldn't resist you any longer. This time, I would give you full disclosure and the choice." I hear the hiss of his zipper and the toilet flush. He washes his hands, and I turn to make eye contact with him in the mirror.

"I love him, Liam," I say in a whisper.

He turns around and leans against the countertop, pulling me to his body. I try to resist, but it's hopeless. "Do you love me?" His eyes are soft and full of hope.

"I...what we have...or *had*...is *different*."

"That doesn't answer my question, Madison." He pulls my face to his, so that I am only inches from his lips. "I think you are too afraid to admit it out loud." His whispered words flutter over me as his lips nearly brush mine. "You don't have to say it now, but one day you will. I'll wait. I can be a very patient man."

He releases me and walks out of the bathroom, shutting the door behind him.

I lock the door and use the bathroom. My eyes are puffy and red. *Shit.* Turning the faucet to cold, I splash some water on my face. Thank God for luxury makeup...I have no mascara tracks or smudges. I pat my face dry with a hand towel and put on my mask.

When I step out of the bathroom, I find him sitting on his bed with two cigarettes between his fingers.

"Still smoking, baby?" He holds them up to me.

God. Yes, I need a cigarette.

"Not since you left. I couldn't...without the memories..." I trail off. "Never mind."

Liam stands and hands me one. "For old times sake. Come on..." he chuckles, holding my hand again.

WE ARE on the top floor balcony. These views of the Empire State building are absolutely insane. The gas firepit is on, but I am still freezing. It is starting to flurry, making the moment even more surreal—almost enchanting.

Liam shrugs off his jacket and wraps it around me. His signature scent envelopes me, bringing a wave of calmness with it. He keeps his cigarette hanging between his lips as he rubs my arms, creating friction.

"Thank you." I take a drag of my cigarette as he watches me intently.

He takes another pull of his own and blows out smoke as he talks. "Does Kil know you smoke?"

I shake my head, exhaling. "He doesn't...I'm sure he will now."

He laughs, a genuine smile forming on his face. "Just blame me. Say I was a bad influence on you."

I slap his arm playfully. "We need to be on our best behavior, Liam. *I mean it.* I don't know how to feel right now, but I know that this," I gesture between us, "is not right."

Liam's smile fades, and he becomes remorseful. "*We are right*, but I get what you mean." He takes one more drag of his cigarette before snuffing it out in the ashtray. I hand him mine, and he does the same.

He looks down at his watch. "Christ. Let's get you back before midnight."

Liam and I are on our way down the staircase from the upper level when we come face-to-face with Chase and his father. I stagger a bit prompting Liam to place a protective hand in front of me. He blocks me with his body, preventing them from coming too close. I realize at that moment what this looks like. I am still wearing Liam's jacket. *Fuck.*

"Alan. Chase." He nods, trying to divert us around them and

back to the safety of the party. He grabs my hand from behind to walk by them.

Chase throws his hand across the banister. His father steps next to him, blocking our egress. Liam's hand clutches mine tighter. You can visibly see his muscles tense through his dress shirt.

"Lemme guess...you two were off *fucking*? Chase says sadistically. "I wonder what Killian would think about this." He eyes the tux jacket I'm wearing, and Liam's shirt that's unbuttoned at the top.

Alan tsks and shakes his head. "What a shame. First, Jack has an affair and finds out he has a *bastard* child..." he spits vitriol at Liam. "then that bastard has an affair with the heir's woman." He turns his head my way.

I can't just stand here and let Liam cause a scene. He is about to snap. I need to say something—and quick.

"Chase is aware Liam and I are old friends from our school bar. Killian is aware of this as well." I lie about the last part. "Liam and I used to smoke out back all the time. And considering I am drinking, and Killian doesn't smoke, he offered me one," I say as innocently as possible.

Alan and Chase don't look convinced.

Crap.

"Thankfully, he was generous enough to lend me his jacket," I add, patting Liam on his shoulder. *He needs to cut it out.*

Chase lifts his arm out of our way but doesn't move. He crosses his arms over his chest and looks directly at Liam. "How much did she *scream* the night you split open my face and fucked her while she was on ecstacy?" he asks menacingly.

Liam lunges and grabs Chase by the throat, bending him over the banister. Alan steps forward to intervene. "Liam, that is *enough*. Take this as *your warning*. At any point, we can tell Killian of your indiscretions."

Liam loosens his grip on Chase's neck. "Quite frankly, *I don't give a flying fuck if you do.* We have nothing to hide, *unlike* you gombeens. Now get the *fuck* out of my face before I tell Jack *exactly* what your son does with our drugs." *Thank God it's just us on the upper staircase.* Liam's voice is echoing down the hall.

He turns his fury back to Chase. "And if you *ever* talk about Madison like that again...plastic surgery won't even be able to fix your face—because *there will be nothing left of it.*"

Liam releases Chase and pushes past him, tugging me down the rest of the staircase. We get to the middle floor, where the bedrooms are, and he bangs a left. The first door on the left is a bathroom. He ushers me in and shuts the door quietly.

My eyes open wide, taking in his appearance. His hands are shaking violently. He looks like he is about to turn around and teach Chase a lesson.

I reach out to place a gentle hand over his. "Liam, it's okay. Maybe we should tell Killian. Come clean. He'll understand. He and I weren't together when you and I..." I taper off.

His eyes meet mine with rage and desire, all mixed into one. If I didn't know him already, that look would terrify me. Instead, it does the opposite.

It excites me.

Thrills me.

My body tingles with anticipation.

He stalks toward me until my ass hits the marble sink, caging his arms around me. "I'm not mad because I am *afraid* Killian will find out—let him. *I'd watch the world burn just to have one more chance with you.*" His declaration turns my mind and heart into putty.

We are nose to nose, and I know where this is going. I press a gentle hand against his chest, to stop his advance. My mouth is dry, refusing to say it.

Liam runs the back of his knuckles along my cheek, then his thumb over my bottom lip. My lips part on impact. He pulls away an inch, his eyes begging me for permission. That is when I see the glow of his digital watch:

11:55 PM

Oh shit.

I grab his wrist and push it toward his face. "We need to go. *Now*."

CHAPTER 25

KILLIAN

THE COUNTDOWN HAS STARTED. Lexi and Conor are wrapped around each other by the stage with the rest of the guests. I scan the tent for Liam and Madison. It's been quite a while since they left for the bathroom. I hope everything is alright.

Just as I am about to grab my phone and call her, I spot my green goddess running my way. Liam splits off and goes straight to the bar.

"I was getting worried. Are you alright?" I ask her, rubbing the tops of her arms.

A nervous smile breaks out on her face. "I'm fine, Kil. I have something to tell you," she says.

Liam approaches behind me and laughs. "She's a closet smoker, mate." He slaps my back. Madison shoots him a glare, then swivels her head to me for forgiveness.

I massage her shoulders, releasing the tension built up there. "Ahh. You and Liam went to smoke after the bathroom." I flip him the bird. "I can find better use for that pretty mouth than smoking a cigarette," I chuckle and kiss the tip of her nose. She does smell like cigarettes, but I don't mind. *I can think of a few ways to persuade her to stop.*

The waitress comes towards us with a bottle of champagne and a tray of glasses. She leaves them on the cocktail table in front of us as the clock ticks down from ten.

10. 9. 8. 7. 6

I slide behind my gorgeous girl and wrap my arms around her waist. I leave a trail of kisses up her exposed neck. She shivers against me, making my cock stir.

5. 4. 3. 2. 1.

HAPPY NEW YEAR!

The crowd goes wild, kissing and jumping up and down. Confetti cannons explode off the stage. New York City is loud and active right now, adding to the riveting moment.

"Happy New Year, beautiful," I whisper in her ear before leaning down to kiss her. Her hand wraps around my head as I deepen the kiss. *Mmm. I can't wait to take her on every surface of my room later.*

Madison pulls away as Lexi comes over and shouts, "Happy New Year!" They embrace and sway back and forth like lovers.

"Love you, Lex. Another year in the books together." She kisses her cheek.

I turn around and pop the champagne, pouring a glass for the small group we have gathered here. Madison helps me distribute them to Lexi and Conor. She smiles shyly at Liam while offering him a glass. He looks like he's in a better mood. Hopefully, he made a better impression on her. Perhaps they are both calmer now that they've smoked.

Liam accepts a glass and leans over to place a kiss on her cheek. "Happy New Year, Madison." He turns around and shakes my hand. "Cheers, brother," he raises his glass.

The dance floor disperses after the band announces the Viennese hour has started inside. *"Latch (Acoustic)" by Sam Smith* begins playing. I clutch Madison by the waist and place her champagne glass on the table.

I twirl her in the direction of the center of the dance floor. Her gorgeous satin green gown flows around her. We glide across the dancefloor as if we have been doing this for years. My hand is at her waist, and her delicate hand is in mine. *Our bubble is intact again. And then it's just us.*

Her chocolate brown eyes are glowing with unshed tears. I spin her out, whirl her around and draw her back to me. Madison releases a little gasp as I dip her over my bent knee. Slowly, I pull her to me and kiss her with all the emotion I have coursing through my bloodstream. I can see our future together.

Many more New Year's Eve Galas.

My ring on her finger.

Her belly swollen with our child.

The song slows to an end and our lips part. "I am so in love with you, Madison. You make me so happy."

"Kil." Liam interrupts our moment.

"It better be damn important, Liam. I'm having a moment with my woman," I laugh. This moment is so fucking light and free of the darkness that looms over us all the time. "Da...he just...we need to go right now," his voice is solemn.

My heart beats wildly in my chest. Madison's eyes turn even glossier. She knows it, Liam knows it, I know it.

Jack Kennedy just died.

"Go to my room when you finish enjoying the party, sweetheart." I clear my throat, trying to remain calm. "I will do my best to come and see you when everything settles down."

"I'll keep an eye on her. You should go, Kil." He squeezes the back of my neck sympathetically. "I'll meet you up there after you've had some time alone with him," he sighs.

I place a firm hand on his shoulder. "He's your father too, Liam."

I'm sure it's just as hard losing Da for him as it is for me. We both got the pleasure of growing up with him. He taught us everything and gave us everything we could ever want. I mean fuck—*he left us a goddamn empire.*

"I know, but you two shared a special bond. And you are next in line. So go. Figure it all out. You know there will be a lot of people waiting on your decisions. I'll make sure Madison is safe and settled in for the night."

"Thanks, brother."

Madison throws her arms around my waist and lays her head on my chest. "I'm so sorry, Killian." I place a kiss on the top of her head. "I love you, handsome. Go. Please don't worry about me," she says adamantly. Her hands grip the lapels of my tux, pulling me in for one last kiss before releasing me and rubbing her thumb along my cheek. I give her my best reassuring smile and leave the two of them on the dancefloor.

I SIT with a double of whiskey at the large round table in my father's office. My tuxedo jacket is draped over the chair behind me. I ditched the bow tie, popped the top buttons on my shirt, and rolled my sleeves up. Sweat beads on my forehead. All eyes have been on me since the second I stepped foot upstairs.

The lawyer is here, along with many of the higher-ups of this organization. Most of them were already here. The other leaders have received word back in Ireland and Miami.

I am blindly signing paperwork, officially taking over ownership of this home and many of my father's other assets. Liam will be up soon to do the same. I'm thankful for him tonight. He is keeping my woman comforted when I can't. Knowing Madison, she is probably feeling uneasy about all of this. My Queen knows that deep down, *I never wanted the power.*

LIAM COMES UP AN HOUR LATER. *A much more sober and put-together Liam.* He's changed out of his tuxedo and into his 'normal' attire: black t-shirt, jeans, and boots. He takes a seat next to me and laces his fingers together, resting them on the table.

"So what's the plan, brother?" Concern is written all over his face. He knows a lot is about to change over the next few days. It will equally affect his life as well as my own.

"I promised to keep Madison's life a nice balance between her world and mine. I plan to keep that promise as best I can." I look up at him from my paperwork.

"What do you need me to do?" he asks as the lawyer places some legal documents in front of him.

"She isn't going to like this—but I need her to stay here in our home. It's the safest, most guarded place. Her presence here tonight alerted everyone that *she is mine.* Madison living back in Connecticut would be a risk I'm not willing to take." I comb my fingers through my hair.

"I'm sure that won't be a problem to arrange," he mumbles, signing the documents with a heavy hand.

"Madison has a J-term to finish in order to graduate. I wouldn't want to derail those plans. The original plan was for her to go home to her off-campus house after the New Year. When the term was over at the end of January, she was going to move home to Long Island—*but that is all about to change.* I'll have her belongings brought here so she is comfortable. Her classes are all online, and I know the professors, so it should work out fine."

"I agree. This is the safest place for her. There are enough men to keep her safe while everything is in transition, and we are most vulnerable," he nods, flipping through the pages with shaky hands.

"I won't keep Lexi from her either. Conor can bring her here if Madison desires. Madison needs to understand that she isn't a *prisoner in this home.* She can leave to go to campus or meet for lunch with family. Whatever she wants. As long as she is with you," I drop the bomb on him. He snaps his head up from his paperwork.

"Me?" He points a pen-held hand to his chest.

"I need to head to Ireland to finish the transition of power." I take a sip of my whiskey. "Da's connections are meeting me at the airport in a few days. You are my second now, Liam. If I die —this all goes to you. In saying that, I need you home to run the Syndicate while I take care of things overseas. Conor will take over the Connecticut business until we settle it all out."

Liam whistles out. "Damn, Kil. You know she's going to put up a fight on that."

"I don't have a choice. And what's worse is I'll need to be there for a few months. Three at minimum," I let out a groan, burying my face in my hands. Just thinking of being away from her for that long breaks my heart.

Liam raises his eyebrows. "Well, shit."

"I hope that this doesn't ruin us...I can't lose her too. In such a short period of time, she has become *my everything.* I hate that she will be thrown into this life like this."

"What is the saying? 'Distance makes the heart grow fonder'?" he laughs, lightening the mood.

"I need a favor from you, Liam." My mood starts to shift to a more serious one.

"Anything. What do you need, Kil?"

"I trust you with *my life.* And now I am trusting you with *hers.* I need you to move back here, Liam. I know you have your own place in Connecticut, but Madison needs round the clock protection."

"You got it. Not a problem." He signs the last document and hands it to the lawyer.

That was easier than expected. I thought he would have put up a fight. Liam has a preference for his home in Connecticut. It's nothing like the city. His place is all woods and trees, and *space*. We are polar opposites when it comes to our likes.

"Thanks, *sweetheart*." I crack a smile as he stands to leave. "Is Madison okay?"

"She is. The girls had some dessert and went back to Lexi's room until you're able to head back."

"I should be wrapping this up soon. Can you let Maddy know she can help herself to my shower? My bathroom has all the overnight items she needs. I'll meet her in my room—well, I guess it's *our room* now."

"Sure." He turns on his boot and leaves.

The lawyer hands me another stack of papers. "Sir, I need you to sign off on the rest of the funeral arrangements. They will be here to take your father's body to the funeral home shortly." He pats my back. "Respectfully, I think you should get some rest after this. It is going to be a long few weeks."

I run a hand through my hair and sign the remaining papers, anxious to get back to my woman. *I need to be inside her right now*. Her gentle touch will calm the storm brewing inside me. The restlessness I feel. The frustration of knowing I won't be around her in just a few short days. The fear of taking over the family business. Of running an empire.

I want nothing more than to show her how much I love her.

I just hope she trusts me enough to leave her for a few months.

CHAPTER 26

MADISON

LIAM WALKED me to Killian's room, letting me know Kil would be back soon. He lingered by the door for a while, making sure I was okay, but something was off with him. He could barely look at me, shifting his weight back and forth. Before I got the chance to ask him what was wrong, he was gone. *Talk about whiplash.* Something important was discussed upstairs, and it's only a matter of time before it comes to my attention.

I'm left alone with my crazy thoughts, no longer in the company of my best friend. Liam said I could help myself to the shower, and I would, but I can't get this dress off without Killian. I don't want to bother Lexi, and I sure as hell wasn't asking Liam for help. I sit on the bed and fidget with my hands while I wait for Killian. My mind is running a million miles a minute. *Did Killian find out about Liam and I? Is this why he was so weird before?*

A gentle knock on the door gets my attention. Killian is standing in the doorway with his arms open wide in invitation. I've never seen him look so disarranged. He is usually so put together. I run to him, and he wraps his arms tenderly around me. The safety I feel there is incredible. No matter what he tells me now, we will get through this.

He kisses my head. "Hi, love."

"Hi." I squeeze him tighter.

We stay like that for a few moments before he releases me and shuts the door behind him. His hands caress my face as he kisses me. He guides me backward to the bathroom, our lips not breaking apart for a second.

When we reach the door's threshold, he begins stripping my dress off me. His hands are not gentle with the material. The noise of ripping fills the space, along with our heavy panting.

"I need you, sweetheart," he whispers against my neck.

"Take me, Killian. I'm yours," I say, pulling his shirt open and running my nails down his chest. He moans and lifts me onto the counter of the double sink.

"Lift your foot," he commands.

He removes each of my heels and then reaches for my garter belt, sliding it to the ground. He is naked within seconds, sporting a huge erection. Killian licks up from the swells of my breast to my neck and latches on. Confident fingers make quick work of the remaining bra and thong.

I am totally bare to him as he slides in between my legs. I wrap them possessively around his hips. Desperate lips crush against mine as his fingers tangle in my hair.

Reaching down, he rubs me, making me slick and raring to go. I don't need more time, I'm ready, and he is *more* than ready. He lifts my ass off the counter and pulls me towards him, lining himself up to my entrance. In one swift movement, he thrust inside me. I wrap my arms around his neck and trail kisses from his collarbone to his ear. He is fucking me slowly and passionately, but I know he needs *more*.

"Don't hold back," I whisper.

"Fuck, you're perfect." He pulls out and places me on the floor, spinning me around to face the mirror. My cheeks are red and rosy. His eyes roam, taking me all in like it'll be the last time he'll ever see me.

Killian pushes my breasts down onto the counter and spreads my legs open. He slides home again, but this time with more powerful thrusts. It's almost too much, stealing my breath away.

"Watch us in the mirror," his deep voice interrupts my immense pleasure.

I lift my head to watch.

His muscles clenching with each thrust.

His hair falling out of place and over his brow.

His strong hands wrapped tightly around my hips.

Sweat drips down his body onto mine. My tits bounce with each movement. Wild curls fall loose around my face and over my swollen lips.

It's the most erotic scene I've ever witnessed.

The pressure of my sensitive clit pressed against the edge of the counter and him slamming into me, is about to unhinge me. I feel my climax building as my legs begin to tremble.

"Come with me, angel," he grunts, close to his own release.

One more thrust and I see stars. The reflection of us in the mirror becomes blurred. "Ahh... Killian. Jesusss," I woosh out.

I press my cheek to the cold marble and try and catch my breath. A second later, his cock pulses with his release. "Fuck, baby." He lowers his head so that it rests between my shoulder blades.

Soft kisses pepper the back of my neck as he pulls out of me. He swivels around to turn the shower on while I peel myself off the counter. Kil reaches out a hand and pulls me under the warm spray. It's exactly what I need right now, soothing my deliciously sore muscles on impact.

"You mean *everything* to me, Madison," he says. His strong hands grip me, pulling me flush against him. "I know it's about to get tough. Just don't give up on me, okay?" Warning butterflies swirl in my stomach at his words.

"I have to leave for a few months after my father's funeral.

It's not something I can avoid," his voice wavers, which breaks my heart.

I look up at him and can't tell if he is crying or if it's water droplets. "I'll come with you. I'll be by your side."

He grabs the shampoo and starts massaging it into my scalp. "You can't baby. It is entirely too dangerous. We are vulnerable right now, more than ever. Until it becomes official that I am the leader of this syndicate, things can become chaotic and risky."

I shake my head in silent protest, but he hushes me.

"It has to be this way, Madison. I promised you that you would be able to continue your dreams, and I intend to make sure they happen. Liam is going to stay here and protect you."

"No! I can take a break and take my classes when I return. I am graduating early anyway!" I shout as angry tears pool in my eyes.

He maneuvers us to rinse the shampoo from my hair while caressing my face between his palms. "This is the only way I can keep you safe. I'm sorry, love."

"Liam is...all caveman-like and irritable." I lie, knowing being around him without Killian is a dangerous combination. *Probably even riskier than going with Killian.*

A rumble escapes his lips before he smiles. "He can be. Tonight he was in a funk, but he's my brother. He'll do anything for you. He would lay his life down for you if it called for it."

He is massaging the conditioner into my hair when I break down. I cover my face in my hands, lowering my face to his chest. "I can't be without you," I sob into his chest.

"I don't want to be either, but you aren't dating a simple man, love. You knew this."

I nod my head. *I did agree to this.* It's my turn to put on my big girl pants and do what I have to for him. *For us.* This won't be easy on him, either.

He lifts my face and bends his head to stare into my eyes.

"There is one thing I ask of you, and I need you to understand just how important it is..." he trails off.

Fuck, this doesn't sound good.

"I need you to move here, to my house. This room is *our* room now. You'll be safe here." His hands land on my shoulders and he starts kneading them.

"Liam and the rest of my men will protect you from any threat. My chefs and housekeepers can assist you with anything you may need." He's still talking but I haven't heard much since he said Liam and I would be shacking up under one roof.

I am in total shock. *Move here? With Liam? Holy shit.*

"Your classes are online, so all of your work can be done from here."

"What am I supposed to tell my family?" I counter.

"Whatever you'd like. Tell them you moved in with me for the J-term because your lease was up. Tell them you went abroad. Whatever will make them question less." He lowers my head back under the spray and massages my silky strands under the water.

"So, I won't be able to go out?" My voice is now shaking at the severity of the situation. This is *real* danger. He is obviously worried about my safety.

"Not at all. You aren't a prisoner, baby. I want you to enjoy New York City. Lexi can even come here whenever she wants. Liam just has to tag along with you wherever you go. I promise he'll behave," he winks at me.

Behave. Ha. Yeah, okay.

Killian hands me a bottle of my face wash. "Did someone get this from my bag?" I cock my head to the side in curiosity.

He starts washing himself, and I can't help but stare at his sudsy, gorgeous body.

"I had my housekeepers purchase all your skincare and toiletries for my house." His eyes are closed while he scrubs his face. "I can feel you staring at me," he smirks.

"I definitely was, Mr. Kennedy." This situation may not be so bad. I've done long-distance before. I can do it again—except this time, I have a *bodyguard*. A brooding, sexy, arcane bodyguard.

He rinses himself off, and I wash my face. I feel his arms wrap around me and his cock twitch against my ass. "We aren't going to get much sleep tonight, Ms. Marrone." His teeth graze my neck as his words ring with an insatiable hunger.

THE FUNERAL WAS INTENSE. So many men and women from all walks of life showed up to pay their respects. Killian and Liam let me attend but kept me wedged between them the entire time.

There wasn't a moment other than using the bathroom where they weren't with me. If Liam had a say, he would have been inside the stall with me.

Damn, bodyguard.

Many eyes followed us as I walked alongside Killian. His arm, his lips, or his hand never left my body. He introduced me as 'his woman' or 'his Queen' to everyone he spoke to.

Liam was uneasy the whole time. I could feel the tension rolling off him—and *not* the sexual kind. It was the kind he displayed on the staircase with Chase and his father—*who were also in attendance.* Their disgusting eyes tracked us everywhere we went. I want to tell Killian about them, but then he would know I was drugged at his bar...and that Liam helped me out. *In more ways than one.*

We end up having an intimate dinner back at the house in honor of Mr. Kennedy. The alcohol has been pouring steadily all night, and the mood has shifted from somber to excitement for their new leader. Killian has been much more relaxed than he was on New Year's. I've been watching him. As much as he was worried about taking on his new role, he is already doing so seamlessly. I see the way he talks to other members and leaders. He was a natural-born leader.

Liam, on the other hand, has been quiet all day. He didn't say a word to me unless he had to. *Maybe he's just as worried as I am about these next few months.*

As the time ticks closer to midnight, my gut wrenches with the thought of Killian leaving for the airport.

The last of the guests are in the main hall saying their goodbyes and well wishes. Liam and I are in the dining room, still nursing our drinks in silence. He pats my leg under the table, eliciting a hushed gasp from me. I turn to look at him —*okay, more like gawk at him.* He just sips his drink, ignoring me as if he didn't just touch me. I wonder if he realizes how shitty this situation is that we are in? I hope that he knows he needs to back off. Killian *chose me*—he *didn't*. It's too late for us to be anything other than friends.

Killian comes back in, breaking our awkward tension. I rise from my seat to wrap my arms around him. He places a brief kiss on my cheek, smelling like whiskey and cigars.

"I love you, Madison. I promise you if we can make it through this, we can make it through anything." He rubs his knuckles along my jaw.

Liam stands, scraping his chair against the floor. "I'll be outside grabbing a smoke." He points to the back patio.

Killian nods. When Liam is out of sight, he lunges for my mouth. This man is putting so much into this kiss.

He *wants* me to remember this.

He wants to imprint this memory into my brain so when I am missing him, I can think of this moment. The moment I realized how much he means to me and how much I *burn* for him.

His tongue slips through my lips and dances with my own. Teeth clash as we claw at each other. His hands are squeezing my ass and lifting my leg up. He rubs himself against me so I can feel how hard he is for me. We go at it for a while, losing ourselves in each other.

The room could be on fire, and we'd never know.

I moan into his mouth and pull his face closer to mine, deepening the kiss. "Let me drop you off at the airport," I beg between kisses.

"I shouldn't..." he nips at my lip, "but I want to spend every last second with you."

Liam clears his throat, and Killian laughs against my lips. "Time's up, love birds." He is leaning against the entryway, one booted foot crossed over the other. His eyes still refusing to meet mine.

Killian turns to Liam and shrugs. "Change of plans. You mind driving me to the airport instead of Conor? Madison is going to come with us. She has a way of getting everything she wants."

Liam's face hints at a smile. He crosses his arms over his chest and smooths his features. "Whatever ya want, Kil. I'll get the car."

THE RIDE there was emotional as hell. I couldn't stop crying. Killian just rocked me in his arms in the backseat. He whispered how much he loved me and that he would come home to me.

My mascara is most likely all over his shirt, and my nose is stuffy from ugly crying. He rubs gentle circles around my back as I try to breathe and calm down. We are standing on the tarmac while they finish fueling the jet. He lifts my chin one last time to give me his own salty kisses and leans his forehead against mine.

"Don't give up on us, Madison. It may get difficult, but I promise to keep in touch as much as I can. Trust me, when I get home, you won't leave our bedroom for weeks." He gives my ass a tap for good measure.

He's such a charmer.

"I won't," I sniffle, placing one more kiss on his lips.

Liam reaches out his hand and pulls Killian into a back-slapping hug.

"Take care of my woman, will ya?" Kil laughs.

"Always."

Killian walks up the steps to his jet, and the flight attendant closes the door.

Liam looks at me—no—*stares* at me. "Ready to go *home*, darling?"

He wraps his hand around mine, but I turn and stomp off to the car.

Looks like we are off to a great start.

CHAPTER 27

LIAM

THE RIDE HOME from the airport is horrible. Madison cries on and off the whole time. I tried everything from music to rubbing her back to offering to stop for ice cream or Starbucks. Hell, I even offered to get her a puppy.

She wanted nothing to do with any of those options.

We pull up to the penthouse, and she swings opens her car door. I reach for her hand and hold it tight, refusing to let her rip it away again. "I promise you it's all going to be okay."

"It's not. How is any of this okay, Liam?" she shouts, her voice cracking with newly shed tears.

"Killian will be back soon, you'll see. It will go by quickly." I try and reassure her even though it's breaking my fucking heart to see her cry for him.

"I'm not talking about Killian! Yes, I'm extremely upset about him not being here. I'm scared as hell for him being away and in danger. But what I'm really scared of is being in this house with you. We...I can't be around you. *It's too much.* But Killian was adamant that you're my bodyguard now. So, I guess I don't have a choice."

I get out of the car and help her out, wrapping a protective arm around her. We take the elevator up to the second floor in silence. Only when we reach the door to her room, does she she turn around to look at me. Much calmer than she was in the car.

"I know I literally just said we shouldn't be around each other, but I don't want to be alone tonight. Can you maybe—I don't know...watch a movie with me or something...just until I fall asleep?"

"Watch a movie?" I chuckle. "What's the *'something'*?" I waggle my eyebrows at her.

She shoves open her door angrily. "Forget it!"

Maddy is about to slam the door in my face when I press my hand against it, stopping her. "How about this—I'll go change into sweats, and you get yourself ready for bed. And please, for the love of God, wear something full coverage," I laugh, but I am dead serious. I can't be around her if she's going to be wearing some sexy pajama set. "Come watch a movie in my room 'til you're ready to fall asleep. I can't be in Killian's bed. *I just— can't.*"

"Fair enough. Thank you. I'll be over in a few," she says in a clipped tone.

Twenty minutes later, I walk out of my bathroom, shirtless and in gray sweats. Madison is cuddled and cozy in a sweatshirt and sweatpants, just lounging on top of my bed. *And damn if she doesn't look good there.* Her hair is still damp and pulled up in a messy bun.

My hunger for her stirs.

Her eyes graze over me for a few seconds before she distracts herself with her phone.

She rubs at her temple. "Why don't you have a shirt on?" Her thumbs fly over her screen as she types out a message, doing her best to ignore me.

"Because I don't sleep in one. Problem, love?" I smirk. *I'm getting to her, and she knows it.*

"So let me get this straight..." she raises her eyebrow. "*I have to wear a shirt, but *you* don't have to?" Her eyes dart up from her text message and scream for a challenge.

"Darling, this isn't a *duel*."

"No, it's not." She crosses her arms over her chest. "You brought a deadly weapon in here," she points at my chest. "And I didn't," she pouts. *It's the cutest fucking thing ever.*

"Baby, your presence here in my room is a deadly weapon. So if this was, in fact, a duel—clothed or not—*you've already won*."

The smile she gives me is incredible. Her cheeks have flushed a beautiful shade of pink. "'Do you want to watch a movie or *something*?'" I quote her from earlier while getting comfortable on my side of the bed.

Maddy smirks at me while shaking her head. A giddy smile graces her face, and her fingers flash across her screen again. I snatch the phone and hold it above me.

"Who has you so distracted? Cause it definitely isn't Killian. And it sure as shit isn't me."

"Liam! Give me my phone!" She lunges over me, reaching for it. Her breasts are pressed firmly against my chest, her leg is thrown over me, and our faces are only a few inches from each other. I tilt the phone to see what she's up to. It's a conversation she is having with Lexi:

> LEXI
>
> How are you holding up girl? Killian left today?

> MADDY
>
> I'm okay. Just going to watch a movie with Liam and try to get my mind off things.

> LEXI
>
> You sure that's a good idea, Mad?

No. I'm not sure. Of course, he just got out of the bathroom in nothing but those gray sweatpants. He looks so hot. We are only on day one. I need you to distract me so I don't do something stupid.

LEXI

Ugh. The gray sweatpants…he wants you to see what he's got under there. To remind you.

MADDY

How could I forget? I've tried.

I'm still affecting her. She feels me grow hard beneath her. Her breathing becomes more shallow—but she hasn't moved off me. She reaches for the phone again.

"Liam. I'm serious. *Give. Me. My phone.*"

I laugh and tease her by lifting it higher. I lower my mouth to her ear. "So you can't forget about our night either?"

She shivers on top of me. "Liam. *Please,* give me my phone." Her voice has grown small and needy.

I hand it back to her but don't let her pull it from my grasp. Her hand overlaps mine. "For the record, I can't get that night off my mind either. *I've tried too.*" I let go of the phone and she moves her body off of me. She slides herself over to the very edge of the bed and brings her knees to her chest.

"So, what are we watching?" I twiddle my thumbs in my hand. My cock is still throbbing for her.

She puts her phone in her pocket and rolls over to face me. "Whatever you want. I'm just happy to not be alone tonight," she sighs.

"No, really." I reach over and pat her leg. "*You* wanted to watch a movie, so you pick."

"Fine. Can we watch *The Vampire Diaries*?

"Sure…" I hesitantly agree. "What kinda movie are we

talking about here? Romance or supernatural?"

"Both." Her eyes light up, and she flashes me a grin. "And it's a show."

I had the staff bring us some popcorn and snacks. We ended up watching a few episodes. Maddy is asleep now, curled into a little ball. I kept watching more episodes because why the hell not—the show's pretty damn good. *I can see why she likes it.* I also can see how eerily similar it is to our situation.

The question is, which brother am I to her?

I WAKE up to Madison wrapped around me like a vine. *Shit.* I must have fallen asleep. She's gonna be pissed I didn't wake her to go back to her room.

Her head is on my chest, legs draped over mine. My morning wood is pressed firmly against her. I run my hand gently up and down her back. Her eyes flutter open, and she looks up at me but doesn't move right away.

Man, I could get used to this.

I feel her tense as her expression changes to one of embarrassment. She tries to scramble out of my embrace.

"Shit. I'm sorry. That shouldn't have happened. I *clearly* thought you were Killian."

"No, you didn't. Your body was drawn to mine, even in sleep," I laugh and ruffle her hair.

She hops out of bed and bolts over to my door. "Well. This was...*fun.* Thanks for keeping me company. I'm sure I'll feel much better sleeping on my own tonight.

"Madison," I say calmly. *She's gonna run.*

"I really would like to hit the gym before my classes start—so —I'll see you later."

I sigh and get up, knowing my shower is going to be freezing cold this morning.

CHAPTER 28

MADISON

AFTER WAKING up sprawled across Liam, I decided I needed to set some *major* boundaries with him. *It doesn't help that I am still so drawn to him.* If Killian and I are going to make it through these next few months, I need to stop letting Liam affect me.

Last night—as fun as it was—can't happen again.

I close the door to Liam's room with my heart beating out of my chest. I need to talk to Lexi about this all. Which means I'll have to ask Liam if she can come over later. We can have a girls' night with some wine in the hot tub. I'm sure she'd love to see Conor too. They really hit it off at the gala. He's been texting and calling her non-stop.

My mind is still racing with thoughts of Liam, even after I brush my teeth and change into a neon pink workout outfit. I grab my headphones off the dresser and make my way downstairs.

Killian's gym has everything I need for my routine—including a mini fridge with water bottles and smoothies. I settle on some cardio first, praying it'll help me blow off some steam. Stepping on the elliptical, I turn on HGTV and shoot Lexi a text:

MADDY

I need a girls' night…if Conor can come get you, will you sleep here tonight? Thinking wine and hot tub. 🥂

LEXI

Hell yes. I'm in.

MADDY

Ok. Let me just run it by Liam. I'll text you the details when I get them.

LEXI

How'd that go last night? You stopped messaging me.

MADDY

He saw our texts.

LEXI

Oh shit. Okay. Tell me everything later.

I place my phone back on the stand and start to focus on my workout.

After twenty minutes, I am dripping sweat and fully engulfed in a show, when someone crosses my peripheral. I don't need to look over to confirm who it is. His lavender and woodsy scent invades my space before he does.

Liam.

I take a sip of my water as he gets on the treadmill next to me.

"Hey there, love," I hear over my music. I turn to look at him, giving him a tight smile. I point to my headphones. Being the stubborn man he is, he pulls one headphone out of my ear by the cord. "*Hi*, Madison," he says all chipper.

"*Hi*, Liam," I mirror him and raise an eyebrow at him. *I know why he's here.*

He starts running. His tattoos are on full display in a black tank top and compression shorts. *Mmm. He is so handsome.*

"Hey listen, can Lexi come over tonight for a girls' night? I was thinking maybe Conor could get her—considering they get along so well."

"Anything you want, *princess.*" His eyes are glued to my breasts. Lust coils in my core. *Why is this my life right now?*

"Thanks," I say powering off my elliptical. I move over to the weights and set up the barbell to do some squats. His eyes watch me through the mirror as I start to do my reps. He slows to a walk and then shuts the treadmill off. I watch him through the mirror as he makes his way over to me, determination written all over his face.

His hand grabs the barbell, gripping it firmly so I can't lower it. "You really should have a spotter when you are doing this." The muscle in his jaw ticks.

"It's barely any weight. I'll be fine." I brush him off and he releases his grip on the bar.

"I'll spot you." His lips curve into a delicious smile. He walks over to face me and runs a strong hand over my waist. "Your form is off too." With a clink, he places the barbell back in place. "Here..." he manipulates my body, "open your legs more like this." He nudges his knee between my thighs, opening them wider. "Good." He lifts the barbell, handing it back to me. "Go ahead. Now, let me see you squat," he commands in his thick, raspy voice.

I do as I'm told, yet he comes closer to me, gripping my waist with both hands and pushing me lower. "Ya gotta get lower, baby," he smirks as I get eye-level with his crotch. *This man is infuriating.* My nipples harden and I feel him staring at me. His hands grip my waist tighter, making me inhale sharply.

"I think I've got the hang of it. Thanks," I say in a breathy voice. He shoots me a wink and then watches me continue my reps.

I finish the last one, realizing I may have been doing squats wrong my whole life. My legs are on fire and shaking. I take a sip of my water and decide I need to get out of here. *I am way too turned on right now.* "I'm gonna go shower—class starts soon." I scramble away, leaving him smiling at my awkwardness.

LEXI and I are in the hot tub on the rooftop patio. We've each got a glass of red wine in our hands. This water feels heavenly on my sore muscles. My legs still are so achy from my workout with Liam. Speaking of Liam, he hasn't been around all day. Maybe he's been avoiding me like I've been trying to do with him.

"What are you going to do about Liam?" Lexi takes a sip of her wine.

"Nothing. We obviously never expected to be in this situation. I'm with Killian now, and he's so good to me. We have great sex. He always makes me feel loved and cherished. I have nothing to complain about." I shrug, take a sip of my wine and sigh.

"I feel like there is a *but*," Lexi pokes for more information.

"*But*...what I feel towards Liam is still very much there. It doesn't help that he knows this too. I can't explain it really...it's just this feeling that makes all the cells in my body vibrate every time he's near me. I do my best to control it but I *can't*. It's like asking someone to hold their breath. They can only hold it for so long before they take a breath."

"I think that you need to figure out what you really want, Maddy. I know how you felt about Liam before he left. You've always been attracted to him. But is it an attraction or is this *something more?*"

As I am about to respond, Liam comes out the sliding doors with another bottle of wine tucked under his arm and a platter of cheese, crackers, and fruit. Lexi looks at him and then back to me. "*It's something more,*" I whisper.

Lexi pats my shoulder. "I think so too. From what you've told me and what I've seen—that man is in love with you."

I let what she said sink in as Liam approaches us. He places the platter and the bottle of wine on the pavers next to us. "Hey, Lexi. Good to see you again."

"You too, Liam. You should join us." *Lexi. What the hell are you doing?*

"I don't want to ruin your girls' night." His warm eyes focus on me. I take another sip of wine and pop a grape in my mouth.

"It's fine. Maybe you should grab Conor too. Make it a whole party," I say sarcastically, narrowing my eyes at Lexi. She starts to blush.

"That's a great idea. I'll be *right* back." Liam practically jogs back to the doors.

I turn to my best friend. "Lexi! *What the hell?*" She just giggles and sinks her head under the water.

LIAM AND CONOR return in their bathing suit trunks with a bucket of beers and some towels. They each crack one open. Liam gets in and sits next to me. He wraps an arm around my head to grab a piece of cheese, popping it in his mouth. Just when I was worried he was going to keep his arm there, he does just that. He snakes his arm back around me, resting it on the pavers.

Conor cuddles up next to Lexi and she places her legs on his lap. He starts to massage her calves. I hope no one else is watching this. *It looks like a goddamn double date.* Killian would lose his shit if he saw this. I look around for cameras but don't see any.

"Calm down." Liam gives my neck a gentle squeeze. "There

are cameras up here but I don't think Killian has time to be monitoring them. Even if he did—what we are doing is completely fine. He told me I need to watch you and I am." *He is definitely taking this whole 'bodyguard' thing a little too literally.*

I nod my head. "Lex, when do you head back to Arizona?"

"Beginning of February," she sighs.

"What are you studying?" Liam asks, taking a swig of his beer.

"I'll be graduating with my Health Science Degree in May. After that, I start my Physician Assistant program.

"I wish you could find a school in New York," I add. I hate that my best friend is across the country.

"Me too," Conor smiles and rubs Lexi's cheek with his thumb.

"I would *love* to come back, but I already got into a program back in Arizona."

"Maybe I'll be able to get some time to come and see you," Conor says hopefully. *He's cute.* The way he looks at Lexi says just how infatuated he is with her.

"I would *love* that," she says standing. "I'll be right back, just need to use the restroom."

"Do you know where it is?" Conor asks, his eyes twinkling with mischief.

"Um...no I don't. This place is huge," she laughs, wrapping a towel around herself.

"I'll show you, angel." Conor wastes no time getting out to *assist* Lexi. That leaves me and Liam alone.

"They won't be back for a while," Liam chuckles. He finishes off his beer and grabs a new one.

"Nope." I finish off the rest of my wine. Liam grabs the bottle and refreshes my glass. His eyes reach mine and they are hungry and inquisitive. "Thanks."

"How are the legs?" His hands strum along the pavers.

"*Sore,*" I admit. "I guess I was never really doing it right." He removes his hand from around my back and dips it into the water. Strong fingers begin to massage my thigh. I can't even help the moan that escapes my mouth. "Ahh."

"I can teach you some more routines if you'd like. We can be gym buddies." He inches his body closer to me, his nipple ring brushing my arm. Liam's eyes are piercing mine now and I couldn't look away if I tried.

He's captivated me.

He moves his hand higher up my thigh into dangerous territory. His knuckles graze my bikini bottom, but it's enough for me to shiver with need. I watch his eyes go to my nipples which are now protruding through the thin fabric.

He leans down to whisper in my ear. "What is it about hot water and *you* that gets me so fucking hard?"

Liam removes his hand and cups my face. His thumb runs over my lips. "Madison. I want you so badly right now. If you were mine, I'd already be buried deep inside you." I clench my thighs tightly together. *It's so wrong that I want that just as badly as he does.*

My rational brain kicks in and I pull away from him. "Liam. We need to stop this. We can't. Killian is my boyfriend. *He's your brother*. There is no chance for us anymore. We need to stop living in the past. *Please*. Just. Stop." He looks wounded by my words. I want to turn around and kiss that scruffy face.

But I can't.

I get out and wrap the towel around me.

"Madison." I hear him say behind me but I don't bother to turn back. Instead, I book it to the house and place as much distance as I can between us.

CHAPTER 29

LIAM

THE LAST FEW weeks with Killian gone have been nothing short of chaotic. I've been holed up in the office going over contracts and working my arse off to run the syndicate in my brother's absence. Madison has done nothing but mope around —when she is actually *outside* of her bedroom. Killian has only made contact with her a handful of times.

She takes her meals in her *room*. Her schoolwork gets done from her *room*. The only time I see her is when she uses the gym once a day—and even then, she avoids me. She told me she would prefer to work out alone.

I check in on her throughout the day, but she hasn't said much to me. She keeps those damn earbuds in the majority of the time, only nodding at my presence.

Enough is enough. I'm putting a stop to this behavior. Her J-term is over today, and it is time to celebrate. I am planning a night out for us at The Triskelion. Her roommate Leah, Carly, Lexi, and her sister Mikayla have all signed NDAs and will be surprising her in the VIP. I want to partake in some of the festivities, so I have arranged for Colin and Kieran to come with us for extra security. *I need this night as much as she does.*

Maddy passes me on her usual route from the gym to the

kitchen to grab an iced green tea. She smiles at me for the first time since our little hot tub night. I let her pass me, wanting to rile her up in the kitchen. It's been too long since I've been able to play around with her.

She has her back turned to me, headphones in, grabbing the freshly prepared tea from the refrigerator. I sneak up behind her and wrap my arms around her waist. Madison jumps at the contact, gasping as she turns around in my arms. Her eyes are wide with fear or perhaps hope that I was Killian.

I snag her headphones from her ears, replacing my arms around her waist again. My hands refuse to move an inch from around her perfect body. She pulls back, trying to put space between us, but I only tighten my hold on her.

"Liam," she puts a hand on her chest. "You surprised me. I thought you were..." she trails off, confirming my theory.

"Sorry, love. Just me." I shrug, masking the pain I feel that she was hoping I was my brother.

"What's this for?" She looks down at our bodies touching. Her sweaty breasts are rising and falling in her sports bra. *Fuck, this woman is gorgeous.* My cock stirs with her in my arms, her seductive scent now mixed with sweat. Her cheeks are stained red from her workout.

"Congratulations on your last day of University, Maddy. I'm so fucking proud of you and the nurse you will become. I mean, I won't be able to trust anyone else but *you* to tend to my wounds from this moment on," I laugh, tapping her nose.

She picks up on our little game of push and pull and disengages her body from my embrace. I let her, not wanting to push her too hard. Quite frankly, I don't even know why I am trying to make things better between us. She's not *mine*. I just have a hard time being anything but absolutely batshit crazy for her. It comes naturally, this pull she has on me. I tried, I really did, to keep my distance and to be respectful, but it's becoming

196

harder and harder. Especially when I see how sad she is. All I want to do is hold her, comfort her, and *love* her.

That's all I've ever wanted since the day we met. To give Madison everything she deserves. To provide her a safe place to come home to. To protect her in my arms when all the energy she exerts on everyone around her is depleted. *Because that's Madison.* Always caring for everyone else until she is exhausted. And she'll never stop. That's her. *That's my girl.* But who's there to replenish her? *It should be me, damn it. It should be me.*

Madison places a straw in her plastic cup and turns to me. "Thank you, Liam. I appreciate that." A genuine smile appears on her face. *I would do anything to get it to stay there.*

She spins around, about to go to her room for a shower, when I grab her arm. Her eyebrow raises—one of my favorite expressions of hers. It's a precursor to her sarcasm and fire that I love.

"Ya gotta stop this bullshit, baby." She pulls her arm away and keeps walking towards the stairs. I capture her again, and she places a hand on my chest, warning me to back off.

"Liam. Stop. I'm fine, and we shouldn't be doing this."

I tilt my head. "What? *Talking?*"

A small smile appears on her face before it hardens with disapproval. Her luscious lips wrap around the straw of her drink. This woman knows exactly how to drive me mad. She knows how her actions affect me. She's saying one thing but doing another. Her heart and mind are at war with one another.

"Classes are over. You are officially done with school. All you do is mope around here, a shell of a woman you used to be. It's because of *him.* I know that. I get it. But you need to shake it off, Maddy. There is so much to celebrate and be happy about." I reach a hand out to run my thumb over her cheek, which has a single teardrop dripping over it. "Let me celebrate you tonight."

She brushes my hand off her face, gently placing it on my

side. "*One* drink and a *cigarette*," she sighs, holding her index finger up. "We can sit by the fire if you want."

"How about we get out of this *fortress* and have a drink and a cigarette in Connecticut? I have to head to the Triskelion for business tonight. We can grab a drink after."

She sips her tea, buying herself time to answer.

I can see the wheels turning. She's contemplating.

"Okay."

"Okay," I say definitively.

"What time do I need to be ready?"

"Colin and Kieran are going to be driving us. I'll come get you from your room at eight."

I leave her with her thoughts, walking to the patio for a smoke.

I KNOCK TWICE on her door and push my hands into the pockets of my black dress pants. The door swings open, and my jaw drops with an inaudible gasp. *She is stunning.*

A tight black, strapless, leather dress clings to her sexy curves. She has thigh-high black boots on and her favorite studded leather jacket. Her makeup is dark and sultry, emphasizing those dark chocolate eyes. The biggest shock of all —her hair is pin straight and *dyed black.*

She's making a statement, and you'd be blind not to notice. *Damn.* My hands itch to reach out and pull her to me. I ball them into fists in my pockets.

"You look absolutely stunning, love."

A shy smile creeps across her face as she steps into the hallway, closing her door behind her. What she does next surprises me. *She hugs me.* Her arms circle around my body, through my open sports jacket, and she lays her head on my chest.

"Thank you." Her body relaxes against mine.

I wrap my arms around her small frame and rest my cheek on her head. She sighs and drags her hands back in retreat but stops over my gun in its holster—her eyes widen. "What the hell, Liam?"

I laugh at her innocence. "Sweetheart, I *always* have one with me. You just haven't ever seen it on my body. It's to keep us safe tonight—if we should need it. You'll be protected, I promise you." I clasp her face in my hands, forcing her to look at me. "Just try and have a good time, will ya?"

She nods, and I place my hand on her back, guiding her to the elevator.

Colin and Kieran are parked in front of the building with the Range Rover. Its bulletproof glass will protect us on our short ride to Connecticut.

I help Maddy into the backseat, sliding in next to her. She smiles but tries to hide it by looking out her window.

"Anything you'd like to listen to, lass?" Kieran asks from the passenger seat.

She leans forward over the center console to hand him her phone. Her elbow brushes my knee, and the static is back between us again.

"This playlist here," she indicates with her finger.

"The Heart Wants What it Wants" by Selena Gomez fills the speakers. The guys laugh, but I focus on the lyrics. She's telling me *something* she can't say out loud.

Colin and Kieran are covering their ears like a bunch of pussies.

"Madison, *please*, with all this girly music. Ya got any other playlists?" Colin groans.

The next song starts, and Miley Cyrus' voice surrounds us, singing her famous *"Wrecking Ball."* Madison has been quietly hurting this whole time. No wonder she has those damn headphones in all day.

The guys groan some more—I'm about to slap the shit out of both of them. I shift my head enough to look at her, but she's looking out the window again with silent tears streaming from her eyes. I slide my hand across the seat and squeeze hers. *I hear you, love. I'm right here.*

"Please, we beg of you, our Queen, put something more upbeat on." Kieran clasps his fingers together to beg.

"One more, and then I'll let you play whatever you want." She leans over to her phone, scans through the playlist, and clicks on *"Red" by Taylor Swift.*

I am about to *lose it.* These lyrics are so deep. Colin and Kieran probably assume this is her way of missing Killian—*but I know better.* I rub my thumb over her hand in mine.

She doesn't pull away like I expect she would. *Does this mean she still thinks about me the way I do of her?* Because if there is still a chance for us, I can't say I can hold back any longer. Brother or not, Madison and I met first. He'll have to hear us out if it comes down to that.

The song fades to an end, and she sneakily wipes a tear away, plasters a smile on her face, and unplugs her phone. "All yours, gentlemen."

CHAPTER 30

MADISON

THE REST of the ride was pretty much silent between Liam and I. Kieran, Colin, and Liam bullshitted here and there about work. My head was spinning the whole time with my feelings for Liam. It feels so good to be around him and not deliberately push him away. I've done that all month. I can't take it any longer.

We pull up to the back entrance of the bar. Liam helps me out and the three of them surround me as we make our way to the door. The two men posted there let us in. Liam's in a great mood, laughing and joking with them. We take the elevator to the ground floor. When the doors slide open, my heart leaps with memories of the first time Killian took me here.

"Ready love?" Liam grabs my hand to lead me to the club.

I nod and follow him in.

"I'll get you set up in a VIP booth. Colin and Kieran will keep an eye on you while I attend some business," he says, guiding me to the cocktail tables and couches on the upper level. "It shouldn't take very—"

"Surprise!" My sister, Leah, Carly, and Lexi all say in unison.

I cup a hand over my mouth and look up at Liam—who has the sweetest grin plastered on his face. One I've never seen on him. I elbow him playfully in the ribs. "You put this together for me?"

He pulls me into him and places a kiss on my head. "I did. You deserve to be celebrated. Tonight is all for you."

The girls come running up to me and hug me, keeping Liam and I in an awkward group hug.

"Madison! I am so fucking proud of you, girl!" Lexi shouts over the bass.

"Nurse Maddy!" Mik says, rubbing my arm.

I release Liam, and Leah runs over to me, pulling me into a hug. "I am in serious need of an update," she whispers while eyeing Liam. He shoots a wink at her.

"I will, but first, let's have a shot," I laugh, feeling so much lighter than I have these last few weeks.

My days are filled with nothing but music that breaks my *fucking heart*, classwork, and confusion. I've been struggling with it all. My heart is missing Killian so much, but if I am being honest, it's not the same longing I felt for Liam when he left.

It's so wrong. I miss Liam more, and he's right in front of me.

I do love Killian. He makes me happy. He makes me laugh. And our sex is out of this world. The reason I'm having doubts about my relationship, is because I never let Liam go. The 'what if' plays too strongly in my mind when I try to cut him off.

Having him around me these last few weeks has been torture. After our night in the hot tub, I did everything to keep myself busy. I couldn't allow myself to slip up around him.

The problem is his energy is magnetic, tugging on mine, even from behind closed doors. It's like he is there when he isn't. I tried music to drown out thoughts of him, but it just made me want him even more. *What a mess we've gotten ourselves into.*

"Are you drinking *tequila*?" Mik asks me as we approach the table. Liam takes a seat next to me. Mikayla looks over at him and then back at me for a response.

"Yeah, tequila sounds good right about now," I sigh. Tonight

I'll enjoy just one night without stopping myself from pining over him.

"I'll have one as well." Liam grabs a shot glass and holds it up.

"You're actually drinking with us tonight?" His eyes answer my question. What I see there sets my chest on fire way more than the tequila will.

"Like I said," he leans down to whisper in my ear, "tonight is *all* for you."

I clench my legs together, feeling the desire build at his words. He smirks, knowing his effect on me, and raises his glass to the group.

"To Madison, the girl we all *love*. You worked your arse off to get here. We are so proud of you. Cheers to being the smartest and *hottest* nurse around," he chuckles.

I almost didn't take the shot like everyone else as I processed his words. My sister and Lexi shoot me a knowing look. I throw my shot back and grab a lime off the table, letting it soothe the inferno in my chest.

"One more!" Leah shrieks, already pouring everyone another round.

Why the hell not?

I take my shot, and Liam slips the lime between my lips. *Damn.* This man is putting me in a dangerous position. I remove his hand from my lips to grab the rind. *He needs to behave.* We are in Killian's club. Not to mention everyone is watching us.

Liam stands and walks over to Lexi to chat about Conor. Carly is already off talking to Colin. Leah and Mikayla waste no time plopping their asses on either side of me.

"How's Killian?" Mik asks.

"I wouldn't know. He's away on business," I say matter of factly.

Leah interjects. "Um...okay so Killian is gone...on *business*... and Liam is..."

"My bodyguard for the night," I finish for her.

Leah grabs both my shoulders to look me dead in the eyes. "Don't play coy with me, Maddy. What are you *thinking*? You told me Liam is Killian's brother. So what the hell are you going to do when Killian finds out you two are secretly pining for each other?"

"We aren't." I shrug, feeling bad about lying to their faces.

"I don't buy that," my sister chimes in.

"Me either." Leah shakes her head. "You could cut your sexual tension with a knife. Anyone can see it."

I flip my hair with my hand, then pour myself a cranberry, club, vodka, and lime. I chug my drink, needing to cool myself off. *The girls have me in the fucking hot seat.* The back-to-back shots are working their way through my system. I am already feeling it and more than ready to let loose.

"Let's dance." I stand, pulling my too-short dress down. Liam turns to look at me. The way he's staring makes me feel like I'm wearing nothing at all.

Lexi runs over and grabs my arm. "Yes! I'm in."

"I'll be watching you from up here," Liam whispers in my ear. His hand glides down my arm before giving my hand a gentle squeeze. Goosebumps flare up at his touch *and* his words.

The girls are dancing and singing in a circle on the dancefloor. The bass is bumping, and the crowd is thick, with others doing the same. Some couples make their way upstairs to the VIP suites, which makes me curious. What is in the other rooms I haven't seen yet? Sweat drips down my chest and into my cleavage. I fan myself, cursing my choice of a leather dress and boots.

The girls and I take two more tequila shots at the downstairs bar and then return to our wild dancing. *I feel so alive right now.* My body hums, and all my worries have vanished. I let the music guide my moves, surrounded by my favorite people. Conor pops into the crowd, and Lexi's face fills with surprise and excitement.

"Hey, Lex." He pulls her in for a kiss. They start separating from the crowd to make out back at our table. Mik, Leah, and Carly went off to do another shot. I don't want to be sick, so I declined. I look up to the balcony for Liam, but he isn't there.

My bladder cries out for help. *Guess it's time to break the damn seal.* I am walking toward the bathroom behind the bar, when Liam comes up behind me and pulls me flush against him.

"Where are you going, baby?" He leans over, pressing his lips behind my ear.

I spin around and grasp his biceps in my arms to steady myself.

"Bathroom," I giggle. *As if that concept is funny.* The drinks are starting to get to me.

"Not without me, you're not." He grabs my hand, leading us back up the stairs. "Come, you can use my office bathroom."

WITH A CLICK, he closes his office door behind us. I take a look around. It's *so* him. Masculine and woodsy with dark walls and a dark oak desk.

I walk to the en suite he has and swing the door shut. He throws his hand up, preventing me from closing it. *Here we go again.*

"Were those songs in the car for *him* or for *me*?" His eyes hold an intensity that could melt me on the spot.

"I need to pee, Liam." I sigh, pushing the door a with a little more force.

"Just tell me. I need to know...it's *killing* me." He releases the door, and I open it again.

"They are about you. *Okay?* It still doesn't change the fact that I am in love with your brother. Or that we are in this fucked up situation, to begin with." I close the door and lock it for good measure.

I finish up in the bathroom and open the door to find him leaning against the desk with his arms crossed over his chest.

"Ready?" I ask hesitantly.

"No. I'm not." He pushes off the desk and marches towards me.

Fuck.

"I can't get you off my mind, Madison," he says, grabbing my face and lacing his fingers through my hair. "You consume me. Every second of every day, your face is in my mind. I want you. *I need you.* And now that you confirmed that you need me too, all bets are off."

He lowers his lips to my neck. It's making me weak in the knees. My legs tremble, and my hands shake with the need to do something about this ache between my legs. I grab his arms, about to push him away, but something else takes over me.

I pull him closer.

"Last chance to leave before I kiss you, baby," he warns. His lips are hovering dangerously close to mine.

I close the distance and kiss him with all the pent-up energy and lust I've been feeling for the last few months. He greedily takes over, forcing my mouth open, and grabs a handful of my ass. I can feel his erection pressing against me. Feeling him hard for me like that is turning me on even more. A moan escapes my mouth, making him go wild. His hands begin to roam recklessly all over my body. They find my breasts and linger there.

Liam picks me up and places me on his desk, stepping in between my legs. "Fuck baby, I've missed you. I've been thinking about this moment for a while now." He holds my face between his palms.

My dress has ridden up and bunched at my ass. He glides his hands up my bare thighs, then one over my soaked lace thong.

"Goddamn, you're so wet." His hand drags the material to the side, and he slips a finger through my slickness. "Your mouth may not say how you feel about us, but this does." He removes his glistening finger and sucks on it.

Holy...

Liam places kisses all over my chest and up my neck. He lingers by my ear, whispering, "we will figure this out, baby." Taking a step back, he tugs my dress back down, and holds his hand out to help me off the desk.

I pause at his abrupt change in direction. *What the hell just happened?*

"I want to fuck you on my desk right this second, Madison. But I know it's wrong. And I know you'll regret it. We need to tell Killian before I can have you again."

Anger floods me. "I...who says I was going to let you? Who says I wanted that?" I get off the desk myself, ignoring his outstretched hand. I'm projecting my anger onto him, and it's not fair. *Of course, I want it. Want him. I'm just mad at myself for wanting it.*

"Oh sweetheart. We both know if I didn't stop—you would have let me." I slap his face and regret it immediately.

He grabs my hand and places it gently against his face. "I know that this whole situation is fucked up. But don't think for one second that I wasn't coming back for you. I made the mistake of losing you once. I won't make that same mistake again. I will tell Killian about us. You just have to admit out loud that you want to be done with him. We can figure this out, baby. It doesn't have to be this way," he says gently. His face is only inches from mine.

"I'm sorry I slapped you." I lower my head, feeling ashamed.

"Don't be. I deserved it. I'm sorry for pushing you. I know you don't want to cheat. I don't want to either. I just can't control myself around you. *You make me crazy.*" He blows out a breath and runs a hand through his hair. "How about that cigarette?" he offers, shifting the mood.

I look up and smile at him, all my anger residing. *He's not wrong.* In the heat of the moment, *I wanted him too.* I wasn't going to stop him. My body was vibrating with the need to feel him inside me again. To crush my lips against his and let him fuck me on his desk. To let myself lose control for once and to not overthink everything. To just be in the moment with him.

We *need to tell Killian.*

I can't do this to him. It's not fair.

THE REST of the night was insanely fun. My girls and I danced our asses off. They even brought out a cake with an enormous sparkler. It's safe to say I am thoroughly wasted and happy.

Liam kept his distance from me after our cigarette. He spent the remainder of the night brooding from the balcony. He may have been physically distancing himself, but his eyes were on me all night. I could feel his frustration and desire without looking at him. *Well, that makes two of us, buddy.*

We are back in the car now, heading back out of town. Colin smiles at me from the driver's seat. "Carly is quite the catch."

"She isss," I hiccup. *Oh great.* It's going to be a *long* drive home.

I must have closed my eyes. Because when I wake up, I am most definitely *not* in the bed that Killian and I share. I look around trying to see where I am. *Where the fuck am I?* My heart starts pounding uneasily. Then I hear Liam's hearty laugh next to me. He's laying down on top of the comforter. Hands behind his head and legs crossed.

"You were about to be sick in the car. We pulled over twice to let you puke, but you never did. The smartest thing was to come back to my place after you fell asleep on my shoulder."

I cover my face with my hands.

Tequila.

"I'm sorry," I whine, my voice laced with shame. *How embarrassing...*

"Don't be. You're cute as hell when you're drunk. And needy too. 'Liam, take me homeee,' he mimics my voice, laughing to himself again.

I look down now that my eyes are adjusted and see that I am in an oversized t-shirt with a raven on it. I throw the comforter off—apparently, I am in boxer shorts too.

"Liam!" I shout and throw the pillow at him.

He catches it and places it back down. "Ya threw up the second you got to the bathroom. A bit got on your dress. I was just trying to help." He holds his hands up in surrender. "I got you cleaned up. You brushed your teeth, had some water, and made it to the bed before gracefully curling into a ball and falling asleep." His lips twitch, holding back another laugh. "It's not like I haven't seen *all of you* before."

"What a hot mess I am," I bow my head.

Liam leans over and lifts my chin so that I look at him.

"*Hot* indeed." He winks. "Are you hungry?"

My stomach decides to growl in perfect timing with his question. He pats it and gets up off the bed.

"Let's feed you then."

His kitchen is incredible. The walls are brick with matte black cabinets and black quartz countertops. Exposed wood beams run the length of the house. A large island with tan leather stools sits in the center. Warm, Edison-style pendant lights hang from the ceiling. Dark hardwoods run from the kitchen to the rest of the house, and forest green paints the walls. It's just like Liam—dark yet inviting. *I love it.*

I sit down on the stool at the edge of the island. "Where are Colin and Kieran?"

He is standing by the stove with his back turned to me. "They went back to the city. I'll drive us home tomorrow. We can take my car."

I spot my purse on the counter and take my phone out to check for missed calls or messages. Liam is rummaging around between the refrigerator and stove, whipping something up. Three texts and one missed call from Killian. *Shit.*

> **LEXI**
>
> Liam was really into you tonight. You can't deny you act differently around him vs. when you're with Killian. He loves you. Read that again! And then delete it. 😊

> **MIKAYLA**
>
> I had a blast with you tonight. Who would have thought the Triskelion was below Schmitty's? Liam made sure we all got home safe...listen whatever or whoever makes you happy... choose it/ them. Life is short. You know this all too well. Xo

> **LEAH**
>
> Missed you girlie. So glad we got to see each other again. Invite me next time you go to the club. It's fucking epic. Liam couldn't keep his eyes off you all night. I think you two should talk about your feelings because damn...I never got to meet Killian but Liam definitely never gave you up.

"What are you smiling about over there?" Liam slides a plate in front of me. "It's not Taco Bell, but it'll do."

I stare at the perfectly prepared *Crunchwrap*. "How did you know I liked Crunchwraps?" I ask in awe.

"I pay attention. You don't think I notice the staff bringing you up Taco Bell for a midnight snack?" He chuckles and takes a seat next to me.

I take a bite and moan loudly. "Oh my God, Liam. This is heavenly." My eyes close as I enjoy it.

When I open them, he is staring at me with a different kind of hunger in his eyes. "You are wearing my t-shirt and boxers.

Moan like that again, and I *will* be taking you back to my bed. I don't care how hungry you are." He swipes some sour cream off the corner of my lips and sucks it off his thumb.

"Killian called," I say over a mouthful of Crunchwrap.

"He called me too. To check in."

I look at him again. "Did you tell him I was here?"

He takes a new pack of cigarettes out from his back pocket and packs them against his hand. "Yes, he knows you're here."

I take a few more bites and push the plate forward. *That was delicious.*

"I should call him back," I say warily.

"Come, let's smoke out back, and you can call him." He grabs a throw blanket off the couch, drapes it over my shoulders then leads me out back.

Lighting up two cigarettes, he hands me one. I inhale deeply before hitting the call button. I throw it on speaker as I pace around the patio. Liam stays where he is by the door, watching me.

His phone picks up, but all I hear is mumbling. "Killian?" I say into the phone. "Kil?" Liam looks anxious. I shrug and hang up. "Maybe he doesn't have service."

I take a few more drags and walk back to him. My phone rings, showing it's Killian. *There we go. Must have been bad service.* Liam mouths to put it on speaker—worry etching his face.

I do, and the sound of female moaning fills the air. "Oh Killian, yes, yes, fuck me harder, yes, just like that."

Liam grabs the phone, hits end, and shoves it into his pocket. He flicks his cigarette and pulls me into his chest, cradling my head.

I start balling. Ugly, hot tears pour from my eyes. My hand is shaking with the cigarette still lit. He takes it and tosses it to the ground, stomping it out. His strong arms hold me tighter, and he shushes me. "I've got you, baby. I've got you."

He guides me into the house and back to his room. He sits down on the bed and cradles me against him.

"I guess I deserve this," I sob against his chest. "We crossed a line tonight, Liam. It's my karma for not being honest with him."

"Stop it now, Madison. Look at me." He lifts my chin. "You are the most amazing woman. He is a *dumb motherfucker*. I don't care that we tiptoed the line a few times. You did nothing wrong. *I did*. I shouldn't have pushed you. You don't deserve this or him, for that matter."

"I need to talk to him," I sniffle.

Liam sighs. "Fine, but *I* am calling him. I have a few choice words to say." He retrieves his phone from the nightstand and calls Killian.

CHAPTER 31

LIAM

AFTER THE THIRD RING, he picks up. "Yeah?" He sounds drunk.

"Killian. What the fuck are you doing, mate? Madison just heard you fucking another woman. She's beside herself," I say, rubbing a protective hand up and down her arm.

"Oh *please*, Liam. Spare me the *bullshit*. Chase and Alan told me about you and Madison. How long has this been going on? Since New Year's Eve?"

I look at Madison. She looks just as confused and shocked as I. "Kil, we met *years* ago. We wanted to tell you, but we were just as shocked to see each other at the gala." I pinch the bridge of my nose, trying to calm down and not ream him out. What he did to Madison was deliberate. He purposely had her hear that to hurt her.

"Wait, what the fuck are you talking about—met years ago?" He sounds more alert.

Madison's eyes go wide, realizing the snakes told him we had some sort of affair after New Year's Eve. Except they failed to mention our meeting first at Schmitty's. Or that his gobshite of a son roofied *my girl*.

"She's the woman I was telling you about, Kil. I didn't

realize you two were dating until I saw her at the gala for the first time. I went to tell her how I felt about her that morning."

The line is silent as he processes what I just said. "Jesus Christ. Why didn't you tell me?" he roars into the phone.

"We didn't want to complicate things, and she had already chosen *you*. We kept our distance and hoped to tell you, but then shit hit the fan with Da."

"Fuck!" he shouts into the phone. I hear a woman whine his name. His voice is muffled as he turns away. "This was a huge mistake, Selena. Go home," he tells her.

"Selena, brother! Really?"

"She flew here to comfort me. One thing led to another...I was hurting and angry. The memories of us flooded to the surface. It was a *mistake*. I shouldn't have done this to Madison. She doesn't deserve it," he groans.

"I also wouldn't trust those *snakes* you call 'family', Killian. Chase is the one who put E in the drinks at the bar. He roofied Madison that night."

"Wait a fucking second. You told me the girl you fell for was named Madelyn."

I look down at Maddy whose face is pressed against my chest. She's curled up into a ball on my lap, looking defeated.

"She was using that name on her fake ID. I didn't find out her name was Madison until after I took her home...that night when I..." I trail off, knowing he knows all too well what I did that night.

Killian sounds like he's crying now. Sniffling and sighing fill the line. "What a fucking mess. We both fell for the same woman, and I just royally fucked it up. Is she there right now? I want to talk to her. I *need* to apologize to her. She has to hear it from me."

Madison shakes her head vehemently. "No," she mouths.

"She's in the bathroom," I lie.

"Liam, I fucking love her. *What have I done?* Just answer me one question. Have you slept together since I've been gone?"

I rub my forehead with my fingers. "No, we haven't."

He sighs on the other end of the line. "*Do you love her?*" he asks quietly.

I look down at my girl. "Yeah. I do, Kil."

The line goes dead. Madison holds me tighter and sobs into my chest. I wrap my arms around her and rock back and forth. "I know. Just let it out, baby."

IT'S NEARLY 4 a.m. when I feel Madison's hand run up my bare chest and over my nipple ring. I look over at her. She's laying on her stomach, watching me. The soft glow from the bathroom illuminates her beautiful face. Poor thing, her eyes are puffy and red. She cried herself to sleep in my arms. I eventually changed into gray sweats and stayed awake next to her, praying Killian won't try and make it up to her.

Her delicate hand travels to the black ravens on my chest. "What do these mean?" She traces the ink with her fingers.

"Ravens represent a lot of things. For me personally, it means surrendering to the truth and letting it set you free. Ravens are about endings, but in turn, about beginnings. They represent transformation—and that all the pain you went through made you stronger." I clasp my hand around hers.

She slides the covers off her, crawls over and straddles me. Her hands wrap around my face as she lowers her lips to mine. "I need you, Liam," she whispers against my lips.

"Maddy, I want nothing more than to make love to you right now—but you're hurt. And that's okay. I don't want our first time—well, second—to be tarnished by what happened. I want you to be sure."

She peels her shirt over her head and places my hands on her breasts.

Fuck. *This woman is my undoing.*

"It's done, Liam. I can't go back to Killian now. Even if I forgive him, it was never really him. I never stopped thinking about you. I loved Killian, but I wasn't in love with him. I am *in love* with you, Liam. I probably have been since the moment we met. There is something about you that is so familiar to me. As if we were together in multiple lifetimes before this one."

Her confession is all I needed to throw all restraint out the window. I roll her over and kiss her. I press my lips along her nose, her mouth, her neck.

I pull her nipple between my lips and suck, making her arch her back off the bed and moan. She drags her fingers through my hair as I trail my fingers lower. Lifting her hips, I remove my boxers off her and toss them to the floor. My erection is digging painfully into her thigh. She runs a hand over it and pushes my sweatpants down.

I reclaim her lips, and the spark between us ignites into something primal and unfiltered. Maddy runs her nails down my back and over my arse as she spreads her legs. I reach between us and gently rub slow circles around her clit.

Her little sighs drive me mad.

I want to take my time with her. I pull her other nipple into my mouth and swirl my tongue around it until it peaks.

"Liam…" she sighs, running her fingers through my hair.

I insert a finger into her warm channel and go in and out of her at a lazy pace. Her soft hand reaches down to stroke me. *It feels so fucking good.* I can't believe this night turned out this way.

"Please." She moves my hand and lines my length up with her entrance. "I need you inside me—and this time, please don't stop," she laughs sweetly.

My lips meet hers again while I slide into her inch by inch. A moan vibrates my chest pressed against hers as salty tears saturate our lips. *She feels so amazing.* The last time I was inside her, I had a condom on—and it lasted two seconds before I freaked out. Now, I get to experience this with her going raw. Taking my time on her.

Ravishing her.

I gyrate my hips, adding pressure to her clit. My thrusts are slow and deep. Her breathing becomes shallow and heavy. With each thrust we breathe each other in. The ebb and flow of making love.

"I've got you, baby. I'll never let you go again, I promise. If my time is ever up in this life, I will find you again in the next one."

Her tears pour more freely, and she raises her hips to meet me thrust for thrust. She wraps her arms and legs around me tightly while kissing my chest.

"I love you, Liam."

"*This* should have been our first time." I kiss her again. I pick up my pace, and she tightens around my cock. "Come with me, baby." I pump into her harder.

"Mmm, Liam, don't stop. I'm so close..." Her hands wrap around the metal bed frame, and her tits bounce as I slam into her.

She clenches down on me, milking me. Her head leans back, and she screams her release.

I follow right after, emptying myself inside her. "Madison, my beautiful girl. I never want to see you sad again." I kiss her lips before rolling over next to her.

I pull her against me and throw the blankets over us.

We both let sleep take us over.

I WAKE FEELING FUCKING AMAZING. My woman is still sleeping soundly, cuddled up against me. My morning wood presses up against her arse, but I ignore it. She could use the sleep. *We didn't get much last night.* I slide out of bed and slip into my sweatpants.

Closing the door with a click, I make my way to the kitchen to whip us up some well-deserved breakfast.

My mum taught me a thing or two, so I plan on making a few things. In no time—I've got the coffee machine on, scrambled eggs made along with pancakes and bacon. I bend over to grab the orange juice from the refrigerator. When I shut the door, I discover Madison leaning against the counter in nothing but my t-shirt.

Fuck. She looks delicious right now.

"Hi." She smiles widely.

Thank God. She doesn't seem to have regrets from last night. "Hi, beautiful."

"I woke up feeling amazing, only to find *my man* missing."

Those two words ring heavily in my ears.

My man.

I've heard those words spoken many times in my fantasies of her. Hearing them flow off her lips is something I'll never take for granted.

"I wanted to feed you. You're gonna need your strength." I kiss her and cage her against the counter. "I don't plan on us leaving the bed the rest of the day."

She lifts herself onto her tiptoes to wrap her arms around my neck. And kisses me harder. "Last night was...extrodinary. *Magical* even."

"I agree, baby. Never in my life have I experienced what I did with you. It's this hold you have on me. I never want to be anywhere but here." I wrap my arms around her.

"Is that coffee I smell?" she giggles.

"Oh yes. I can't have a cranky, hungover woman on my hands." I kiss her nose again and grab a mug from the cabinet above her head. "Cream and sugar, right?" Madison nods as I pour some coffee and add a bit of each. She reaches for it gratefully, pulling the steaming mug close to her chest.

"How is your house stocked if you are never here?" Her eyebrow raises as she takes a scalding sip. How she doesn't burn her taste buds off is beyond me.

"I have a housekeeping company that keeps the basics stocked. They clean the fridge and pantry if I am gone for extended periods of time," I shrug, pouring my own cup of black coffee.

I reach down to the warmer and pull out the little spread I made us.

"Sit." I point to the lit fireplace. There are cushions, blankets, and place settings lining the floor.

We take our seats, and I let her grab what she wants. She never ceases to amaze me. She takes a ton of bacon, some eggs, and two pancakes, drizzling syrup over all of it. Most women would take a tiny bit of eggs and one slice of bacon. That's why I love her. She's not afraid to be herself—*especially* around me.

The both of us dig in. When we finish, she refuses to let me lift a finger. She loads the dishwasher and wipes the countertops down.

I summon her with my finger to come back to the fire and sit with me. I pat the spot between my legs. She sits back down, crosses her legs, and lays against me. I kiss the back of her head and wrap my arms around hers, enjoying the warmth of the fireplace and the static running through us. The wood crackles, and so does the desire between us. She leans her head up to look at me, and I claim her lips.

Twenty minutes later, we are laying naked on my living room floor with a fleece blanket tossed over us. Our breathing is light and in sync. I rake my fingers through her hair as tears prick the back of my eyes. *I am one lucky man. My mum would have adored her.*

CHAPTER 32

MADISON

WE ENDED up spending the entire weekend at Liam's. Neither of us was really in any rush to get back to Killian's house. *It still doesn't feel real.* Only a few days ago, I was in a relationship with Killian, and now...well...I'm not quite sure what Liam and I are. *It's complicated, I guess.*

Killian introduced me to his entire syndicate and associates as 'his woman'. And now we are....over. I know that. *I can still hear his ex-fiancée's voice climbing to ecstasy, the slapping and the moaning.*

I am no saint. Let's be clear about that. I understand that I walked the line with Liam; that we crossed boundaries we shouldn't have. That I slept with him only a few hours after that phone call. The difference is—I wasn't trying to hurt Killian. It doesn't make my actions right. What Killian did to me was meant to deliberately hurt me. I guess he is like 'Darth Vader' *after all*—I was just too naive to see it.

Where do we go from here?

How do we navigate this moment?

Will Liam and I ever be able to be in a 'real' commitment after this?

The high I was riding all weekend is starting to buzz out, and reality is creeping in. Dread pools in my gut at the thought of going back to Killian's. But we have to. It's the safest there.

I am staring out the car window, trying not to cry. We are in Liam's car driving back to New York City. I sigh loudly and scroll through my phone. Killian hasn't touched base with anyone.

Liam places a hand over my phone and clicks the screen off. "It's no use worrying about him right now. Baby steps, sweetheart. When he comes back, we will deal with him together."

"Yeah," I mumble and turn back to sulk out the window.

"Hey. Don't do that. Don't shut me out. I know this is uncomfortable, and you're still hurting. But please don't push me away. We are meant to be together, Madison. You said so yourself."

I turn and look at him. *He is so handsome.* His features are now screwed into a look of worry and anxiety—and it's my fault. *I put them there.*

"I'm sorry if I am making you anxious. I don't mean to. It's just—this isn't navigating a 'simple' breakup. This is so fucking complicated." I put my head into my hands. "*Ughh!*"

His strong hand caresses my thigh, and he gives it a gentle squeeze. "I'm not worried about *us*, love. There has been a car tailing us since we left the house."

The blood drains from my face. "What?"

"It's fine. I've got two of our men from the Triskelion catching up with us as we speak—for added security. Nothing will happen to you. Not on my watch."

I wrap my shaking hand around his, holding onto it for dear life. *Oh, God.*

Liam keeps looking in his rearview and swerving in and out of lanes.

"Fuck," he growls right before our car gets slammed into from behind.

The car swerves toward the shoulder, but Liam regains

control. He hits the accelerator, and I lurch back against my seat. The car behind us hits us harder this time and we veer off the road, flipping into the ditch off the highway.

I didn't even realize I was screaming until Liam grabs my face, forcing me to look at him. *Are we...are we upside down?* The airbags deployed, and I think we are trapped. *Oh fuck.* I feel warmth dripping down my face.

"Stay with me, baby. I'm going to get you out. *Don't fucking move.* Just try and stay still." His voice is soothing yet commanding. He unbuckles himself and climbs out of his window. Gunshots ring out, and instantly I freeze in fear.

"No. Liam! No!" I scream out.

My door opens. A man in a black mask unbuckles me and drags me out of the car. He puts a knife up to my neck as he pulls me to stand. I can feel the sharp metal digging into my carotid. One wrong move and I'll bleed out.

That's when I see Liam. A gun is pushed up to his head by another masked man. "Get the bitch on the floor." The man holding Liam shouts. He has a very familiar voice.

I've heard it before.

"I'm going to make your man here watch as I *fuck you.*" The man holding me threatens loudly. Liam's face becomes contorted with rage.

Wait a fucking minute. *It's Chase.* I've heard him do interviews a thousand times at the stadium. I struggle to get out of his hold. Chase presses the knife deeper into my skin, drawing some blood superficially. *Adrenaline courses through me.*

"I should have killed you when I had the chance," Liam slams his elbow into Alan's nose, and the gun clatters to the floor. He grabs it and shoots.

Chase wails and falls backward on impact.

The knife drops from his hand, and blood splatters on my face. *His blood.*

Then it all happens in slow motion.

Chase pulls out Liam's gun from the front of his pants and shoots as Liam runs toward me. Liam drops to the ground and doesn't move.

"No... No! No! No!" I scream.

I stare at Liam's lifeless body. *He can't be dead. He's just unconscious.* In the corner of my eye, I see Alan running back toward their SUV. *Goddamn, coward!* Remembering the gun, I spin around to Chase behind me. *He isn't going to shoot me.* He dropped the gun and is grabbing his shoulder, writhing in pain. Blood pours from it and stains the snow.

I make a decision in that moment.

I grab the gun next to Chase and retrieve the knife he had against my neck, placing it in my back pocket. My hands shake as I aim the gun at him.

"Get up," I seethe. Chase looks up at me with wild eyes.

I jump at the sound of more gunshots going off in the distance. It sounds like it's back up the hill by the highway.

"I said, get the fuck up!" I reposition the gun more firmly in my hand, letting my finger hover over the trigger. Chase stands slowly, all while laughing maniacally.

My heartbeat is so loud it wooshes in my ears.

"I would do as the lady says," a deep anguished voice says from behind me. Liam's bloodied hand gently grips my shoulder. He runs it down my arm to take hold of the gun. I don't let go, realizing I'm in shock right now.

"It's okay, love. I'll take it from here. Let go, baby." He grips the gun and pushes me behind him, shielding me. His shirt is drenched in thick blood. Looks to be a chest wound—but I can't be sure until I get a better look at him.

Liam aims the gun at Chase, who is still laughing. "Well isn't this a turn of events? I wasn't going to *kill* her, Liam. I was hired by Killian to shake her up a bit. He knew you would intervene, and that was our chance to kill you."

Chase's eyes start to widen in fear now. He starts backing up, raising his hands as best he can.

"I never ordered *any* of those things," a deep voice booms from behind us. "Time for your games to be over. You've fucked with *my family* enough." Killian steps next to us with his gun raised and aimed at Chase.

Another shot rings out.

This time Chase goes down and doesn't get back up.

Killian walks over to stand over his body. Liam turns to me, covers my ears, and presses my face to his body. Killian puts two more bullets into Chase as I scream. My body begins to shake violently.

Everything becomes fuzzy after that.

Killian walks over to us, his eyes taking in Liam holding me. Liam stumbles twice and collapses to the floor, pulling me down with him. I scream and scream some more as Killian pulls me off him. I kick and thrash to no avail. He ends up throwing me over his shoulder and putting me in the backseat of his Range Rover.

He slides in next to me, wrapping his arms around me and pressing my face to his chest. The hold he has on me is strong. It's preventing me from getting out of the car. Colin jumps in the driver seat and pulls into traffic as I beat my fist against Killian's chest.

"Liam! We need to go back for him. Liam! Liam! Killian, let me fucking go. *I hate you*! Let me go. Just let me go," I sob.

He only holds me tighter to his chest.

I feel my fists going numb. I start to get weaker. It travels, and my vision becomes tunneled before going black.

"Liam."

CHAPTER 33

MADISON

I WAKE up feeling disoriented and nauseous. I sit up and take a look around at my surroundings. I'm in bed and not just *any* bed—I'm in *Killian's* bed. Memories of the accident come flooding back. I cover my mouth as another vicious wave of nausea attacks me.

The shower is running and the door is closed. I attempt to slide out of bed to investigate when I realize I am attached to a fucking IV. I don't care—it won't stop me from finding out about Liam. *I need to get out of this bed!* My mind refuses to think of the possibility he didn't make it home. I need answers. *Now.*

With every movement my body aches. My muscles scream at me to just sit still—*especially my stomach.* I take a quick inventory of the rest of my body. Glancing down at my arms, I discover they are covered in bruises and scratches. I run my fingers over my throbbing forehead. There is a large bump there, accompanied by several stitches near my hairline.

The shower turns off, and I scramble to get up. I am unsteady on my feet and fall to the floor. The door opens, but I can't see who it is over the bed.

"Madison?" Killian calls out, his wet feet squeak over the hardwoods as he makes his way over to me. A look of sympathy plays across his face. He reaches down with nothing but a white towel around his hips to help me up. "I've got you. Come on, let's get back in bed." His strong arms pick me up off the ground, gently placing me back on the mattress. He throws the covers back over my legs and puts an extra pillow behind my back.

"*Where is Liam?*" I narrow my eyes at him.

He sits next to me and takes my hands in his. I rip them away from him. *Fuck him.* My heart is going to explode out of my chest with anticipation. Water droplets drip off his hair onto the comforter.

"Where is he?" my voice pitches, preparing for a breakdown.

Killian grabs my hands again, this time more firmly. He places a kiss against the one with the IV in it.

"He's *alive*, sweetheart. We are lucky that we have a fully functioning operating room here. Some of the best surgeons are on our payroll," he winks. "He's recovering nicely. Lad took a nice bullet to the chest—missed his heart and lung by a few inches and got lodged into his shoulder. *He's one lucky bastard,*" he chuckles.

I release the breath I was holding and hug Killian. I don't know why I am seeking comfort in his arms right now, but they make me feel safe. *He did help save our lives, after all.*

I guess I should be thankful.

He takes a breath and releases it, stroking my hair. "For a minute, I thought I lost you both," his voice cracks. "Liam was in critical condition. It was very touch and go. He lost *a lot* of blood."

I pull back to look at him, my anger simmering down—now that I know Liam is okay.

"When I got you safely in the car, you wouldn't stop hitting me and screaming for *him*. I was *never* going to leave him behind, sweetheart. Even if he died right there."

He brushes gentle fingers over my wound. A pained look crosses his face. "Your head injury looks worse than it is. It's a few stitches from the glass. A plastic surgeon took care of that one, so the scar shouldn't be too noticeable when it fully heals."

Kil reaches over and lifts my shirt a few inches, revealing a few bandages over my abdomen and one over my belly button. "You injured your spleen in the crash—luckily, it was repairable, and they didn't have to remove it. The doctors are confident that it shouldn't be an issue for you in the future. I made sure they did it laparoscopically."

I run a hand over the bandages. *Holy crap.* I must have been out of it since last night.

"Thank you for helping us. How did you even know we were there? And why are you back home so soon?" I tuck my shirt back down and lace my hands together in my lap.

"I came home before your celebration—I was planning on surprising you. Liam still thought I was in Ireland, but I managed to finish everything over there as quickly as possible. Right before I was about to leave for the Triskelion, Alan and Chase called to tell me their little story." He pinches the bridge of his nose and bows his head. "Selena texted me to congratulate me, and that's when I told her to get on a plane to New York." He runs a hand through his damp hair and lets out a shaky breath.

"When I spoke to Liam that night, I realized how badly I had fucked up. I was on my way to his house to come and talk to you when Ryan and Conor called me frantic. They were already on their way to you, but they didn't know how bad it would be..." agony laces his voice. "Your phone pinged your location, so I knew how to find you."

"You've been tracking me?" My anger begins to boil.

His eyes find mine again. "I do have a tracker on your phone, yes. I never used it before last night though. Madison, *I swear to you.* I know you aren't happy with me right now—I'm seriously ashamed of myself," he admits, rubbing my leg through the comforter.

"I understand now how...*complicated* our situation has

become. I really hope we can work through this. I do love you, Madison. I was hurting and stupid and acted out of spite with the wrong information in my hands."

He reaches for my hand, but I pull it away closer to my body. Tears line my eyes. I swipe at the liquid angrily.

"I forgive you, Killian. But I can't move beyond what has already transpired. If I am being completely honest with you, I was wavering on my feelings from the beginning. Because of how things left off with Liam. Never in a million years did I expect to see him at the gala, let alone discover that he's your *brother*."

Killian reaches over to the nightstand to grab a tissue. I take it from him and wipe my eyes.

"Selena and I were a lot like you and Liam. We met a few times at our father's events as young adults. We had always felt a spark but never really acted on it. One day my father approached me, telling me we were to be wed in two years' time. So we dated and got to know each other as best we could. And we found that we genuinely enjoyed each others presence."

I look at him and his eyes have softened. Finally, he is opening up to me about Selena. "Our sex was ..." he looks up for approval to continue. I nod my head. "The sex was *amazing*. It was passionate and wild. We couldn't keep our hands off each other. Then her father pulled the plug on the whole thing right before our wedding. Tensions rose within our families, and we became enemies."

"What happened after that?" I am now invested in hearing more of his story.

"I loved her...or I *thought* I did. So we secretly kept in touch, until one day she stopped returning my calls. I've never told *anyone* that before," he smiles softly at me.

Killian lays back on the bed with his arms behind his head. He looks at the ceiling as he speaks. "I realize that perhaps we were just in love with the *idea* of us. The sex and the thrill of being forbidden lovers made us crave each other more. But *that's not love.* My point is—you and I started something real. Something with a solid foundation. You and Liam...you both want each other right now because of the thrill of not being able to have each other."

I sit silently, digesting what he just said. "You're wrong," I whisper.

He turns his head to look at me. "What you just explained about Selena sounds a lot like love to me. That is how love *should* feel. It should make you feel on edge. You'll be ready to take a new leap of faith or risk—just to be around them." I smile, thinking of how Liam makes me feel and feeling extremely blessed that he's alive right now.

"When they aren't around, you feel like you can't breathe. It's like your soul left right along with them. That's how I felt when Liam left for his assignment in November. I was completely destroyed. When you left to go to Ireland, I was hurt. I was sad. But I wasn't feeling like half of my soul went with you. I'm sorry, Killian." His lips form a thin line at my confession.

"Do you remember how you felt when Selena finally ended things with you?" I push for him to understand.

Killian sighs, running one hand up his chest. "Yeah, I felt like nothing else mattered after that. I felt like I could go the next seventy years alone and not give a fuck."

He turns over and leans on his elbow. "Then I met you. You made me feel alive again. You made me feel something other than anger and loss. You opened my heart back up again, Madison. I mean that. "

"And how did you feel when Selena met you the other night?"

"I was *hurting*, I told you. So seeing her was like a sight for sore eyes. So many of our memories came back in full force. She comforted me, and we got drunk...then one thing led to another."

"That's not answering my question. How did you *feel* knowing she came all that way to be with you?"

"It felt good. Damn it, Madison. What are you trying to prove here?"

"That we can fall in love multiple times in our lives, but sometimes we can't control the timing of when we recognize that."

"So you are saying that I've been in love with Selena this whole time. And only recognized it the other night when we reconnected? I hope you don't think I settled for you because I didn't." He looks confused.

"I don't think you settled for me. In the same way I didn't settle for you after Liam. I think our hearts just found familiarity and healing within each other, and we called that love. *Which in a way it is.* Love is when you are willing to do anything to see that person happy. To make them feel stability and safety. Plus, the sex was *hot*," I laugh, trying to lessen the blow.

He rubs his chin, contemplating what I said. He crawls up the bed and puts two hands on each side of the pillow I'm laying on. He leans down, gentle enough not to touch my body with his.

"Does this make your heart race for me, love? What if I kissed you right now? Tell me that you don't miss me at all. Or that if I was Liam right now, you wouldn't be by my side."

His eyes peer into mine as he continues his speech. "I *know* I fucked up, but that doesn't take away from the fact that we *do* love each other. I hear what you are saying about Selena. And perhaps Liam has you all fired up—*for now*—but you can't deny we still share *something* here."

His nose and lips hover over mine. *My heart does race.* I wish it didn't. He places a tender kiss on my lips then gets off the bed.

"Think about us for a little while. Don't throw this away. I'm not mad about you and Liam...I *understand.* You don't even have to decide between us now, but I am still in this. Your reaction to me just said it all—so don't count me out *just* yet."

He strides into his walk-in closet to change. I guess he is trying to be respectful.

"I want to see Liam, *Vader*."

Kil walks out with only a pair of gray sweatpants hanging low off his hips. He is towel-drying his hair as he walks over to me, rolling his eyes.

"Let's go, princess. I'll take you to him."

He helps me out of bed and makes sure I am okay holding on to the IV pole unassisted.

"You said you hated me in the car last night. And I *deserved* that. But hate can be out of passion too—which means I still have a chance."

His remorseful look makes me unsure of exactly what I still feel toward him. It's not hate...but is he right? Do I still *love* him the way he thinks I do? I know with certainty it is different than what I feel for Liam. With Liam, it was something I felt the whole time, even if I only recognized it later. With Killian, our love grew over time.

I slide my feet into the slippers he left by my bed, and we make our way slowly down the hall. I wince and stop a few times but suck it up.

I need to get to Liam.

"Sir." Kieran pulls Killian aside, whispering in a hushed tone. "Selena is here. She says she has nowhere else to go that is safe. What should I do?"

Killian walks back to me and reassuringly rubs his hands up and down my arms. Bending down on his knees, he takes my hands. Worry is etched onto his face.

"I'm still in the race. *This changes nothing.* I'm just giving her a safe place to stay while we try to find Alan. Apparently, he's been working with her family to retaliate against us. She never wanted anything to do with them after the wedding was called off."

"You still love her," I whisper while smirking at him and patting his face gently.

He stands and pulls my face to his, wrapping his lips around mine for a second time. "You're wrong. I just want to make sure she's safe. I love *you*. As I said, I'll give you time, but I'm not giving up."

Killian turns to Kieran, "Take her to a guest room upstairs. I'll be there shortly."

We take the elevator to the upper level and enter through a big wooden door. The room is set up on one side like a hospital room. The other half has another door that opens into a small operating room.

Liam is sleeping. An IV is in his arm, and his shoulder is all bandaged up and in a sling. They have him hooked up to oxygen. I have to say he looks peaceful. *I'm sure he's on a lot of pain meds.*

"I'll let you two *chat*. Here, come sit." Killian helps me into the recliner next to Liam's bed. "I'm going to check up on our new *guest*."

CHAPTER 34

LIAM

THEY HAD to sedate me when I woke up. I kept ripping my IV out and attempting to find Maddy. Killian reiterated over and over that she was okay, but I needed to see her beautiful face for myself. Once the drugs kicked in, I couldn't fight it any longer; my body betrayed me by giving in to sleep.

I peek through one eye. I already heard my woman walk in with Killian. *I'm curious as to which guest he is talking about.* As soon as he leaves, I turn and flash her a smile.

"Hey there, beautiful." I immediately take notice of her stitches. *Christ.*

Madison reaches for my hand, places my palm on her cheek and holds it there. Tears pour from her eyes, and silent sobs roll through her.

"I thought you died. *Twice.* Twice in one night, I watched you go down."

"It's gonna take a lot more than a bullet to take me away from you, baby." I rub her lips with my thumb. "Are you okay? I see you got some stitches there."

"My head is fine." She moves her hand to lift her shirt, revealing a handful of bandages. "My spleen, on the other hand, tore. They repaired it, and I am expected to make a full recovery."

The corner of her lips goes up in a smile. *How could she be smiling right now?*

My eyes glaze over in horror. This was the *exact* reason I didn't want her in this life. Why I put her safety over my need for her.

"Stop." She gives my hand a gentle squeeze. "I know what you're thinking. *Just stop*. It could have happened to me at any point in my life. A car accident, a bad fall...I could get mono," she shrugs.

"But it *didn't*, Madison. This happened as a direct result of my life corrupting your innocent one." I pull my hand away from her. I'm fucking livid at myself and at Killian for bringing her into this world. She shouldn't be with either of us.

"You saved me, Liam. *You took a goddamn bullet for me.* I'm safe with you, and there's nowhere else I'd rather be. So cut the shit. I love you. I'm not going to let you push me away because you think that's what's best. When you left me standing in my bathroom, you didn't give me the option to choose. You just took part of my soul with you. Now that I have it back, I feel *complete*. I'm not letting you walk away with it again."

I groan. "I don't *want* to. You're the woman I love. The woman I want to spend the rest of my days with. You're the woman who will give me the most beautiful children. I'm just so fucking sorry you got wrapped up in all this. Give me one more day. I'm going back to my room. You can stay with me there."

Her eyebrows scrunch, and she remains quiet. "Where have you been staying?" I clench my jaw, already knowing the answer.

"Killian has me in his room." She looks down at her hands.

"Of fucking course he does. Has he said anything to you?" I search her eyes for the truth she is shielding me from.

"Just that he isn't giving up on me. He thinks we will work it out and that what you and I share is more of a '*want what you can't have*' rather than love."

"Do you believe that?"

"Not at all. I told him he's got it all wrong. I think what he and Selena have is the kind of love you and I share. What Killian and I have is love...it's just the sort of love you feel when your needs are met and you are simply happy."

"So...you told him you're over?"

She sighs and shakes her head, once again not looking at me. "He didn't exactly get that part."

"He will when I speak to him. I'm sorry you had to talk to him alone. I should have been there when you had that conversation." I bring her palm to my lips and kiss it. "Who is this special guest Killian speaks of?"

Her eyebrow raises and I know she's about to tell me something interesting. "It's Selena. She's here for refuge. From what Killian told me, her family and Alan have an alliance—they are trying to retaliate against your syndicate. That's probably why Alan wanted to keep me alive." Her body shakes with fear. "They must have wanted me for ransom or worse."

"Alan is still *alive*?" His name drips from my lips like venom.

"They are looking for him."

Gunshots go off somewhere down the hall. I move as quickly as possible, realizing what a fucking big mistake it was for Killian to take in Selena. *She's like a Trojan Horse. How could Killian not see that?* I rip my IV out and unhook the oxygen from my nose. As I leap off the bed, pain radiates up my left shoulder. I pull Madison up with my good arm, and she winces.

Being as gentle as I can, I hustle her into the bathroom and down onto the lid of the toilet seat. "Sit there and don't move. I swear to fucking God, Madison...*don't follow me.* Just stay here until I come back." I lift her chin and lean over, smashing my lips to hers. Her fingers cling around my neck, trying to get me to stay.

As much as I would love to stay here, forget all our worries, and fuck her against the wall of this shower—I can't. We need to be *alive* in order to do that. With all the energy I can muster, I pull away from her and shut the door.

I grab my gun off the nightstand and crack the door open slowly; throwing the lock, I pull it shut behind me. I pad down the hallway to the commotion in the guest room. Colin, Kieran, and Conor are running up the staircase. We all group together and push open the door with our guns raised.

Alan is dead in a pool of blood, and Killian is on his knees with Selena cradled in his arms. I take the gun from him and kneel, patting him on the back.

"Kil, what the fuck happened?"

"Alan was in the room with her when I walked in. He had a fucking gun to her head!" he shouts. "It's done now. He and his son can rot in hell for all I care." He rubs small circles over Selena's back. "Kieran, scan the entire house and check for security breaches. That arsehole must have been here since we got home."

Kil, it's okay. I'm okay." Selena tries to calm him.

"There will be a meeting in twenty minutes to discuss our security moving forward," he scowls, eyeing all of us.

"Colin, take Selena to one of our guest rooms in the main hall and stay with her until I get there," he continues.

Colin helps them up and walks a crying Selena out of the room.

Killian squeezes my good shoulder and looks me dead in the eyes. "Just so you know, I am *all in* with Madison. I'm not giving up on us. I fucked up and I will spend every second trying to make it right. I know you love her, Liam. But so do I." He walks towards the door. "This incident doesn't change a goddamn thing."

I spin around—*fucking livid*. "It's not up to us, Killian. It's up to her."

He turns around to face me and stretches out his hand to

shake mine. "We'll let *her* decide then. There won't be any bad blood between us once she does."

"She already chose. I'm sorry, Kil. You and Madison are done. She wants to be with me."

"That's not what it seemed like when her lips were on mine earlier," he smirks before leaving the room.

I KNOCK on the bathroom door before I open it. "It's just me, baby. We are safe now."

She leaps at me, wrapping her arms around my neck. I flinch, but it feels so fucking good to have her in my arms again. I push through the pain and cradle her head in my hands, crushing my lips against hers.

"Alan is dead," I say between kisses. "Killian just shot him."

"Alan was in *this* house?" she asks incredulously.

"Yeah, we are going to be reorganizing security around here. Clearly, there was a major breach. Killian is ready for heads to roll."

"Is Selena okay?" she whispers her name as if she is in the next room.

I laugh. "She's fine. A little shaken up, but she's used to this. Her dad *was* the head of the Cuban mob in Miami." I look down at her hand. You took your IV out?"

A sly smile spreads over her face. "Yeah. I wasn't going to be attached to a pole if someone happened to get in."

I kiss her forehead and pull her to my side. "You are something else."

"I think *you* are. You ripped your IV out and went all caveman on me," she giggles. It is so nice to be able to hear that laugh and see that smile again. The last 24 hours have been such a nightmare.

"Can I ask you something?" I ask more seriously now.

"How about we get you back in bed, and then you can ask me," she deflects.

"No way in hell am I staying in this room after tonight. *We* are going back to my room. Just answer me one thing. Did you kiss Killian earlier?"

She tenses beneath me, already answering my question.

Fuck him. He's playing games now.

"He kissed me," she admits. "It's when he told me not to give up on him."

"I think you need to set him straight, baby. We'll do it together. He thinks you will give him a chance to make things right."

"He is probably not in the best mood right now." *Why is she making excuses?*

"Madison. *Look at me.* Are you going to be giving him another chance? You keep deflecting."

"I'm tired, Liam. Let's just go to bed. Tomorrow I'll be able to figure it all out. I don't know where my head is at." Her words are like a slap to my face.

"I can't watch you be with him. I already did, and look where that got us. It's either him or me," the words fly out of my mouth.

"Liam..."

"I can't even believe this," I say, shattered. "Ya know what? Why don't you sleep in the guest room tonight and think on that. Maybe we all need a bit of space." I storm off to my bedroom.

IT'S after midnight when my door cracks open. I see her silhouette in the doorway from the hall light.

"Liam...can I sleep with you, please? I don't want to be alone," she whispers at the threshold of my door.

"Don't want to be *alone,* or do you actually want *me*?" I grumble.

"I want you," she says with finality.

My heart leaps at that. I've felt like complete shit since our conversation. I shouldn't have left things off that way. I didn't mean them. I would wait an eternity for her. This situation sucks in general. From the looks of things, she was done with Killian. *I want to know what changed earlier.*

"Come here, sweetheart," I say, patting the bed.

She walks over, and gets under the covers, laying her head on my good shoulder. Her hands come up and settle over my raven tattoo.

"Endings lead to new beginnings. And the truth sets us free. Tomorrow we will tell Killian that it's *you*, Liam." She starts crying, so I rub her arm, letting her know I forgive her. I shouldn't have been so intense earlier.

"We are a team. We will make it through this." I kiss her head as she snuggles in closer to me. "I promise."

"I'm sorry I made you think you were only an option," she sniffles. "You aren't. I was just confused that he wanted to fight for me. Especially with Selena here. When he kissed me...I still felt something there...and that scared me even more."

"I think that perhaps you're right. We *can* love two people at the same time, but in different ways."

"I do love him. It doesn't consume me the way it does with you. When you hurt, I hurt. When you want to ravish me, I want to devour you. When we aren't together, I feel this darkness sink over me. It's why I was listening to such depressing music and keeping to myself when Killian was gone. *It wasn't for him.* Not having you and you being so close wrecked me."

I kiss her with all that I have. Maddy just verbalized what I have felt for her since I met her. She climbs on top of me, only wearing a short black satin nightgown. She starts to pull my sweatpants down, but I stop her.

"Baby, you can't. You're still healing. I don't want to hurt you."

"That's why I'm on top." She winks at me and continues to push my sweats to my calves. Madison lifts herself, lines me up with her slick opening, and sinks down slowly. Taking me inch by inch. My beautiful girl is so much tighter this way. I keep my good hand wrapped around the top swell of her arse.

She moves slowly, riding me, running her hands erotically up her stomach and over her hardened nipples. "That's right, baby. Ride that cock." Her pace picks up slightly, and her breathing becomes labored. I feel her wetness building and her walls wrapping tightly around me.

"Fuck, Liam...this is so deep," she moans. I pull her hands behind her back and lift my hips up to meet her movements.

"Ahh. I'll never get over the feeling of you inside me," she sighs.

I release her hands and move my hand between us. Using my thumb, I rub circles over her clit. She tilts her head back. Gorgeous, silky hair pools down her back.

"I'm so close, Liam."

"Me too, baby." We are both about to come when the door practically flies off the hinges, slamming against the wall. A very pissed Killian stands in the doorway.

"I guess you made your choice then." His eyes pierce Madison's.

FEBRUARY 2014

CHAPTER 35

KILLIAN

THE WEEKS PASSED US BY. We all have been coexisting awkwardly in this house. Work has kept Liam and I extremely busy. We have continued to receive increasing threats from the Cubans, especially after I sent Alan's head in a box. My priority right now is to increase our security here. I recruited more men from other areas of our syndicate to come to New York.

Madison has done a great job at avoiding me. Liam insisted he take her back to his house in Connecticut after I stormed in on them. We had a screaming match in the hallway until Madison broke it up. Ultimately, I had the final say. I wouldn't allow either of them to leave. I am the leader of this Syndicate, and Liam knows my word is final.

Call me a masochist—but the truth is—everyone is safer under one roof than spread out. Our resources are in New York. I don't want to split them between Connecticut and here. Liam's home is not as equipped for an attack as mine. With the updated security, we should all be very secure here.

If I am being completely candid—and even a bit childish—I was hoping Selena's presence here would make Madison a bit jealous. Perhaps it will make her realize she does still want me.

Liam is someone who caught her eye. It may be thrilling now, but it will burn out. Madison and I run deeper than that. She just needs time to process this all.

TODAY IS VALENTINE'S DAY. I thought it would be a nice gesture to get everyone together for dinner. I have the chefs preparing an intimate candlelit meal for the four of us. I highly doubt Liam is going to be okay with this. I figured I can get Madison on my side while he is out.

I knock twice on Liam's door with a dozen green roses in my hand. Madison opens it and looks down at the flowers in a heart-shaped box. She eyes me cautiously.

"Hi..."

"These are for you, a peace offering." I hand her the roses that remind me of her. "I know Liam is busy all day. I just wanted to chat with you *alone* for a minute."

Her eyebrows scrunch together. She doesn't trust my intentions, and I suppose I understand why. *I just need to make her remember us again.* She places the flowers on the dresser and then steps into the hallway. Her arms cross over her chest, covering her hard nipples. I smile inwardly, knowing I still affect her.

"What would you like to discuss?" She attempts to hold eye contact with me.

"How would you feel about dinner tonight for the four of us—"

"Kil, we shouldn—" I stop her from interrupting me by placing my hand under her elbow. "Just hear me out. Okay?"

She briefly glances down at her arm before finding my eyes again. "Are you and Selena an *item* again?" Her eyebrow raises in question. *Ahh, there it is.* The hint of jealousy.

I rub my fingers over my chin hair. "She would love to be. I'm just taking it day by day. You did say that she and I still have desires for each other. Perhaps I should try exploring them again."

She shifts her weight and thrums her fingers along her arms. *I'm getting under her skin.*

"That's great. I'm happy for you, Killian. She and I have spoken a few times since her arrival, and I really like her." She steps back, and my hand falls off her arm. "Listen, I wanted to thank you for letting me stay here…after everything. I know it's been awkward. I never got to tell you how sorry I was that you found out the way you did." Her eyes search mine for something. *What that is? I'm not sure.*

"It's fine. I acted immaturely, barging in like that. When I heard you two going at it, I was upset. I knew you would go to him when you asked for space. I just didn't expect to hear you fucking him after I kissed you in the hallway." I shrug like it's no big deal—but it was. *I was gutted.*

"I'm sorry, Killian. It's all my fault. I should have never continued engaging with you online while I was still hurting from Liam's loss. I wasn't over him. I just thought by moving on, especially with someone who had gone through similar heartbreak—that I would forget him."

"I understand," I sigh. I don't blame her. *No one saw this coming.*

"You and I created something beautiful. I don't regret the months we had together. And I won't let them be tarnished by this whole situation. I just hope we can all move on from this. You and Liam have such a great relationship. I would never forgive myself if I ruined that for you both," she says softly.

I reach for her again. Then pull back, thinking better of it.

"Liam and I are fine. We talked about it like men and agreed there would be no bad blood. And for the record, I don't hate you. You'll always be the one who brushed the soot off my heart and shined it back up."

A small smile forms on her face but doesn't reach her eyes. "What time would you want us for dinner? I can talk to Liam about it when he comes home."

"Figure around eight. We can have dinner and some drinks. The chefs are making us a special meal for Valentine's Day."

"That should work," Madison nods in agreement.

"I would like to try and get this household to be a little less hostile and work on being a family again."

"I hope for that too." She grabs the flowers off her dresser and tries handing them to me. "You should give these to Selena. Don't let her slip away again, Kil."

My heart falls in my chest, knowing she wants me and Selena to work out. I take the flowers and rub her cheek with my thumb. "Alright. Thanks, love. I'll see you both at dinner."

I KNOCK on Selena's door. She opens it in nothing but a red satin bathrobe and a playful smile on her face.

Her hair is wet. She must have just gotten out of the shower. I always loved how she looked with no makeup—natural dark hair and tanned skin.

She's sexy as hell.

Excitement fills her features as she takes in the flowers in my hand. I step into her room and close the door behind me.

"Happy Valentine's Day." I lean down and kiss her cheek, placing the flowers in her hand. *I feel like a dick for not getting her anything.*

"Thank you, Killian. These are beautiful." She walks over to her nightstand and places them down before taking a seat on the bed. Selena pats the space next to her, inviting me to join her.

I hesitate for a moment. Being near her and a bed could be a bad combination. We've never been able to keep our hands off each other. I can already feel the sexual tension sizzling between us.

"I won't bite," she giggles.

I close the distance and sit next to her, leaving a bit of space between us.

"I wouldn't mind if you did," I laugh, falling back into our old ways.

"You never told me what happened between you, Liam and Madison. I assume after our night together and the accident, that things didn't work out for you two. Madison has been sleeping in Liam's room...so are they officially together? That doesn't seem like the Liam I know."

"They didn't cheat on me like I thought they did." Her face falls. She knows I had only used her that night as pain relief and a way to get back at them.

"Oh." She plays with a nonexistent piece of lint on her robe.

I take her hand and lift her chin to look at me. "I shouldn't have done what I did to either of you. I hurt Madison, and now I hurt you. I'm sorry, Selena."

"It's okay, Kil. I forgive you. I know you loved her. But I don't regret coming to see you that night. I missed you so much. Any chance I got to be with you again, I took selfishly," she says sheepishly. My cock twitches at the memory of Selena and I together, but I try to ignore it.

"Liam and Madison met before she and I believe it or not. We never knew we were talking to the same girl. Liam left for an assignment—" I stop myself from saying where. "And he was going to win her back when he got home, but discovered we had started dating. It's a mess. To answer your question, yes. Liam and Madison are together now."

Selena moves closer to me and places a warm hand on my face. "I miss you, baby. *I miss us.* Maybe we were meant to come back together. Our timing was just off." She sits up on her knees and brushes her lips against mine. My hand runs up her back, and my fingers lace into her hair. I pull her to me and kiss her lightly.

She straddles me, and her lips part, inviting my tongue in. It's a foreign feeling. Madison and I had amazing sex. It was always heated and passionate between us. The way I feel with Selena is like free falling. You don't care if you have a parachute or not. You just jump and enjoy the moment for what it is...*and that's what I do.* I open her robe and trace my fingers over her lace bra. She rocks on my lap against my erection. When I latch my lips over her neck, she moans and pulls me closer to her.

"It's always been us, baby. Why can't you see that?" she whispers breathlessly.

I need to stop. I'm not ready for this. *My mind wanders back to the look on Madison's face the night after the accident when I leaned over her in my bed.* I free my lips from Selena's and close her robe, gently sliding her off me. I stand and brush a nervous hand through my hair.

"I'm trying to make peace with everyone around here. Come to dinner with Liam, Madison, and me tonight."

Selena looks confused at my whiplash of emotions, rubbing a finger over her swollen lips. She stands and wraps her arms around me, laying her head on my chest. "It's okay to feel unsure, Kil. I'm willing to wait and give you the time you need to get over her."

I press a kiss to her head and walk towards the door. "I'll come grab you at eight." A lone tear slides down my cheek as I click her door shut. I have a feeling my plan is about to backfire on me.

CHAPTER 36

MADISON

IT TOOK a lot of convincing for Liam to agree. He was much more malleable after we re-enacted our first time in the shower —which was everything it should have been—and more. I'm extremely impressed with his ability to fuck me against the shower wall after having a bullet lodged in his shoulder. He is recovering unbelievably well, pushing through PT like a beast. He still gets sore, but his range of motion is way beyond what it should be for only a few weeks post-op.

I am blow-drying my hair when he walks up behind me and leans down to place soft kisses on my neck.

"I love you, baby." He places a sweet kiss on my temple. "I was planning on getting you the tattoo you wanted, but this will have to do for now." He reaches in front of my neck and places a black diamond raven necklace there, securing it. The gorgeous raven overlaps the triskelion—which I still haven't taken off. I guess, in a way, it's symbolic. *My past, present, and future transformations.* I move my hand over Killian's necklace, prepared to take it off, but Liam places a hand over mine.

"Leave it on until you're ready. I'm not looking to destroy every good memory you had with him," he smiles gently at me in the mirror.

I turn the blow dryer off and place it down on the counter. My hair is shiny and full of volume. This look always makes me feel sexy and confident. Lately, I've been feeling sexier than ever. Liam makes me feel proud of my own body. He's always reminding me that in, his eyes, I am perfect. I wrap my arms around my man and capture his lips in mine.

"I love you too, Liam. *So much*. It's beautiful."

"I'm sorry I couldn't get my favorite tattoo artist to do an at-home session," he says remorsefully.

"It's okay, babe. I want my own raven tattoo someday, but I'm willing to wait," I sigh, tracing my fingers over his tattoo. I place kisses from one end to the other, dropping my head lower and down his trail of hair. I stop at his boxer briefs and drop to my knees on the bath mat. With confident hands, I tug them down, letting them fall to the floor. I look up at him and run my tongue over his length from base to tip.

"Jesus, Madison." He places a hand on my head. "What did I do to deserve you?"

WE ENTER the warm candlelit dining room a few minutes past eight. Killian and Selena are nowhere to be found. I turn to Liam, and he shrugs.

Being a gentleman as always, he slides my chair out and I sit, throwing the red cloth napkin over my lap. Liam takes his seat next to me, looking extremely uncomfortable. I stare at him, admiring how handsome he looks all dressed up. The chef walks in, pulling my attention away from him.

"Can I grab you both a drink?" Her eyes linger on Liam while she talks.

"Is Kil—Mr. Kennedy going to be joining us soon?" I ask her.

Her lips twitch. She nods her head, eyeing Liam again and

pouring us some water. "He'll be in shortly. He had some *business* to attend to." Her voice is laced with innuendo.

"Thank you, Lainey." Liam flashes his perfect smile at her. Her eyes soften when he says her name. She places a hand on his shoulder and squeezes, lingering a bit too long for my liking. *Am I missing something here?*

"Actually, I'll have a glass of Prosecco, please." I smile sweetly at her. I'm feeling jealous for more than one reason. Tonight's environment is making me on edge. I said I was happy for Killian to try again with Selena...so *why don't I feel happy right now?* I also never realized the chef had a thing for Liam. I need to ask him later if they were ever together.

Liam, noticing my shift in behavior, leisurely runs his hand over my thigh. "I'll have a double of my favorite whiskey." He glances up at Lainey before turning his attention back to me.

"I wanted to do something special with you tonight. I planned on taking you for a night swim."

"We still can. How about after dinner?" I take a sip of my water.

"Have you ever swam naked in a heated rooftop pool?" He waggles his eyebrows at me.

"I can't say I have," I laugh. Desire stirs in my core at the thought of it. It's amazing how just his laugh and the mention of our bodies connecting again soothe me. *This green-eyed monster has got to go.*

His hand creeps higher up and under my dress as the chef comes back with our drinks. Bold fingers skim under my panties, lightly brushing my sensitive, exposed skin. Lainey must notice and makes herself scarce.

"Did you two ever have a thing?" I eye Lainey walking back to the kitchen.

Liam's hand stops its exploration, and his face becomes stoic. "No, baby. Not at all. She has shown interest in me, but I never mixed our business relationship with pleasure. You have nothing to worry about there." I relax, knowing it's more one-sided than anything. I need to calm down. *Jealousy is an ugly bitch.*

Killian makes his grand entrance with a blushing Selena. He has an arm wrapped around her and his hand at the curve of her ass. Liam removes his hand from under the table and gives the back of my neck a gentle squeeze.

"Sorry to make you two wait. We *lost track of time*," he smirks as his eyes drill into mine.

Oh, Killian. What game are you trying to play? And why is it working? I want Liam. I chose Liam—I mean, it wasn't even really a choice. *It was always him.* So why am I still feeling anything toward Killian right now?

Killian slides the chair across from Liam out for Selena to sit and takes his seat across from me. Like a hawk, his eyes travel from my face to the new addition around my neck. He grabs the glass of water in front of him and takes a few sips.

His eyes blaze.

They find mine and hold them captive. He nods his head ever so slightly, acknowledging the presence of his necklace still on my neck.

Part of me wants to take it off this second to prove a point, but I have to behave. We are trying to play nice tonight, and I refuse to sink to Killian's level.

Lainey comes in to take everyone's orders for dinner and brings Killian and Selena their drinks. Another staff member comes in with a tray of soup and salad. The soup smells delicious and is one of my favorites—*french onion.* I would say it was just the chef's choice, but then the salad is placed down, and it's green goddess. *My other favorite.* I look up at Killian, and he shoots me a wink. I angrily spear a piece of avocado onto my fork and take a bite. Kil stifles a laugh into his napkin. I would roll my eyes at him, but Liam is watching our interaction now.

"Liam, I was so happy to hear from Killian the news that you are biological brothers." Selena smiles and tosses her hair over her shoulder, revealing a hickey.

My blood boils.

What are we, teenagers? *Deliberately leaving hickeys to be spiteful.*

Killian's games are going too far now. I said he should be with her and I meant that. He doesn't need to shove it in my face. This whole situation is a disaster waiting to happen. He's an ass for using Selena as collateral damage in his stupid games.

"It was a surprise to both of us. I have always felt like a brother to him, regardless."

"I'm happy for you, Liam. I don't think I've ever seen you this smitten before." She looks at me with a gentle smile on her face.

Liam wraps his hand around mine and gives it a gentle squeeze. "You definitely haven't. I've never felt this way about anyone before. And damn, Sel. It's nice to see your face around here again. I always knew you and Killian would find a way back to each other," he chuckles, taking a sip of his soup.

The next hour goes by *painfully* slow. The three of them talk about their past adventures together. I drink about an entire bottle of Prosecco—not saying much. Liam and Killian took turns glancing my way, gauging my reactions to their stories.

We are standing in the corridor, saying our goodnights. Dessert was delicious—a dark chocolate mousse cake. I had to hold back a moan at how decadent it was. Selena did the opposite, moaning and sucking on the fork after each bite.

Liam shakes Killian's hand and thanks him for the dinner. Selena comes over to me and pulls me into a hug.

"Madison, we really should hang out more when the men are busy at work. We might as well make the best of it while we are on lockdown. I'd love to get the chance to get to know you better."

I pull back from her embrace and do my best to smile at her. I feel Killian's intensity on my back. "I try to go to the gym once a day. I could use a workout partner," I offer.

"Yes! That would be great!" She seems so cheerful and genuine. It's not fair of me to be projecting my insecurities on her. I need to put aside my jealousy and try to give this girl a chance to be my friend. *We may even be family one day.*

Killian comes up next to her and drapes an arm around her shoulders. "Ready to head up, Lena?" He looks at her with lust hazing his eyes.

"*More* than ready." She winks at him.

"Thank you for a lovely dinner, Killian," I interrupt their flirting. I smile at him, and his eyes flash to my necklaces again. I am about to turn to Liam's outstretched hand when Killian reaches for my new necklace, holding it between his fingers.

"Liam always loved ravens." He releases it and kisses Selena's temple, guiding her upstairs.

I let out a silent breath before I grab Liam's hand.

LIAM LEAVES to go to the pool first, telling me to meet him there in fifteen minutes. I am wearing my new black bikini—the kind with a revealing thong bottom. Liam couldn't hold back his excitement when we got back to the room. The bikini was on the bed, surrounded by rose petals. Normally, I wouldn't wear something so revealing—but with Liam—I feel daring and bold. The fluffiest black bathrobe is wrapped around me. Liam got himself a matching one too. *Which he looks freakin' adorable in.*

I check my phone, and my fifteen minutes is up. I'm more than ready to spend some alone time with my man.

I pass Selena's room at the end of the hall by the elevator and stop short. I'm *not* trying to eavesdrop—but it's hard not to hear the bedframe hitting the wall. The sound of moaning and slapping seeps from under the door. Killian grunts and Selena sighs, "fuck baby, I missed this so much."

I've heard enough and press the button to the elevator with impatience.

Click. Click. Click. Come on!

I tap my foot while I wait. One of the staff must be using it on the main floor. I contemplate taking the stairs. Selena's door opens, revealing the both of them in their own set of bathrobes. I give them a quick smile. My gaze goes back up to the elevator arrows. With a ding, the doors open, and I get in—grateful for an escape.

Then the worst possible scenario happens.

They both get in with me, laughing and giddy in sexual afterglow.

"Hey, Maddy," Selena giggles again.

"Madison, where are you off to? We were just about to use the hot tub—you're welcome to join us." He winks at me and his lips twitch.

I want to smack that smug look right off his face. He knows where I am heading.

"Killian!" Selena smacks his shoulder. "Girl, you're hot. I mean *super* hot. I'm just not into threesomes. No offense." *Translation—he's mine, bitch.*

"None taken." I tap my foot and cross my arms over my chest, ready to get off this damn elevator.

I book it down the hallway when we reach the top floor. "Have a nice night," I shout over my shoulder.

I open the patio doors, so absorbed in what just happened, that I barely take notice of Liam sitting by the fire. Rose petals and candles form a heart around him. Clear votives with floating candles surround the pink-colored pool. Swirls of steam rise off the top. Liam has a bottle of champagne and two bubbling glasses sitting on the table near the fire pit.

A smile forms on his face as I approach him. He stands and

tugs the lapels of my bathrobe to pull me closer to him, placing a sweet kiss on my lips. "Happy Valentine's Day, baby."

Tears prick my eyes. "Liam..." I take another glance around. "This is all so perfect. You set this up?"

"I had some help, but yes, it was all my idea." His voice is full of pride. And it should be. This is beautiful and so thoughtful.

I capture his lips in mine again and wrap my arms around his neck. He picks me up and cups my bare ass in his hands. They are cold but welcomed against my too-hot skin. My tongue traces along his lips. He growls against mine in response.

"I can't wait to strip these off you, but I will say—I am *loving* these bottoms—or lack thereof." He gives my ass a nice squeeze." All mine," he whispers.

Liam places me down on the couch and takes his place next to me. He hands me a glass of champagne. My smile widens at how sweet he is to have put all this together. We clink glasses, our eyes roaming over each other hungrily when the sliding door opens. His eyes dart over to it, and he instantly becomes tense.

Killian and Selena walk out with cocktails in their hands. "Aw Liam, I always knew you were a big old softie!" Selena sing-songs.

"Nice touch, brother." Killian nods to the pool. "We were about to use the hot tub. Mind if we join?"

Liam grumbles next to me and whispers, "so much for getting you naked under the stars."

I run a finger over his lips, ignoring Killian and his rude interruption.

Take a fucking hint, dude.

"Maybe they'll take the hint if we pack on the PDA," I snicker and place a loud kiss on his lips. I was cordial during dinner. All bets are off now.

"Ya, no problem. Just close your eyes if we decide to get down and dirty in the pool," he teases Killian.

Selena and Kil walk over to the far side of the pool and

remove their robes, tossing them onto a nearby lounge chair. They waste no time sinking into the spill-over spa. Selena sits in Killian's lap and lays her head on his chest.

Liam finishes off his drink and runs his hands through his hair, sighing. "I'm sorry, baby. I feel like he's been purposely playing games all night. We don't have to stay here. We can head back to our room."

Fuck that.

I straddle him, and kiss him like my life depends on it. "No way. I want you to make love to me in that pool. There is something sexy about the idea that someone could be watching us," I say giddily.

He chuckles against my lips. "Ya. Killian and Selena will be the ones watching us."

"Not if we scare them away." I grind myself against him. "Mmmm," I moan loudly against his lips.

Liam undoes the tie to my bathrobe and shimmies it down my shoulders. He dips his nose between my cleavage and inhales deeply. "Fuck, I love how you smell. Your perfume drives me wild." His cock twitches underneath me, making me clench my thighs tighter around him. *I need him inside me more than ever right now.*

Kilena needs to get lost. *Now.*

"I need you," I whisper in his ear.

He groans and yanks my robe all the way off. Determined fingers untie the strings of my bikini top. I cover myself as he removes it and tosses it aside. He stands abruptly, and throws me over his good shoulder, slapping my bare ass.

"Liam, don't you dare!" I'm laughing and flailing, enjoying our fun.

His lighthearted laugh booms into the night air. He runs full force along the pavers to the deep end and jumps in. We break the surface of the water, and I wipe the hair out of my eyes, laughing hysterically.

"Liam, you asshole. You haven't changed a bit!" Selena shrieks with laughter from behind us. Now soaked.

Killian is the complete opposite. His face could be carved from stone, looking royally pissed—and wet. He wipes the water off his face, throwing Liam the bird.

Liam wraps his needy fingers around my waist and swims us up against the wall. I wrap my legs around his hips. He cages his muscular tattooed arms around my head, shielding me from them. My arms circle his neck as he brings his lips to mine. We make out, not giving a fuck about the nearness of Killian and Selena.

The two of them start talking in hushed tones.

After a few lingering moments, I see them stand to get some towels.

Liam laughs and places his lips against my neck. "I knew that would work," he mumbles against it.

"It definitely did." I roll my hips against his erection.

MARCH
2014

CHAPTER 37

LIAM

IT'S insane how quickly weeks turned into months of us being on lockdown. The Cubans have been quiet while we have more than tripled our recruits. Killian felt confident enough to lift the mandatory lockdown today.

What perfect timing. Today is Madison's birthday.

I planned a weekend getaway to Vermont for us to get some much-needed *alone time*. It'll be just the two of us in a cozy cabin overlooking the mountains. Madison is ecstatic. She's already packed and ready to go. I need to finish up a few contracts and we are set.

I plan on asking Killian if we can use the jet, but I'm not sure if I'll be getting Jekyll or Hyde today.

Having Killian's room next to mine has been horrendous. He and Selena have been going at it like rabbits. If he isn't working or at the gym—he's fucking her multiple times a day. I'm so ready to get Madison the fuck away from here.

I can't say I blame him.

If I wasn't so busy with my work, I'd be doing the same thing. Madison has been studying for her NCLEX. As much as I'd love to distract her, I know how important it is to her. She's been super stressed out and anxious over it. Her graduation ceremony is approaching on May 1st. Her goal is to pass her test before she graduates so she can take a position at a hospital in New York. We have many connections here. She could choose any hospital she wants...but she doesn't want or need our help.

Maddy wants to discuss looking into hospitals in Connecticut too. We both would love to move back to my place. I'll do whatever she wants—I'll sell my place in Connecticut and get us a larger space in New York if she prefers to work here.

Life's been getting back to normal. I think Killian is finally coming to terms with the idea of Madison and me. He has played fewer games over the weeks, but I still catch his eyes tracking Madison when we are around him.

He and Selena still haven't made things official—at least—I haven't heard anything. Madison goes to the gym with her a few times a week, and she hasn't mentioned anything to her either. *Poor lass.*

I am going over a contract in the upstairs office when Killian knocks on the door. I look up from my paperwork. "Hey, Kil."

"Hey, *sweetheart.*" He's back to joking with me again. *Maybe he is finally healing after all this.* He takes a seat at the table and folds his hands on the wood.

"What's the craic?" I lean back in my chair.

"So, Selena mentioned she and Madison were talking about your trip this weekend. She's been holed up here like the rest of us...I was hoping we could join you for Madison's birthday celebration. Don't feel pressured. She's just been nagging me to get away."

I focus on my paperwork for a minute, buying myself time to contemplate.

"Yeah, I don't see why not. We have the space. There are two master bedrooms and a basement with bunks. Conor is coming for added backup. We could always have Kieran come if you guys join."

"Perfect. We should take the jet. I'm surprised you didn't plan on using it. It's half yours now."

"I completely forgot about that. My mind was all over the place on New Year's. I was blindly signing paperwork. I'll have to remember to make an appointment with the lawyer and go over everything again," I laugh.

He stands and taps his knuckles on the table. "I'll let the pilot know. Selena's going to be thrilled."

MADISON WAS fine with them joining us. She and Selena chatted the entire flight there. Those two have very similar personalities. Honestly, they've been getting along great. Killian and I discussed work as usual while the ladies discussed our weekend plans.

The house is *incredible*—a luxurious cabin overlooking the mountains. The rooms are cozy and intimate. Each room has a private balcony with hot tubs. The kitchen is fully stocked with snacks, meals, and drinks. *Oh, and coffee. Can't forget that.*

Madison looks around in awe before leaping into my arms. She plants a huge kiss on my lips. "Oh Liam. Thank you! This is going to be the best birthday weekend!"

She slides off me, and she and Selena scurry off to look for Prosecco.

"Let's get this party started!" Selena hollers down the hall.

I shake my head and retreat out front to light a cigarette. Killian follows and leans against the back of the car.

"Those two seem to be getting along well." He stares back at the house.

I take a drag and blow out the smoke slowly. "Yeah, who would have thought," I sigh, agreeing with the weirdness of our situation.

"She seems stressed lately. What's been going on with her?" His eyebrows come together in concern.

"Maddy has been studying for her NCLEX." I pull another drag of my cigarette.

"Ahh," he nods.

I take a few more drags before I put it out in the ashtray on the porch.

We bring the bags in, dispersing them into our rooms. We are only here for a weekend, and the girls packed two huge suitcases each. I take a moment to look around. It is quite lovely here.

I wish it had been just the two of us.

Killian and I walk into the living room a few minutes later and sit on the couch. The girls are already drinking and have managed to find the sound system. They are blasting 90's music and dancing around the kitchen. It's nice to see my woman having a good time. She deserves it after everything she's been through. The same goes for Selena. She seems happier and less anxious this time around. But there's something there I don't fully trust...and I can't put my finger on it.

Madison makes two cocktails and brings them over to us. She hands Killian his then walks over to hand me mine. Dark hair brushes my face as she leans down to place a kiss on my lips. That kiss and her eyes hold a promise of all the naughty things we will do later. *I look forward to it.*

We enjoy a nice evening by the fire pit out back. All of us are drunk and laughing, finally relaxing after weeks of stress and awkwardness.

Selena stands on wobbly feet. "I think I drank a little too much," she hiccups. "I am gonna call it a night."

Killian stands to walk her back when she places a hand on his shoulder, making him sit back down in the wooden Adirondack chair. "Stay." She kisses him. "You're having fun. You never get to just relax."

"I'll make sure she gets back okay." Kieran stands, placing a hand under her elbow to stabilize her. The walk back to the house is short but I know Killian would feel safer knowing she gets back there okay. Conor is back at the house, keeping an eye on it—and probably sexting Lexi.

And so there were three.

"Ugh, we should have brought more Prosecco," Maddy giggles. She is holding up the empty bottle and dramatically pouting.

I decide Killian isn't a threat anymore and offer to go get it for her. "I'll get another bottle. Kil ya need anything while I'm up?" I look at him. He's deep in thought, looking into the fire. "Kil," I say a little louder.

He looks up at me and shakes his glass. "Another double would be grand if you don't mind."

I grab his glass and kiss the top of Madison's head. "Are you cold, princess? Do you want me to grab a blanket too?"

"That would be aaamazing. Thanks, babe."

CHAPTER 38

KILLIAN

I STARE AT MADISON. The fire is casting a warm glow onto her beautiful face. She is mesmerized by the fire, not saying a word. I wish I knew what she was thinking. I decide this may be the only chance I get to talk to her without Liam or Selena around.

"Happy Birthday, gorgeous." I smile at her from across the fire pit.

She looks over at me with half-lidded eyes. "Thanks, Kil."

I lean over in my seat and place my elbows on my knees. "Are you happy, sweetheart?"

"I am. *Are you?* You and Selena seem to have hit it off again," she rolls her eyes. "I can hear you through the walls."

"As I've said before, the sex with us has always been great. I'm still a little hesitant to make it official."

"Why? She loves you, Kil. I can see it in the way she looks at you."

I sigh loudly and scrub my hands over my face. Can't she see why I won't make it official? Madison always knows how to make me feel vulnerable around her. She'd be a nice tool for enemies—with how easily she can extract information without even lifting a finger.

"Because of you. I have tried to accept that you're not mine anymore. To accept that I lost you. But...if I'm being honest, I miss the hell out of you."

She plays with the necklaces on her chest, still wearing mine.

"I–I miss you too, Killian. But not enough to make me change anything with Liam. I'm sorry, that's probably not what you wanted to hear." She shifts uncomfortably in her chair and stares back into the fire. "I miss the sweet Killian. The one who took his mask off around me. You've put your walls back up around everyone again. I can't take these games you play with me. They hurt." She wipes away a tear.

I get out of my seat, keeping an eye on the backdoor—I don't want to disrespect Liam. He and I got back to a good place. I need to have one last conversation with Madison about *us* before I fully let her go. I crouch down next to her and hold her hand in mine.

"Why do you still wear my necklace?" I look up at her chest.

She uses her free hand to grab the triskelion between her thumb and middle finger. "I couldn't take it off. It didn't feel right."

"Where do we go from here, Madison?" She looks into my eyes, and more tears fall from her face. Her hand slides out from my grasp. She reaches around and unclasps the necklace, placing it in my hand and gently folding my fingers around it.

"I think I am always going to love you, Killian—but I don't think we are right for each other. I still care about you. So fucking much. But I can't give all of myself to Liam when I am holding onto pieces of us. We've got to let each other go if we ever intend to move on and find happiness again."

She gets up and wipes the tears from her eyes. Her intoxicating perfume invades my space as she places a gentle kiss on my cheek. Then before I can say anything else, she walks back to the house.

I look down at the necklace in my hand and rub the moisture from my eyes.

"Goodbye, Madison," I whisper to myself as I tuck the necklace into my jeans pocket.

Liam comes back to the fire after a little while. He hands me my drink and takes his seat back by the fire.

"Madison went to bed. She said she was tired and not feeling well. I have to ask because she looked upset, and I didn't want to push her...did you guys talk about something?"

I nod and sip my drink, leaning back in my chair. "We just needed some closure. She gave me the necklace back." I look at him to gauge his reaction.

He sips his drink and nods his head. "I noticed she was only wearing one when she came in. Are you okay?"

"I'm better now. Listen, I'm sorry for the games I was playing these last few weeks. It was childish of me."

"I understand why you did, Kil. It's not a normal situation we got in. I think we *all* needed our fair share of closure." He raises his drink to me. "So...what does this mean for you and Selena?"

"I need to make it up to her. I've been a dick, using her as a way to ruffle Madison's feathers. Don't get me wrong, there absolutely is still a spark between us that never went away. But I haven't been going out of my way to make her happy. She deserves to be loved the right way." I take a sip of my drink, letting the booze soothe my racing mind. "I'm just afraid to get close to her again. We ended off in such a bad way. I never want to feel that way again. When she stopped seeing me, my world felt empty. I felt empty. And now, after losing Madison too, I don't know if I have it in me to open my heart again the way she deserves."

"I think you do. Selena is still here, isn't she? *She loves you, Kil.* Now that you took a step back from the Madison thing, it will be easier to see how much you love her too."

THE REST of the trip was very nice. We ventured out to some orchards, played board games, and drank some more. Selena and I got the chance to spend time by ourselves Saturday night.

We started in our hot tub and ended up on the floor by the fireplace. It was romantic and different from our usual marathon of quick dirty sex. I think my conversation with Madison last night officially closed the chapter on us. Part of me wants to keep fighting. She told me she still cares—but I know I shouldn't. Plus I feel like perhaps Madison was right about Selena. We do have something really special.

Selena still loves me and wants me to be vulnerable around her. I just have to let myself open up to her. Madison was always in the back of my mind. It's become easier to fall back into things with Selena in a more romantic way after last night.

A gentle hand caresses my chest. I wrap my hand around hers. "What are you thinking about, baby?" she whispers.

I kiss the top of her head and wrap the comforter tighter around her. "I haven't been very fair to you these last few weeks. And I'm sorry about that. I was still getting over everything and not giving you the attention you deserved."

"I know you were. Something changed in you today. What happened?" She runs her hands over my face, tracing my nose and lips with her finger.

"Madison and I had a conversation last night. She and I are both ready to leave everything in the past. I guess we each got the closure we needed."

Selena nuzzles into me and closes her eyes. "I'm glad, Kil. I like Maddy. She's smart, she's sweet, and Liam certainly loves her. I've never seen him so happy before."

I nod and pull her body closer to mine, not feeling the jealousy flare up as much as it used to when the two of them were mentioned.

"They both are truly happy. And you make me happy. I want you to be mine again, I know I've kept you waiting for a while. That is—if you still want me."

I feel her smile grow wide against my chest. She looks up and kisses me with so much passion. It brings back the feelings I had that were buried deep beneath the surface. *The feelings I had when I would do anything for her.*

"I know this sounds silly...but even when you were with Madison...I still felt like I was yours," she says against my lips. "You never stopped being mine."

We stay silent, listening to the fire crackle next to us. I massage her scalp until her eyes gently flutter closed.

"Killian, you've always been it for me. Since we were younger, I always knew one day we would be together. When my dad broke off our engagement, I felt like I had died inside." She opens her eyes, revealing so much pain. "I refused to come out of my room for months. I couldn't eat. I had lost so much weight. I was practically a zombie. When we got a few opportunities to connect again, I felt alive. My body has always been so in tune with yours. It was like we didn't need introductions again. We just fell back into the same rhythm. My father found out about our meetings. He threatened to not only kill you—but he would start a war with the Tri-State Syndicate if I ever saw you again. So I ghosted you. I'm so sorry, Kil. I was just so scared he'd kill you. I chose to be miserable rather than have people I cared about at risk. You know I love your family like my own."

Tears fall from her eyes, and I rub gentle circles on her back, taking in all that she said.

Holy shit. She wanted me the whole time.

I'm so glad we ended that motherfucker's life. He was a piece of shit father and a dirty corrupt leader. I need to tell her this— *but now's not the right time.*

I roll her over and enter her slowly, making love to her again.

MAY
2014

CHAPTER 39

MADISON

TODAY IS THE DAY! I walked for graduation with my peers and friends. My family was all there in the crowd as well as Liam, Killian, Selena, and some men from the Syndicate. They all shouted as I walked across the stage to receive my diploma. I thought I would die from embarrassment. The dean said a nice sentimental speech about the community's hope for Chase and his father's safe return. They went 'missing' after a charity hockey game.

Killian and Liam set up a nice dinner for my family at a steakhouse back in the city. They rented the whole place out just for me. At times, I still can't believe this is my life. I wouldn't trade it for anything. I've never felt more myself than when I'm with Liam.

There is one problem, though. *My family still thinks I am dating Killian.* I wanted to set the record straight, but everyone agreed it would be best to tell them in a few months.

My dad is chatting away with my sister Mel, mom is drinking and talking with Killian, and Liam is sitting with my sister Mikayla—looking extremely uncomfortable. *He looks like he could use an out.* I walk over to them to see what they are talking about.

"Liam, is my sister chewing your ear off?" I mouth, "I'm sorry," behind her back. The corner of his lips goes up, and he nods.

"Actually, I was just telling Liam that I don't believe this whole charade you all are putting on," she says sweetly as she takes a sip of her wine.

I laugh. "What are you talking about, Mik?"

She lowers her voice, "I know you and Killian aren't together anymore. This guy over here—" she jabs a manicured thumb his way "—goes nuts every time he places a hand on your lower back. He's tried jumping out of his seat a few times when Killian kissed your temple. And Selena over there—she's honestly super sweet, has been puppy dog eyes for Killian the whole night. So... Liam, Maddy, care to tell me what's going on?"

Oh Mik. Always so fucking observant. I haven't told anyone except Lexi that Liam and I are together. I am about to respond when Liam does it for me.

"She and I are together. As you may know already, it's a complicated situation. We thought it would be best not to make a big thing about the timing of it all with your family."

Mik takes another sip of her wine. "I agree. Mom and Dad would think you were being a slut." Liam cringes at her verbiage.

"Jesus, Mikayla. Thanks so much for that," I glare at her.

"You know I don't think you are. I know your whole '*once upon a time*' with Liam. I'm happy for you guys. Don't worry. I won't say anything." She pretends to lock her lips and throw away the key. Liam visibly relaxes across from her.

He gets up from his chair, excusing himself, and guides me by my arm toward the bar. "I know we all agreed to pretend tonight, but if Killian kisses your face one more time, he's going to end up with a broken jaw," he growls.

I lean over and kiss his cheek. "I need to use the bathroom," I whisper, looking around. Everyone is busy talking. Not one person is paying attention to us other than maybe Mikayla.

"Mind coming with me?" I smile seductively at him. He catches on and practically drags me down the hall.

He pushes the door open and slams it shut, flipping the lock. His big hands pull my face to his lips as he presses my body against the door. "Fuck, Madison. I want you right now."

"So take me," I counter between kisses.

He unbuckles his belt and undoes his pants, freeing himself from his boxers. He pulls my lace underwear down and lifts me. My arms circle his neck, and my legs wrap around his hips. He moves my dress out of the way to slide his fingers between us. I moan into his mouth loudly.

"Might wanna keep it down if you don't want to explain to your family the truth," he laughs against my neck.

I'm already so wet. That's what he does to me—with just a look and a simple touch. Not being near him and feeling his eyes track me all night had me ready for him. Feeling his hands on me set me over.

He locks his lips over mine, tasting like whiskey. Moving us away from the door, he carries me over to the wall. Not a second later, he enters me.

God, he's so hard right now.

He isn't gentle either, and I don't want him to be. He slams in and out of me. My ass slaps the tiles with each thrust. Grunts fly off his lips as he nips at my neck and then runs a tongue over it to soothe it.

"You are mine, Madison. I can't wait for the day we can tell everyone. This was absolute fucking torture."

"Ahh. I know, babe. I promise to tell them in a few weeks. Ahh...fuuuuckk," I mewl into his shoulder as his pace picks up. My walls clench around him and I am about to explode.

"I love you so fucking much, baby."

He holds my lips captive as I ride out one of the most amazing orgasms ever. Liam follows right after me, emptying his release inside me.

We are both panting and trying to catch our breaths when he places me back on my feet. I grab some paper towels to clean up the mess when he restrains my wrist.

"Leave it. I want you to feel me there when you're on his arm." An inferno blazes in his eyes. *Or is that my own eyes reflecting in his?* Because right now—I am ready to abandon this party with him.

Liam leaves first, kissing me hard one last time before he goes. I'll follow a few minutes later, so no one gets too suspicious. I fix my lipstick in the mirror and tidy my hair. My face and chest are flushed, and my eyes are gleaming. This man has changed my whole world. Where I was once a shell of a woman, I am now alive and confident in myself again. Liam worships me. He is always pushing me to see myself through his eyes. I couldn't be more thankful for him.

Selena approaches me on my way out of the bathroom. "I need a cigarette desperately. Killian doesn't like me smoking. Think we can sneak out for one?" She shoots me a wicked smile.

"I could use one too," I laugh and link arms with her.

"I bet you could!" She winks at me. "Public bathroom sex is so hot."

We pass Liam at the bar with my sister. The two of them are doing a round of shots and laughing. Looks like they are doing better than before. Killian is in deep conversation with my dad. We easily walk out the front door. We should have at least one bodyguard, but we're literally right out front. I grab my crossover bag, retrieving my pack of cigarettes and lighter. I hand her one and the lighter after lighting my own.

"I'm sorry this is so awkward tonight. I plan on telling my family in a few weeks," I say remorsefully. "I'm sure they will be supportive. It's just a lot to take in and explain."

"It's fine. I wish I could say I get it—but I don't. My dad ended my engagement with Killian a few years ago, as you know. He was shot and killed a few months ago in Miami. They think it was gang-related." She takes a quick drag and blows out.

I wonder if that was when Liam was in Miami?

"I'm so sorry," I rub her arm.

She takes a longer drag this time. "Don't be. He had it coming, honestly. Our relationship was never great. So, how are things going with Liam?"

I smile at her. "It's been amazing. He has been more than good to me. I don't think I have ever felt this way before. I can see my whole life with him, and I can't wait. He's my forever. I know that whatever comes our way, we can handle it together."

"That's how I feel about Killian. I'm so happy we get to be with two amazing men, and I'm really happy we got so close these last few months. Liam was always irritable and noncommittal when we were younger. It's crazy to see how soft and sweet he is with you. I've never seen him act this way around anyone, let alone a woman."

"I'm really happy we became close too. We need another game night soon. I thoroughly enjoyed myself the other night."

"Killian was such a sore loser. We got back to the room, and he kept going on and on about how he thought Liam was secretly taking money from the *Monopoly* bank," she laughs.

I glance inside to see everyone sitting down at the table again. "We should head back in." I toss my cigarette into the sand bucket by the bench. Selena follows suit.

We are walking toward the front door when a black truck screeches to the curb. Two masked men jump out and grab Selena and I. I kick and thrash, trying to slam my elbow into my attacker's nose or groin—but it's no use. They drag us both into the car. I try screaming for Liam until a gloved hand covers my mouth.

The last thing I see before they slide the truck door shut is Liam's horrified face through the glass. He's already on his feet, but it's too late. The door shuts, and the smell of sweat and rust fills my nose. I claw and punch as Selena kicks and screams next to me. I feel a pinch in my neck, and my attempts to escape become less and less likely.

I've been fucking drugged. Again.

My eyes flutter closed, and the world goes black.

ACKNOWLEDGMENTS

The journey of writing this book has been thrilling and nerve-wracking all at once. I loved writing the different perspectives of the characters. Hopefully, you all did too. I would like to thank my husband for dealing with me being absent after he gets home from work. Most nights I was up until 4 a.m. writing. I also would like to thank my mom for providing financial support to help get my book started. This has always been a goal of mine—and also very personal to me. Big hugs to my family and friends for peer-reviewing the book and giving me the best feedback. Lastly, I would like to give a huge shout-out to my talented cover artist as well as interior designer, Emily at Quirky Circe Book Design. The book is beautiful, and seeing it come to life has been a dream come true! To you reading this—thank you for giving my book a chance. I hope you'll stick around for the rest of the series!

ABOUT THE AUTHOR

Luna Everly is a new indie romance author who would like to share the fantasyland she has in her mind with the world. This dream world consists of strong sarcastic men, who are grounded by their smart sassy heroines. Add a bit of suspense, impossible decisions, and amazing besties to the lives of these characters-- and you've got yourself quite the adventure to go on. Grab the tissues for emotional ups and downs and a fan for some seriously steamy moments.

As a Pisces, Luna often gets lost daydreaming. When she's not lost in thought, she's spending time with her husband, daughter, two rescue dogs, and her clingy cat Loki. Luna enjoys cooking, game nights, getting lost in a good book, self-care bubble baths, and even the occasional marathon of Call of Duty with her husband. You'll never find her far from her cup of coffee--or multiple cups for that matter.

Luna Everly is a pen name. She currently resides in New York with her family.

GET SOCIAL

authorlunaeverly.com

Facebook
https://www.facebook.com/profile.php?id=100088486166891

TikTok
https://www.tiktok.com/@authorlunaeverly

Instagram
https://instagram.com/authorlunaeverly

info@authorlunaeverly.com

* Subscribe to my newsletter to stay up to date on new releases and giveaways.

* Follow along with my blog to keep up with me and my wild adventures.

www.ingramcontent.com/pod-product-compliance
Lightning Source LLC
Chambersburg PA
CBHW070312260626
47160CB00003B/813